Ron Fortier's
BROTHER BONES
SIX DAYS OF THE DRAGON

AIRSHIP 27 PRODUCTIONS

An Airship 27 Production
airship27.com
airship27hangar.com

Cover and interior illustrations © 2013 Rob Moran

Editor: Ron Fortier
Associate Editor: Charles Saunders
Production and design by Rob Davis
Promotion and Marketing Manager: Michael Vance

ISBN-13: 978-0615919355
ISBN-10: 0615919359

Printed in the United States of America

10 9 8 7 6 5 4 3 2 1

ROMAN LEARY

DAY ONE

*B*rother Bones is going to get you.

What? What the hell? Stay away from me!

You think you're going to get away with what you did? What you did to my little girl?

I didn't do anything to your kid!

Liar!

Dammit, lady! Back off, will you! Weren't you paying attention in there? Case dismissed! No evidence! None! Now, leave me alone!

You're never going to be alone again, you murdering bastard. His shadow's going to be with you everywhere you go.

Can somebody please get this woman away from me!

My little girl's going to point you out to him. That's him, she'll say. He's the one. And then it'll be all over for you.

Leave me alone!

"You think we should go up there and check on him?" Benny said.

Mick and Pete looked up from their cards. "What for?" asked Mick. He was in the middle of a hot streak, and didn't want the game to be interrupted.

"You didn't hear him just then?" Benny asked.

"I did," said Pete. "Sounded like he said, *leave me alone*. Something like that."

"He's just having a bad dream," Mick said. "There's no way to that bedroom except through here. Did you see anybody walk by? I didn't."

Benny wasn't convinced. "I dunno…"

"Listen, kid," Mick said, "we're being paid to keep his sorry ass alive, not hold his hand and sing him lullabies. As far as I'm concerned, the little creep deserves every nightmare he gets. If he wasn't rich as Creasy, we wouldn't even be here."

"Croesus," said Pete.

"What?"

"You meant to say, rich as Croesus."

"Well, excuse me, Professor Pete. Tell me, if you're so damn smart, how come you've been losing all night?"

Pete frowned and looked at his cards.

"Now, where was I?" Mick said. "Oh, yeah, if this guy wasn't loaded, he couldn't have afforded to buy protection from the Shilohs."

"How much do you think he's paying them?" Benny wondered.

"A damn sight more than they're paying us, you can believe that!" Mick said. He shook his head at the injustice of it all. "I can't figure out what he's so scared of, anyway. He already bought off everybody who could've hurt him. Making that evidence disappear must have cost a fortune."

"Yeah, but some things aren't for sale," Benny said. "That little girl's mother would skin him alive, if she could. Did you see her outside the courthouse this afternoon? She was really giving him hell."

"I saw," Mick said. "Can you blame her? Maybe she's the one he's afraid of."

"I know what's got him spooked," Pete said.

The other two looked at him. He stared at his cards and scratched his chin.

"C'mon, Pete," Mick said. "You gonna keep us in suspense all night?"

Pete lowered the cards. "He's afraid of Brother Bones."

Henry couldn't seem to get away from the woman. Where was the car? There was supposed to be one right here, waiting to whisk him away to his townhouse where he could lock the doors and close the blinds against these clamoring fools.

He gave up and started running. He couldn't bear another second of the woman's presence, couldn't stand to hear another word from her mouth. He ran around the corner and was astonished to find the street completely empty. How was that possible? It was the middle of the day, and this was one of the busiest intersections in Cape Noire.

Except now it wasn't day. Henry blinked his eyes. The sun was gone, and he was staring down a darkened street illuminated by dull, yellow lights and a wan sliver of moon. He began to feel cold and damp. He looked down, and discovered that he was clad only in his pajamas. His feet were bare, and the grit on the asphalt dug painfully into his soles. A cool breeze wafted by, pressing his night-clothes against his body and tousling his thinning hair.

Across the street, about a block away, something moved in the shadows.

Henry strained his eyes. What was that? It looked like…

It was a little girl. She stepped into the dim circle of light cast by the corner streetlamp.

Henry stared at her pale features, and he felt a cold knot of fear form in the pit of his stomach. "It can't be," he whispered.

The girl pointed at him. She looked over her shoulder and addressed the darkness. "That's him," she said. "He's the one."

☗ ☗ ☗

"Brother Bones?" Mick said. "Are you kidding?"

"Nope," said Pete. "The woman outside the courthouse told him that Brother Bones was going to get him."

"She did? I didn't hear that."

"He told me about it later. He'd never heard of Bones, so I told him the story."

"What story? Don't tell me you filled his head with that crap about Tommy Bonello."

Pete shrugged. "Well, he asked…"

"Who's Brother Bones?" said Benny.

The other two looked at him. "You don't know?" Mick asked.

"I just moved here a couple of months ago," Benny said. "Is he one of the big bosses?"

Mick and Pete exchanged a glance. Mick sighed and put down his cards. "Go ahead and tell him," he said. "I know you're dying to."

Pete turned to Benny and smiled. "Okay, young man," he said, "here's the story. Once upon a time there were two brothers, Jack and Tommy Bonello. They were twins, good-looking guys, but mean as hell. They were the toughest pair of stone killers in Cape Noire, but then something happened…"

☗ ☗ ☗

As Henry watched, someone else came walking out of the shadows. It was a tall, powerfully-built man clad in a long black coat and a large slouch hat. The face beneath the hat was a grinning white skull. A pair of pitiless black eyes gleamed inside the sockets, glaring at Henry.

Gasping, panic-stricken, Henry tried to run, but his legs wouldn't cooperate. They stubbornly remained rooted to the spot. How could this be happening?

The man in black advanced until he was only a few feet away. Henry could now see that the face wasn't really a skull, just a mask. He would have found the knowledge reassuring, if he wasn't persuaded that behind the false face lurked something infinitely worse.

Henry's mouth worked, but no sound came out. Was he really going to die here? This wasn't the way his story was supposed to end! It wasn't fair!

"You're right," the man said. His voice was a grinding of granite, the sound of a stone sealing a tomb.

"Right?" Henry said, finding his voice. "What do you mean? Right about what?"

"It isn't fair," said the man. He lifted his arm. In his hand was a silver-plated .45 automatic. He leveled the gun at Henry's head.

"If it was fair," said Brother Bones, "you would be suffering a lot more."

The gun exploded in Henry's face.

💀 💀 💀

"Jeez," said Benny. "Did you hear that? That dream he's having must be a real doozy."

"If he needs help, he'll ask for it," Mick said.

"I guess you're right," conceded Benny.

"Of course I am," Mick said, glad the kid was seeing the light. He was disappointed the game had fizzled out, but it was probably time to wind it up anyway. You could only win for so long before tempers began to fray and you had a fight on your hands. Also, though he would never admit it, he enjoyed listening to Pete tell the old stories. Pete was really good at that sort of thing. In another life, he could have made it big on radio, instead of being just another thug in the Cape Noire underworld.

The kid looked at Pete. "Let me see if I've got this straight," he said. "Tommy Bonello comes down with a case of religion, or something like that, and gives up the life to go join a monastery. His brother Jack finds out, and decides that he's not gonna stand for that. So Jack takes a few guys up there and kills Tommy, along with all the other monks."

"That's right," Pete said.

"But then Tommy came back," Benny said.

Pete nodded. "He came back as a spirit. He killed Jack, and took possession of his body. Now he walks the streets of Cape Noire, trying to make up for all the evil he did in life by avenging the innocent."

"Innocent," Benny said, "like the little girl that our guy killed."

"He's not *our* guy," Mick said. "He's just *a* guy, who happens to have pretty deep pockets."

"Not deep enough," said a harsh, grating voice.

Henry lay in bed, shivering. His silken pajamas and Egyptian-cotton sheets were drenched in sweat, but he made no move to escape them. Rather, he pulled the sheets up to his chin and held them there. He caught a glimpse of himself in the mirrored ceiling, and felt a pang of embarrassment. He looked ridiculous, like some little kid frightened of the boogeyman.

Through the crack in his bedroom door, he could hear the muffled voices of his guardians drifting up the stairwell from the room below. The drone of their conversation was comforting. He found himself hoping they would talk all night.

The men below began to shout. Henry sat up. Why were they doing that? Were they arguing about something?

There were two gunshots, followed in rapid succession by three more. Then came more shouting and a crash of furniture and breaking glass. Someone screamed.

Silence.

Henry still held the sheets to his chin, but he was no longer embarrassed. There was a thump, followed by a loud creak, then another and another. Someone was ascending the stairs.

Thump, *creak*. Thump, *creak*. Thump, *creak*...

Now they were at the end of the hall. The heavy footfalls, muffled by the plush carpeting, came closer and closer to Henry's door.

The hinges squeaked as the door opened. In the darkened hall stood the figure of a man. He was clad in a long black coat and a large slouch hat. The face beneath the hat was a grinning white skull.

"Your name is Henry Oliver," said the tombstone voice. "You raped and murdered a ten-year-old child."

Henry's response was pure reflex, honed by a thousand rehearsed denials. "I didn't do it," he said. "No one can prove that I did. There's no evidence."

"You're wrong" the man said. "There's a witness."

From behind the long black coat stepped a pale little girl. She pointed at Henry.

"That's him," the child said. "He's the one."

Brother Bones raised his arm, and leveled a gun at Henry's head. Sometimes dreams do come true.

Two blocks from Henry Oliver's townhouse, a DeSoto sedan sat parked in a darkened side street. The driver, a wiry redhead in his mid-twenties named Bobby Crandall, was relaxing behind the wheel, his elbow resting out the open window. To the casual observer, Bobby would have seemed little more than a kid, but in his young man's face were a pair of old man's eyes, aged before their time by sights no man should see.

He was halfway through his second cigarette when he heard the shots. They were muffled and distant. He wouldn't have noticed them if he hadn't been listening for them. He glanced at his watch, and decided he had time to finish his smoke before his roommate returned. It wouldn't be long, though. The dead travel fast.

Sure enough, he had just taken a final drag when he heard approaching footsteps. The rear passenger door opened, and Brother Bones stepped into the car. "Take us home," he said.

Bobby started the car. "Run into trouble?" he asked. "I heard a lot of shooting."

"There were some men," Bones said. "I had to hurt them, but they're still alive."

"What about Oliver?"

Bones' eyes met with Bobby's in the rear-view mirror.

"Never mind," Bobby said.

Bobby drove slowly through the quiet streets until he came to the cold water flat he shared with Bones. They went inside and Bones, as he always did, immediately headed for the spare bedroom he stayed in whenever he wasn't on one of his violent errands. He paused by the door and spoke without turning. "Are you going to the casino?" he asked.

"Yeah," said Bobby. "I'm working graveyard a couple of nights this week as a favor to Larry. I told him I'd be late. He said he'd find someone to cover my table until I came in."

"What made you so sure I wouldn't need you for the entire night?"

Bobby shrugged. "I know you, Bones."

"I suppose you do," Bones replied. He walked into his room and closed the door.

Bobby took his time driving to work. He had been a night-owl all of his life, and he always enjoyed traveling the early morning streets. Perhaps it was the illusory sense of having the city all to himself that he liked. It appealed to his loner's heart. That delicious, desert-island frisson was soon banished by the approaching lights of Five Corners.

As in all big cities, there were some places in Cape Noire where the tide of humanity never receded. One of these spots was Five Corners, the bustling red-light district at the heart of Mid-Town. Rising from that heart, like a stake trapped in the chest of a tenacious vampire, was the venerable Tinsley Tower. The oldest hotel in the city, the Tower had once been the pride of Cape Noire. Now it was mainly a prop for garish billboards and neon signs, its windows overlooking a cauldron of licentious humanity.

Bobby never went to Five Corners, but he frequently skirted its edges on his way to the Gray Owl Casino, another place where bright lights and desperate desires never dimmed. It was here that he made his living as the most popular blackjack dealer on the floor.

Bobby pulled into a parking space, and as he was getting out of the car he was struck by an odd realization: Bones hadn't once crossed his mind during the entire drive.

It was a small thing, but it bothered him somehow. There was an efficient and accomplished killer—who just happened to be a zombie—sitting in his flat, and Bobby had been able to forget about him the moment he had left him behind. What did that mean?

"Jeez," Bobby whispered to himself. "I guess he's just a normal part of my life now. When did I get so used to him?"

It certainly hadn't been that way at the beginning...

Bobby was barely nineteen when he landed his job at the Gray Owl. The work suited him, and he would have been happy to do it for the rest of his life, but the crooks that ran the place had other ideas. They were in the middle of a bloody and protracted gang war, and they were in dire need of cannon fodder.

Bobby was pressed into the service of some hard and dangerous men. His skill-set soon expanded from dealing cards to driving fast cars. Unfortunately, he didn't drive well or fast enough, and one terrible night he found himself tied hand and foot on a warehouse floor, looking up the barrel of a gun held by a handsome killer named Jack Bonello.

"Sorry about this, junior," Jack had told him. "You just happened to be in the wrong place at the wrong time."

Then, against all odds, fate dealt Bobby a winning hand, and it was handsome Jack who went bust. Even as Bonello was squeezing the trigger, a gust of cold wind came roaring through the confined space, as if a magical window had been opened to the Arctic. Carried on the wind was an agonized wail, the cry of some unspeakable horror being born full-grown into a world of bloodshed and misery.

Bobby, his eyes wide and dry with terror, watched in mute astonishment as an ethereal copy of Jack Bonello floated into view.

"What am I supposed to be, Tommy?" Jack shouted at the ghost. "Scared? You think you can scare me?"

Bobby certainly thought so. Despite his bluster, Jack Bonello was clearly frightened out of his wits. The ghost let him mouth off a little more, and then it must have gotten tired of listening, because it plunged one of its spectral hands into Jack's chest and stopped his heart. As went the hand, so did the rest of the body, and soon the ghost had completely disappeared into Jack Bonello's corpse.

Then the corpse began to move.

Bobby had been struggling with his bonds from the very moment he had been captured. Now, the sight of Bonello rising to his knees drove the young man's efforts into a frenzy. His feet and hands were raw and bleeding by the time he managed to work the last knot loose. Shaking with fear and pain, he scrambled to his feet and was about to break into a desperate run for the door, when a voice from beyond the grave commanded him to stop.

"Run and you are a dead man!" roared the voice. "Heed my words, Bobby Crandall!"

The warehouse door couldn't have been more than fifty feet away, but the distance seemed to elongate before Bobby's eyes. It might as well have been fifty miles. No matter how fast he ran, he knew he would never get away. His heart sinking into a maelstrom of despair, Bobby turned to face the walking dead man.

Tommy Bonello—and it was certainly him now, wearing his brother like a hand-me-down suit—advanced on Bobby, his hand outstretched and pointing as if in accusation.

"I have saved your life, Bobby Crandall," he said. "Do you understand that?"

Bobby managed to gasp out a feeble affirmative. Bonello's finger hit his chest, pushing him back a half-step.

"Good," said the dead man. "Never forget it. From this day forward, your life is mine to do with as I please. In this manner you will remain in good health. Cross me once, and you will die."

Bobby's mind was reeling. He felt dangerously close to hysteria, but he managed to choke down the crazed laughter that was bubbling inside of him. He forced himself to look into the monster's eyes, and to speak in a calm, if uneven, voice. "Right, Mr. Bonello," he said.

The dead man grabbed Bobby by the ear and leaned in close. "Jack Bonello is gone," he said. "My name is Brother Bones."

"Are you gonna stay out here all night?" someone said.

Bobby flinched. He looked up to see the beautiful face of his sometime girlfriend, Paula Wozcheski. She was dressed in the standard issue outfit for a cigarette girl at the Gray Owl; high heels and a black bustier that could throw even the best player off his game.

"Easy there, lover," she said with a laugh. "You look like you've seen a ghost."

Every day of the week, Bobby thought, and he laughed, too. "Shouldn't you be inside?" he asked.

"I was just cooling my heels in the break room," Paula said. "I happened to be looking out the window when I saw you drive up."

"Is that so?" Bobby said. He opened the car door a little wider. He reached out to Paula, and gently pulled her to him. "Tell me, who's covering my table?"

"Marco," Paula said.

Bobby pushed up her bustier and began kissing her midriff. "Has he been having a good night?" he asked.

"I think he has," Paula whispered.

"Good," Bobby said. "Then he won't mind waiting a little longer."

Paula made a shuddering exhale by way of reply, and sank into the car.

For the second time that night, Bobby forgot all about Brother Bones.

"They say Brother Bones did it," said Officer Calvin Byrd.

Lt. Dan Rains, Chief of Detectives, considered this statement with resigned dismay. "They're really sticking to that?" he asked.

"Like glue" said Byrd, and then he chuckled. "You should talk to the kid, the one named Benny."

"What about him?"

"He can't figure out if he's terrified or honored. I think he'll be telling the story to his grandchildren."

"I guess it's not every day you get your ass kicked by a legend."

"Not at all," Byrd said. He looked over at the couch where the three battered hoodlums sat, nursing their wounds. "So, what do you think really happened?"

"I'd like to know the same thing," said a soft, feminine voice.

Dan closed his eyes and sighed. "How long has she been standing behind me?" he asked.

"Not long," replied Byrd.

"Is there a particular reason you didn't tell me she was there?"

"I didn't want to make her mad. I'm kind of sweet on her."

"Go find something else to do."

"Yes, sir, Lieutenant. Right away, sir.

Dan turned and looked into the midnight blue eyes of Sally Paige, crime reporter for the Cape Noire Tribune. They were the same height, so he was able to keep a level gaze. Her beautiful features were framed by a cascade of raven black hair that spilled from beneath a snap-brim fedora. The weathered hat was a perfect match for the old trench coat she draped over her lean, but shapely, form. The masculine clothes should have made her look like a rumpled tomboy, but instead they lent her a peculiar sort of steely glamour.

Dan glanced at his watch. "It's three in the morning," he said. "Don't you ever sleep?"

"No rest for the wicked," she said with a smile. Her glistening red lips made Dan think of wet strawberries.

"You're making wicked look good," he said.

"That's cute, but it's not exactly the quote I'm looking for."

"Okay," Dan said. "Here's one. 'This is apparently a gangland slaying.' "

Sally arched an eyebrow. "Are you kidding? You actually expect me to write that down?"

"You can write whatever you want, but if you quote me, the statement had better read, 'This is apparently a gangland slaying.' "

Sally nodded in the direction of the bruised and bleeding goons. "That's not the story they're telling."

"How do you know that?"

"I keep my ears open."

Dan shook his head. "Those men are the victims of a violent crime.

They're in a state of shock. They're apt to say anything."

"Hey, Mick," Sally called out. "Are you in a state of shock?"

"Huh?" Mick replied.

"See?" Dan said. "He's so upset he can't even understand a simple question."

"Let me talk to him for five minutes," Sally said. "I'll calm him down."

"Five minutes with you would make him the exact opposite of calm. Would you mind following me outside? It's nice and cool out there, a beautiful night for an off-the-record chat."

Dan gently took her arm and walked her to the door. After they were out the stoop, he offered her a cigarette, which she accepted. "How do you know Mick?" he asked as he gave her a light.

"I know every two-bit thug in this town."

"Then you must know who Mick and his buddies work for."

Sally nodded. "They used to work for old Robert 'the Bruce' Shiloh, but now they take their marching orders from his college-boy grandson, Edgar."

"That's right," Dan said. "Now, here's the part where you can help me. Do you have any idea why Eddie or the Bruce would give a damn about Henry Oliver?"

Sally held up her hand and rubbed her thumb and forefinger together.

"Not a good enough reason," Dan said. "They've been rolling in it since Eddie turned around the Bruce's old bottling company. That thing was just a Prohibition front, and a lousy one at that. Now it's a million-dollar enterprise."

"Have you tried that stuff they're making?" Sally asked.

"What? That *TenaciTea* crap?"

"It helps you hang in there," Sally said, quoting the ads with a laugh.

"It makes you want to puke," Dan said, "but people can't seem to get enough of it, for some ungodly reason. Which brings me back to my main point. Eddie Shiloh has taken a crooked business and turned it into a legitimate goldmine. He's on his way to being the richest man in Cape Noire, and without breaking a single law…that I know of. Why would he risk screwing it all up by getting involved with a creep like Oliver? It just doesn't make sense."

"Maybe I can get him to explain it."

Dan looked at her, letting his eyes ask the question.

Sally grinned. "I have an interview with him day after tomorrow."

"He's willing to talk to a crime reporter?"

"He is if she's filling in on the society page. Our young soda-pop king is the most eligible bachelor on the West Coast, in case you didn't know."

"I didn't know. Have *you* gone out with him?"

"That kid? Give me a break. Believe it or not, he did make a half-hearted pass at me at a fund-raiser a few months ago."

"You weren't tempted? He's awful rich…"

"Money isn't everything."

"So I've been told. Do me a favor, willya? Give me a call after you talk to him."

"Oh, come on, Dan. As the Great Detective once said, 'I am not an agent of the police.' "

"I'm not asking you to be a spy. I just want you to help me understand the kid."

Sally considered it. "Okay," she said, "you'll be hearing from me. But you owe me one, got it?"

Dan offered his hand, and they shook on it. There followed a moment of silence as they both retreated into their thoughts. After a minute or two, Sally turned her eyes to Henry Oliver's bedroom window. "Was it really Bones?" she asked.

"Brother Bones doesn't exist," Dan said, studying his cigarette.

"Yeah, but was it him?"

Dan slowly nodded.

"They should give him a medal for this one," Sally said.

"Are you going to say that in your article?"

"Nah, I don't do opinion pieces. I only report the facts." She gave Dan a wink. "This is apparently a gangland slaying."

"Awful late for you to be out, isn't it, Mr. Elliot?" Bobby asked. He was nearing the end of his shift, and was surprised to see Preston Elliot, Cape Noire's most famous radio personality, taking a place at the empty table.

"I've been burning the midnight oil on this new show, my boy," Elliot said. "I've got a lot riding on the premiere."

Bobby considered the man as he shuffled the cards. Elliot was ordinarily perfectly coiffed and dressed to the nines, but tonight he looked worn, red-eyed and haggard. His thin moustache was untrimmed, his cheeks were dark with stubble, and the lines of his suit were broken by more than a few wrinkles. Bobby, who liked and respected Elliot, found the overall effect disconcerting. It was like catching Zeus in the middle of a three-day bender.

"Are you sure you're okay?" Bobby asked.

"More than okay," Elliot said with smile. His rich baritone, familiar to millions, sounded unusually shrill. "I'm keyed-up! Excited! Our new program is going to be the biggest thing to ever hit the airwaves! I can practically taste it!" He smacked his lips, tasting it. "Now deal, my boy, deal. I need to let off some steam!"

Bobby obeyed. Elliot's play was erratic and reckless, a far cry from his usual, thoughtful style. What the hell was wrong with the man?

After about thirty minutes of wretched decisions, Elliot threw up his hands and said, "Enough! Someone stop me before I kill again!"

"Whatever you say, Mr. Elliot. It's time for me to go anyway."

"Go? You mean, you're off work now?"

"Um…I will be soon," Bobby said.

"Meet me in the café! I insist you let me buy you breakfast!"

"I don't know about that, Mr. Elliot. Management really doesn't like for the dealers to associate with—"

"Oh, to hell with all that," Elliot said. "If Larry Kent has a problem with it, tell him I said I'd never darken the door of this place again if you wouldn't join me."

Bobby hesitated for a moment, then gave in. How could he turn down such a unique opportunity? There were people in Cape Noire who would kill for a chance to break bread with Preston Elliot.

Twenty minutes later, Bobby Crandall was enjoying a hearty breakfast in the company of one of the most respected men in radio. Elliot was a little more himself now. His eyes had softened, and his voice had regained some of its typical warmth and confidence. "I made a complete ass of myself out there, didn't I?" he said with a rueful smile.

"Well…I wouldn't say that, Mr. Elliot."

"Of course you wouldn't. You're too polite."

"You were just having a bad night," Bobby said. "It happens to everyone."

"No, it wasn't that," Elliot said. "The plain truth is, I'm strung out from lack of sleep. I've been on the go for more than twenty-eight hours straight. I made the mistake of trying the sponsor's product yesterday, and I've been wired as a hummingbird ever since."

"What product?" Bobby asked.

"TenaciTea, my boy. It helps you hang in there. From a noose."

"I don't understand."

"That makes two of us. One bottle of that soda packs more punch than three full pots of coffee. Scratch that, four pots. I don't know how you kids drink the stuff."

"I don't drink it," Bobby said.

"Good for you, but don't tell anyone I said that. Without TenaciTea, I never would have been able to get my new show off the ground. Say, that's a pretty good pun! Maybe I can incorporate it somewhere…"

"What's this new show you keep mentioning?"

Elliot gawked at him. "You don't know about it? Have you been living in a cave?"

More like a tomb, Bobby thought.

Elliot leaned forward. He looked as if he were about to draw Bobby into a fantastic conspiracy. "My boy," he said, "in five short days, WXYZ will broadcast the debut episode of 'The TenaciTea Midnight Mystery Show', created by, written by, produced by, and starring none other than yours truly."

"Sounds exciting," Bobby said. "What's it about?"

"It's a thriller starring a ghoulish vigilante who operates right here in Cape Noire! He acts as a law unto himself, avenging the innocent and punishing the guilty. His name is…*Brother Bones!*"

"Brother Bones?"

"Yes!"

"You're doing a radio show about Brother Bones?"

"Yes!"

"Oh."

"Isn't it brilliant? I can't believe no one thought of it before me. I say, Bobby, are you all right? You look pale all of a sudden."

"I'm fine. If you don't mind me asking, what's Brother Bones like? In your show, I mean."

"Well, by day he's a dashing millionaire named…hey, that's a nasty cough, son. Are you sure you're okay?"

"I'm fine, really. A dashing millionaire, you say?"

"Yes, yes, a debonair man-about-town named Thomas Bonaparte. By night, he dons a skull mask and becomes a black-clad creature of darkness who strikes terror into the hearts of criminals!"

"Sounds like a busy guy. Does he…um… have anyone to help him out? Like an assistant?"

"Absolutely! He has an entire team of operatives, real colorful types. They're completely devoted to his cause, and he repays their loyalty by supporting them in lavish style."

"Lucky operatives," Bobby said.

Elliot laughed. "Aren't they, though? I have to confess, I enjoy writing those characters a lot more than Bones. He can be a bit of a Johnny One Note, what with all that obsessive grousing about justice and vengeance."

"I guess it could get old after a while," Bobby said.

"Let's hope the audience doesn't think so, at least not for a few years. Frankly, I think they're going to love it. I know I do! There is one thing that bothers me, though…"

"What might that be?"

"The sponsor wants Bones to pitch TenaciTea at the beginning and end of every show. I understand their perspective—they want to get their money's worth, after all—but I think it just kills the whole mood. Why would a guy like Brother Bones wax rhapsodic about a lousy soft drink? It's completely out of character."

"I'd have to agree with you on that one."

"Great minds think alike," Elliot said with a grin. "Well, I believe we could both use some sleep. Did you enjoy your breakfast?"

"I'll never forget it."

"Good! We'll do it again sometime."

"I hope so," Bobby said.

Dawn clawed at Cape Noire with painted red nails. The City of Night resisted the sun, clutching at every scrap of darkness, clinging greedily to every shadow, before finally giving in from sheer exhaustion.

In the dusty spare bedroom of Bobby Crandall's flat, Brother Bones stirred from his seat, went to the window, and closed the blinds. A creature of darkness in life, he was now even more so in death.

He settled back into the worn and tattered chair he occupied whenever he wasn't performing his grim duties. His powerful muscles relaxed, and his head slowly tilted forward until his chin rested against his chest. He was the consummate image of peaceful repose, but the image was misleading. Brother Bones was at rest, but he was not at peace. His mind was constantly filled with a deafening jangle of discordant memories. They crashed and clanged inside his skull, showering sparks as they collided, revealing in the brief flashes of light one scene after another of blood and pain and cruelty.

Here was Harry Beest, his old mentor in the ways of murder, teaching him the finer points of the garrote.

Here was his first contract kill, a grocer who refused to pay protection money.

Here was a vagrant he had beaten to death for no reason he could recall. Here was the girl at Sadie Levine's bordello…

The girl who had thanked him…

He and Jack had been sent to Sadie's on a simple mission; kill every living thing in the house. They smashed through the place like hell-bound trains, but then something happened that sent Tommy off the rails. One of the girls—young, pretty, and shot to pieces—looked up at him with her dying eyes and said, "Thank you."

Baffled, he leaned closer, hoping she would say more, but by then she was already gone.

Why did she say that?

He told himself that he had misunderstood her, but he knew that he hadn't.

Thank you.

He tried to brush it off, but he couldn't.

Thank you.

It stayed with him. Day after day it echoed between his ears, keeping away sleep and ease and whatever passed for happiness in his life. Soon her voice was joined by others, a constant chorus of sad and broken souls. *Thank you*, they said, over and over, louder and louder.

Thank you, Tommy.

Thank you for freeing us from our lives.

Thank you for killing us.

One day, it occurred to him that he was going insane. This terrified him, as he was unequipped to handle any problem he couldn't solve with a gun. Completely at a loss, he turned to the last person on Earth anyone would have expected Tommy Bonello to seek out; a priest. The man's name was Father Dennis O'Malley.

Tommy unburdened himself to the old man. His confession went on for hours, a catalog of crimes that flowed from his mouth like a stinking black deluge of death. When he was finished, he looked into the priest's eyes, and recoiled at what he saw there. Father O'Malley was just too honest. He couldn't hide the revulsion or the horror…or the pity.

"Are you sorry for what you've done?" the priest asked.

Tommy wasn't sure. Did he truly regret his misspent life? Or did he only regret what he was going through because of it?

Thank you...Thank you...Thank you...

The priest held out a hope. "But if you agree to what I am going to suggest," he said, "it will mean the end of this life of killing. The man you are will have to die."

Tommy agreed without hesitation, and then he ceased to exist. He passed through the healing waters, and was reborn as Brother Michael, a permanent resident of the monastery at Mt. Serenity. He was a somber man with haunted eyes, and his sleep was deep, though often disturbed by whispers from the restless dead.

He worked, and prayed, and was content, and one day he was seen by someone who recognized him.

And the day after that, his brother Jack came calling.

Jack brought an entire death squad with him, as if he were attacking an armed and hostile force, rather than a dozen helpless monks. Tommy begged him to spare them. "It's me you want," he said. Jack agreed and shot him in the head. Then he killed and burned all the others.

Tommy's death spared him the sight of his brothers in spirit being slain by his brother in blood, but it was no consolation. He found himself floating in a strange, inchoate netherworld of endless misty silence. He looked down at himself, and discovered that he no longer had a body. He tried to speak, but he no longer had a voice. Intangible and incorporeal, he had been reduced to a single, infinitesimal mote of consciousness, and then cast adrift in a dark and limitless void.

Is this Hell? he wondered.

No, someone replied. *Hell is far, far worse.*

From out of the emptiness, a figure appeared.

Hello, Tommy, said the girl from Sadie Levine's. Her lips did not move as she spoke, but her voice rang in his mind with painful clarity; a crystalline sound so exquisite that hearing it might have been fatal for a living man.

Hello, girl, Tommy replied. Have you come to thank me again?

The girl surprised him by smiling. *It is you who should thank me*, she said. *I have been sent to make you an offer.*

I'm listening.

If you accept, you will be allowed to return to the fallen world. There, you will be neither alive nor dead, neither man nor spirit. You will become an instrument of divine justice, existing only to protect the innocent and punish the guilty.

How will I know who's who?

I will guide you.

And if I refuse?

As I have said, there are worse things waiting.

Not much of a choice.

It is more than what you gave me.

True enough. All right, I accept.

I knew that you would, said the girl. *Prepare yourself. This is going to hurt.*

That's okay. Hurt is all I know.

The girl smiled again, and then she sent Tommy screaming back into the world. The first thing he saw was his brother Jack, pointing a gun at some helpless kid.

The boy's name is Bobby Crandall, said the girl. *He is an innocent. Save him.*

Jack turned to face Tommy. His expression held an extraordinary mix of amazement, malice, and stupidity.

That's how I must have looked to the girl on the night she died, Tommy thought, and even in his spirit form he felt sickened by the epiphany. He considered the killer before him; a vicious bastard who was, in every way that counted, a perfect reflection of himself. He studied the man, and discovered that he did, in fact, know more than hurt.

He knew sorrow.

And he knew rage.

Bones' reveries were broken by a flicker of light that danced at the corner of his eye. He turned and regarded the candle that rested on the stand beside his chair. It had, of its own accord, sputtered to life. He watched the tiny flame caper at the tip of the wick. This was, for him, a familiar sight. It was an omen that always heralded the arrival of...

"Where are you, girl?" Bones whispered. "You always follow the flame."

The room was suffused by a white and gold radiance, and the girl was before him. Bones gazed at her expectantly. Now she would reveal to him some travesty, give him a name, and he would take care of the rest.

He waited.

The girl said nothing. Her head was cocked to one side and she was frowning in concentration, as if listening for something she couldn't quite hear.

Bones grew restive. "What is it, girl? Why have you come to me?"

Her eyes met with his. *Something is about to happen.*

"Something's always about to happen. Could you be a little more specific?"

The Dragon is coming.

"What dragon? What are you talking about?"

There is much that is concealed even from me, said the girl. *I can only offer you this warning. The Dragon is coming to Cape Noire, and death is following in his wake.*

"Is that all you can tell me?" Bones asked.

The girl gave him a silent, inscrutable stare.

Bones, though annoyed by these Delphic ramblings, did not press her. By what right could he demand more? He was, if nothing else, a stoic.

Be wary, said the girl. *Be watchful. Remember what I have said.*

Then she was gone.

Bones shook his head. A warning that only made sense in retrospect wasn't a warning at all. Why did the girl trouble him with this nonsense?

"The dragon is coming," he said. "Fine. Let him come. I'll be waiting."

Bones heard the front door of the flat swing open, then footsteps as someone entered. *Bobby's back*, he thought. The young man passed by the bedroom door, twirling his key-ring on the tip of his finger and whistling a popular tune. Bones found a strange satisfaction in these mundane sounds. It was good to know that the boy was home. That he was close by if needed. That he was safe.

Bones closed his eyes, relaxed, and drifted back down the Styx into his private Hell.

In a luxurious office in a newly renovated building overlooking the Old Town docks, a tense young man was considering the facts as reported by Sally Paige.

"*This is apparently a gangland slaying, said Lt. Dan Rains,*" Edgar Shiloh read aloud. He lowered the morning edition of the Cape Noire Tribune and frowned at the man sitting across from him. "Does he really believe that?"

"No," said Officer Calvin Byrd.

"Then why did he say it?"

"He doesn't have much of a choice. The official line on Brother Bones is that he's a myth, a campfire story for gangsters. Rains couldn't talk about the guy even if he wanted to, which he doesn't."

Edgar drummed his fingers on the surface of his expansive desk. The desk, like the office, seemed a little too big for him. Come to that, Edgar's entire life seemed too big for him, at least to Byrd's way of looking at things.

Byrd had been selling information to Edgar for almost a year, and in that time he had come to like him fairly well, but never to respect him. "Little Eddie," as Byrd had secretly dubbed him, was a bright, energetic kid with a scholarly bent. He might have gone far as an historian—the career he had, in fact, trained for—but he would never make it as crime lord. The very thought made Byrd want to laugh. Eddie was just the sort of wispy, bookish introvert that Byrd had spent his entire childhood stomping the crap out of. A man like that could never command the respect—or inspire the fear—necessary to run a successful mob. If it didn't run counter to Byrd's own interests, he would counsel the boy to get out of the rackets altogether. Why bother with street-level crime when you owned something like TenaciTea?

As it happened, Byrd had guessed the answer to that particular riddle very early on. Eddie could make millions off of syrupy beverages, but it would all count for nothing without the respect of Robert Shiloh. Why Edgar idolized the old goat was anybody's guess, but the fact remained that he *did*, and if being a heavy hitter in the Cape Noire crime scene was what it took to get a pat and a smile from "Gramps," then Eddie would keep swinging until he hit something.

Little Eddie spoke. "Did you know my company was sponsoring a radio program based on this man, this 'Brother Bones' character?"

"I've heard the ads," Byrd said.

"So who is he, anyway? They say that he's some sort of zombie."

"So the story goes."

"You don't believe it?"

"Give me a break," Byrd said with a chuckle. "What am I, a little kid?"

Edgar laughed, too. "No undead avengers in this town, huh?"

"Not even one."

Edgar leaned forward and lifted an ivory-handled letter-opener from his desk. He idly twirled it in his hand like a small baton. "Do you know who Harry Beest is?" he asked.

Byrd, flummoxed by this odd turn in the conversation, simply nodded. "Everybody's heard of the ape-man," he said.

"The ape-man," Edgar said. "Why do they call him that?"

This was a rhetorical question. The grim fate of Harry Beest was a well-known Cape Noire legend. Beest had been Boss Topper Wyld's hard right hand until he committed the sin of getting up close and personal with Wyld's teenage daughter. As punishment, Wyld kicked Beest into the clutches of a scientist named Bugosi, who in turn subjected him to a surgical procedure as incredible as it was perverse.

"They call him that," Byrd said, "because his brain got transplanted into the body of gorilla."

"Have you ever actually met him?"

Byrd hesitated, then said, "No." Did the lie show on his face? He hoped not.

"Do you believe he's real?"

"Of course I do. He runs the biggest mob in Old Town. Although you're starting to give him a run for his money."

Edgar acknowledged the compliment with a smug little nod. "Tell me this, Byrd," he said, "if you can believe in a gorilla gangster, why is it so hard to believe in a killer ghost?"

Byrd shook his head. "That's apples and oranges," he said. "Beest is the product of a medical experiment. There's nothing supernatural about him. He's not the boogeyman, and neither is Brother Bones."

"What is he, then?"

"He's a vigilante with a gimmick. He's built up a legend around himself that gets the job half-done before he even shows up. Personally, I think the guy's a genius. Crazy as hell, but a genius."

"So, the bit with the skull mask is just…"

"Psychological warfare," Byrd said. "Like how the Scots used to paint themselves blue before going into battle."

Edgar brightened at this, just as Byrd knew he would. Sprinkling the conversation with that kind of pseudo-intellectual crap was a sure road to the kid's favor.

"That makes a lot of sense," Edgar said, "but why is he killing criminals in the first place? Isn't he supposed to be a crook, himself? I heard that he used to be a hired gun in the Wyld mob."

"He *used* to be," Byrd said, "but something changed him." He turned a palm up. "There's no man more righteous than the fallen man reformed. Just look at Saint Paul."

Edgar liked that one, too. Byrd silently congratulated himself. Then he had a thought, and decided to go for the trifecta. "I think that Bones sees himself as a modern-day Lionheart," he said, "driving the heathen from Cape Noire."

Edgar was beaming. He pointed the letter-opener at Byrd. "You know, I really think you're on to something. That theory explains so much about–"

He was interrupted by the phone. He answered it, then held it away from his ear as an explosion of profanity came bursting from the ear-piece. He put his hand over the receiver.

"Gramps," Edgar whispered to Byrd. "He's just found out about Oliver."

Byrd tried to look sympathetic, but he could feel a smile pulling at the corners of his mouth. The tinny voice of Robert "the Bruce" Shiloh sounded like the yapping of a tiny bulldog trapped inside the phone.

"Who the hell did you send down there?" barked the dog. "The goddam Little Rascals?"

"Now, take it easy, Gramps. I've already fired those guys and—"

"You *fired* them? You dummy! If I were still in charge, I'd have killed them all before breakfast! And I would've kicked your ass, too, just for good measure!"

Edgar grimaced. "Gramps, you're not being fair."

"Fair? Henry Oliver paid us a fortune for protection, and you couldn't keep him breathing for twenty-four hours!"

Byrd could practically see the spittle flying out of the phone. It was all he could do not to laugh.

"Gramps, there's no need to –"

"Shut up! What are people going to say about you, now? Would you like me to tell you?"

"Gramps, your heart—"

"Shut up! They're going to say that you can't honor your commitments! They're going to say that you're a worthless candy-ass who can't—"

"Gramps, you have to calm down. Remember what the Professor said about—"

Professor? Byrd wondered.

"Don't remind me!" shouted the Bruce. He then erupted into a coughing fit so intense that Byrd thought the old fart might crack a rib. After a moment, he recovered and resumed his wheezing rant. "I'm so tired of that condescending prick I could scream! He's all talk, just like you! You and your big words and big ideas! You walk around putting on airs like some goddam captain of industry, and meantime some nutcase in a mask makes you look like –"

Edgar hung up the phone. He looked at Byrd, his eyes a tempest of anger and humiliation. "You thought that was funny, didn't you?" he said in a quiet voice. "I could see it on your face. *Ha-ha, he's really tearing him a new one*, that's what you were thinking."

Byrd's face flushed. "I wasn't –"

"Don't insult my intelligence."

Byrd kept his mouth shut.

"He didn't really mean it, you know. It's the medication that makes him like that, that makes him talk to me like…" Edgar let the sentence hang. He dropped the letter-opener and slowly turned in his too-large chair. He gazed out the window at the gulls and the freighters and the murky, brackish water.

Byrd stared at the back of the chair for a minute. Was he being dismissed? He didn't really want to ask, but he didn't care to just sit there in silence, either. Also, there was the small matter of his fee. Unlike the public library, Byrd didn't share information for free.

"You're still here?" Edgar said.

Byrd grew irritated. What kind of childish crap was this? If Little Eddie wanted to sulk because of a dressing-down from Bobby the Bruce, he could do it after taking care of business. Maybe it was time someone explained the facts of life to him.

"Eddie," Byrd said, "I'm going to shoot straight with you. You're a smart kid, but brains never took a man to the top of the rackets in this town. They play a part, sure, but you need something else, something…"

"You don't think I'm man enough to run this mob," Edgar said.

I sure as hell don't, Byrd thought, but he said, "I wouldn't put it that way."

"How would you put it?" Edgar asked, low and soft.

"Frankly, Eddie, I don't think you've got a thick enough skin for this kind of work. Maybe you should stick to selling pop."

Edgar turned the chair back around. The tempest had faded, and been replaced by a cold stillness. He was holding a gun, and the gun was pointed at Byrd.

"Edgar?" Byrd said.

"Thanks for the advice, Byrd. I'm going to shoot straight with you, too."

Bethany Timms was working on the third draft of a letter for Mr. Shiloh when she heard a strange *pop* sound from behind his closed door. This startled her. Mr. Shiloh's office was sound-proofed. What could have happened in there that was loud enough for her to hear?

She glanced at the typewriter, and felt her blood run cold. The distraction of the sound had caused her to make a typo. She unrolled the paper, folded it, and put it in her purse. It was probably a futile measure—

EDDIE GAZED OUT THE WINDOW AT THE GULLS....

Mr. Shiloh counted the sheets of letterhead at the end of every day—but it was worth a try. Maybe, just once, he would forget to check.

The intercom on her desk buzzed, and she almost cried out, so frayed were her nerves at the realization of her mistake.

"Yes, Mr. Shiloh?" she said, leaning toward the speaker. It wasn't necessary for her to do that, but Mr. Shiloh had been specific in his instructions. *Always put your mouth close to it*, he had said. *I want to be able to hear your lips move.*

"Mrs. Timms, call Howard and tell him I need a cleanup in my office. Ask him to come through the private entrance"

"Yes, sir."

"After you've done that, call Bill Fraley at WXYZ and tell him I want five minutes of air time tomorrow at noon. I don't care what it costs."

"Yes, sir."

"And Mrs. Timms…"

"Yes, sir?"

"One more thing…"

Bethany's mouth went dry. "Yes, sir?"

"There's a mistake in this letter you've drafted to the Chamber of Commerce."

"I…I'm very sorry, sir."

"I know you are, Mrs. Timms. Please report to me at four-thirty for discipline."

Bethany's jaw was clenched so hard she thought her teeth might crack.

"Are you still there, Mrs. Timms?"

Bethany could not bring herself to reply. Then she thought of her little ones, and how much they depended on her.

"Mrs. Timms?" His voice was low and soft. It was the warning voice. The one he always used when he was about to explode.

She thought of her late husband, and, as she often did, prayed to God that he could not see her now. She made herself say the words: "I will report to you at four-thirty, sir. I will…accept whatever discipline you feel I deserve."

"Excellent," said Mr. Shiloh, and the intercom went dead.

Edgar sighed, leaned back in his chair, and regarded the dead man. It was probably a mistake to kill Byrd, but Edgar couldn't bring himself to regret it. It was enough that the cretin had sat there and smirked all through Gramps's tirade. To then turn around and insult him, accuse him of weakness…that was just too much.

There was a faint tapping at the private entrance. "Come," Edgar said. A pot-bellied man wearing gray coveralls and black cheaters waddled into the room behind a cart of cleaning supplies. The man blanched when his eyes fell on the sight of Byrd's mortal remains.

"Well, don't just stand there, Howard," Edgar snapped. He pointed at the crumpled body. "Get that trash out of here."

Howard gawked at Edgar. His eyes looked as large as a pair of silver dollars. He blinked and shook his head, visibly composing himself. "Yes, sir. Um…What about the chair, sir?"

Edgar scratched his chin. "Did the bullet exit the body?"

Howard took a deep breath. He stepped over to the corpse and gave it a gentle tug. Byrd slumped forward and tumbled to the floor. "The chair isn't damaged, Mr. Shiloh. It's just…soiled."

"Then I guess you should clean it up."

"Yes, sir, Mr. Shiloh," Howard said, and he went to work.

Edgar rolled his eyes. Howard's timid stupidity was almost as irksome as Byrd's insolence. Edgar swiveled his chair so that he wouldn't have to look at the man. He wanted to just get up and leave, but there was too much work to do. Not that anyone would thank him for his diligence. Quite the opposite, actually. *You and your big words and big ideas!*

"And my big profits," Edgar muttered. "You forgot those."

Why didn't Gramps appreciate anything he ever did? Why couldn't he comprehend the scope of Edgar's achievements? In his mind, the echo of Byrd's taunting voice replied that brains alone just weren't enough. *Maybe you should stick to selling pop.*

Edgar clenched his fists until his fingernails nearly drew blood from his palms. He had to fight the urge to get up and kick the cop's body around the room. Then he remembered his four-thirty appointment and settled down. A session with Mrs. Timms was the perfect thing to calm his nerves and clear his head. He was looking forward to it already.

His private line rang. He turned and reluctantly lifted the receiver, half-expecting another stream of vitriol from Gramps. "Hello?" he said cautiously.

"Mr. Shiloh, this is the Professor." The familiar voice, smooth as oiled metal, was laced with a vaguely European accent that Edgar had never quite been able to pin down.

Edgar straightened in his chair. "Do you have some good news for me?"

"Oh, yes. I have the final test results for the second-generation TenaciTea formula. It is, I am pleased to say, *twice* as addictive as the current product."

Edgar slumped. "That's good," he said, without enthusiasm. "Even better than we had hoped."

"Yes, also, we can proceed with your grandfather's operation in three days."

Edgar stood up. "Are you serious?"

"Of course I am serious. Why would I jest about a thing like –"

"Forget it! It's just a figure of…Listen, if there's even the slightest possibility that you're going to have to postpone again, then I need to know right now. I can't get his hopes up and –"

"Seventy-two hours, Mr. Shiloh. Perhaps even less. You have my word. Why don't you come by the laboratory this evening? I'll walk you through the procedure and introduce you to your grandfather's…host."

Edgar grinned. "Good enough," he said, and cradled the phone. He fell back into the chair and laughed aloud. He glanced at the desk, and his eye fell on the mistake-free letter Mrs. Timms had prepared for the Chamber of Commerce. He grabbed it, wadded it up, and tossed it through the air. It bounced off the back of Howard's head and fell neatly in the wastebasket.

It was going to be a good day, after all.

☠ ☠ ☠

A few blocks from the offices of the Shiloh Bottling Company was a shop on the ground floor of one of the oldest buildings in Old Town. A sign outside the door proclaimed it, *The Antiquarian Book Shoppe*.

Inside the small, dusty shop was a small, dusty man with thick glasses and a scruffy van dyke. If anyone were to look at him closely, which few were inclined to do, they might have discerned the lean and hungry child of the streets he had been in his youth. That feral boy was still there, lurking in the occasional glint from a pair of sea-green eyes, but the lad was well-concealed by graying hair and middle-aged paunch.

The man's expression was impassive as he sat quietly behind a cash register that, like him, dated from the previous century. His bland exterior, however, was belied by a nervous tension that coiled inside of him like a watch spring.

It's almost lunch-time, he thought, casting an anxious glance out the dingy plate glass window. *She's usually here by now. I hope she's all right. Good Lord, what if something's happened to her? There's no reason anyone would even tell me! I'd never know!*

The object of these agitated thoughts was a girl named April Moon. She had wandered into the shop one day looking for used textbooks. As she was browsing around, she noticed a chessboard on a corner table, the pieces all in place. "Do you play?" she had asked.

"Not for many years," the shopkeeper replied.

"My father taught me," she said. She regarded the board for a silent moment, then said, "Would you like to play a game with me sometime?"

He gave a nonchalant shrug. "I usually close the place for lunch. If you come back tomorrow at noon, you can show me how well your father taught you."

In the intervening months, the game had become an almost daily ritual. At first, the shopkeeper had viewed it as a mere courtesy to a friendly customer. At least, that's what he told himself. But as time passed he grew increasingly fond of the girl, and the lunch-time game had become a ray of sunlight in the gray doldrums of his normal routine. For the shopkeeper, a day without April Moon—as today was threatening to be—was a dark day indeed.

He absent-mindedly began to chew his thumbnail. This was the only outward sign he gave of the turmoil he was feeling. He had almost worried the nail to the quick when the small brass bell attached to the front door rang. He fairly leapt from his chair at the sound, but his heart sank when, instead of his young friend, a well-dressed man with swept-back silver hair stepped into the shop. He took in the surroundings with undisguised disdain.

"Are you Arthur Sinclair?" asked the well-dressed man.

"I am" said the shopkeeper. "May I help you?"

The man opened his mouth, but before he could answer, the bell chimed once more. A young, cream-complected blonde wearing a Cape Noire University sweater and a long black skirt stepped into the store. "Hi, Sinclair!" April said brightly. "Is the board already set up?"

Sinclair maintained his façade of drowsy indifference, but beneath it his soul was singing. The song was cut short by the well-dressed man. "Do you know this fellow?" he asked the girl, cocking a thumb at Sinclair.

"We play chess almost every day," April Moon said with a grin.

"Do you, now?" He turned to Sinclair. "Chess," he said, infusing the word with amused disgust, as if it were a thinly veiled euphemism.

Inside of Sinclair, the watch spring tightened.

The blonde's grin slipped a little. "Maybe I should come back later…"

"Oh, no," said the man. "Please stay! I'd like to have a witness for this."

Her grin disappeared completely. "I don't think—"

"This will only take a moment, April," Sinclair said. He settled his eyes on the well-dressed man. "I'm afraid you have the advantage of me, Mister…?"

"You don't need to know my name. What's important is this." The man reached into his coat and produced a small, leather-bound and gilt-edged volume. He lifted the book as if he were about to deliver a sermon from it.

"This item," he said, "was purchased from you by my wife for the sum of three hundred dollars. She presented it to me as a birthday gift. She was told by you that it was a first edition of the memoirs of Sir Edmund Merridewe."

"Yes, I remember that sale."

"You, sir, are a damnable cheat."

Sinclair's green eyes flashed. "I beg your pardon," he said.

"You may beg all you please," said the man, "but you'll get no pardon from me, you swindler! How dare you try to pawn this off as a first edition! I demand that you take back this trash and grant me a full refund at once!"

"Sir, you are mistaken. That book is an authentic first edition. If you wish to sell it back to me, well, I'll be glad to make you an offer…"

"Oh, so that's the way it's going to be, is it? Well, I suppose we'll just have to get the police involved in this matter!" The man looked at April, then back at Sinclair. "I'm sure they'll be interested in hearing about your sharp practice and your *chess games* with this young girl."

The watch spring snapped. "No need for all that," Sinclair said in a mild tone. "May I see the book?"

The man stalked forward and held the book in Sinclair's face as if it were a loaded gun. Sinclair reached up and took hold of the man's wrist. For a moment they were frozen in tableau, then the man's face blanched and he wrenched his hand away. He rubbed his wrist and goggled at Sinclair. "What did you just do?" he said.

"Don't worry, Chester," Sinclair said. "I didn't hurt you."

"You damned well better not have, you…What did you just call me?"

"I called you Chester, as in Chester Bunyan Banks, which happens to be your name."

"What kind of trickery…?"

"Not trickery," Sinclair said, wagging a finger. "The only trickster here is you. You know very well that book is the genuine article. You came in here hoping you could bullyrag me into giving you cash for it so you could buy your mistress a diamond bracelet."

Chester gaped. His jaw seemed to have become disconnected from his skull.

"You should be ashamed of yourself," Sinclair said. "I can't believe that a hero of the Great War would stoop to such tactics!"

"The war?" Chester croaked.

"Yes. You were a sapper in the 115th Engineers. When you came home, you parlayed your skills into a successful construction business."

"You must...You must have recognized me... "

"As an arrogant jackass? I certainly did. However, I will give you a bit of helpful advice. That little 'problem' you've been experiencing lately? It would go away if you'd lay off the sauce."

"What?"

"Remember what Shakespeare said about alcohol, 'It provokes the desire, but it takes away the performance.' Just because they finally repealed the Eighteenth Amendment doesn't mean you should drink the town dry, Chester."

Chester turned and began to stagger toward the door.

"And try not to eat so much bacon," Sinclair called after him as he left.

After the door was shut, and the little brass bell had fallen silent, Sinclair turned and looked into the pale blue eyes of his young friend. She stared at him for a moment, then burst into a loud peal of musical laughter.

"Oh, that was incredible!" she said, clapping her hands. "How did you do that? Can you show me how to do that?"

Sinclair could not help but smile, even though in his heart he was sure he had just made a terrible mistake.

"I'm afraid there's been a mistake," said Gerhard Krause to the pudgy young bellhop.

The boy turned to the dapper German with a nervous, slightly pained expression. Rivulets of perspiration ran from beneath his hat, presumably from the strain of carrying Krause's heavy bags. "Mistake?" he said.

Krause, not unsympathetic, gave a smile which softened his

otherwise sinister mien. Out of sheer whimsy, he wore a monocle and a Mephisophelean goatee that made him look like a *Fastnacht* devil. The effect was enhanced by the burnished black walking stick he swung by his side. It was all a bit too theatrical, perhaps, but the women seemed to like it. "We're at the wrong door," he gently informed the lad. He pointed his stick at the end of the hall. "I'm staying in the Presidential Suite."

Babbling a stream of apologies, the boy made haste for the correct room. Krause, chuckling to himself, followed in his wake. Then he stopped in mid-stride, his features a mask of baffled amazement.

Someone in this city just made use of the Insight, he thought.

But how could that be? He would be aware if any of the others were in Cape Noire, wouldn't he? They were all on their way, he knew, but none of them were here yet. He would have staked his considerable fortune that he had been the first to arrive.

Then it must be someone else, he thought. *And it was definitely the Insight. That feeling—that tug at the consciousness—is unmistakable.*

Krause closed his eyes and concentrated. An image began to coalesce in his mind. Books. Row upon row of books. A library? No, it was –

"Are you all right, sir?" the bellhop asked. He was standing by the open door, waiting for Krause.

"What? Oh, of course. Forgive me, my friend. My mind wandered for a moment. Tell me, do you know if there are any bookshops near here?"

The boy's eyes widened. "Several," he said with a grin. "Do you like to read? I love to read! I'm a writer myself, actually! I'm trying to sell a script for a radio show to –"

Krause raised a hand to stem the tide. "Please," he said. "I am thinking specifically of a shop specializing in used and rare titles."

The boy shook his head. "I'm sorry, sir. I'm afraid I'm not sure…"

"Never mind, lad," Krause interrupted. "It is of no importance."

The boy looked as if he wanted to continue the conversation, perhaps hoping to steer the topic back to his writing endeavors. Krause was too distracted to feign interest in the ambitions of sweaty bellhops. He cut the boy off by passing him a generous tip as he stepped over the threshold.

After the door was closed, Krause crossed the room and opened the blinds on a picture window which afforded a panoramic view of the city. *Magnificent*, he thought as he surveyed the spires and canyons of concrete and steel. *It's like a beautiful young wanton! Depraved and amoral, but oh so tempting…and so vulnerable.*

"If only you knew the danger you were in," he said, addressing the whole of Cape Noire. "You may rest easy, though. My brothers and I, we will protect you.

"We will save you from the Dragon."

A little after five o'clock, Howard the cleaning man, his shoulders slumped and his head hung low, exited the offices of the Shiloh Bottling Company. As he made his way through the crowded streets, a transformation began to occur. Behind the black cheaters, a hardness came into his eyes. His spine straightened, his shoulders squared, and his diffident waddle strengthened into a purposeful stride.

Moving at a brisk, energetic pace, he traveled for six blocks before stopping at a telephone booth in front of a drug store. There was a poster in the store window of a gleeful young boy popping the top on a bottle of TenaciTea. Was there a touch of madness in the boy's smile? A hint of desperation in his eyes? Howard decided that there was, and the thought made him chuckle as he dialed a number from memory.

After a few rings, a voice as rough and deep as the bottom of a gravel pit came on the line. "Yeah?"

"It's Howard, sir."

"You got some news for me?"

"Edgar killed Calvin Byrd."

"Are you kidding?"

"I'm afraid not. I spent most of the afternoon getting rid of the body."

"That crazy bastard! What did he do that for?"

"I don't know, sir. The best I can figure is that Cal insulted him somehow. He's a touchy kid, and violent as hell. I've told you the things he does to his secretary."

"Yeah, the little pervert!"

Howard smiled to himself. The boss sometimes revealed a puritanical streak when it came to other people's bad behavior. Nonetheless, his disapproval was sincere, and Howard happened to share it. There were just some things a man shouldn't do to a woman.

At the other end of the line, the boss was still grumbling. "I'd like to beat that punk from Hell to breakfast! You know how long it's going to take to find another cop as useful as Byrd was?"

Howard shrugged. "I'm guessing two or three hours."

"At least!"

"I do have some good news, though…"

"You found the books?"

"They were in a safe hidden behind a painting of Napoleon. I've made copies of everything. The entries are encrypted in a substitution cipher, but I'm sure I can crack it."

"How long will that take?"

"No more than a couple of days. By the end of the week, I should be able to tell you anything you want to know about Edgar Shiloh's finances."

The earpiece rattled with simian laughter. "Good job, Howard! Let me know when you've got something to show me."

"I will, Mr. Beest. Count on it."

It was well after sundown when Edgar Shiloh unlocked the door of the large townhouse he shared with his grandfather. He placed his hand on the knob, then hesitated. He stood there until his driver, Lewis, called out to him from the car. "Are you okay up there, Mr. Shiloh?"

Edgar looked over his shoulder at the man. Lewis Toole was one big bruiser; a dull-witted but completely reliable ex-pug with a flat nose and ears like a cauliflower garden. Edgar regarded him with the sort of detached affection that one can sometimes feel for a neighbor's pet. "It's okay, Lewis. I've just got a lot on my mind."

"Well, whatever it is, it's nothing you can't handle, Mr. Shiloh. You're the smartest guy I know."

"You think so? Someone told me today that brains weren't enough."

"Like hell! The guy who said that, he must be really stupid."

Edgar grinned. "He certainly was. Take the rest of the night off, Lewis. You've earned it."

Edgar remained on the stoop until Lewis had pulled away, then reluctantly opened the door. The house was dark save for a dim red flickering that emanated from an open door at the end of the hall. The hiss and crackle of a blazing fire echoed off the walls, making Edgar feel as if he had entered an antechamber of Hell.

I'll bet he's had that thing burning all day, Edgar thought. *It's going to feel like an oven in there.*

He briefly considered attempting to slip upstairs unnoticed, but decided against it. Better to get it over with now. Besides, he had an ace up his sleeve that was guaranteed to put a smile on the old man's face. Well, almost guaranteed.

Steeling himself, Edgar marched down the hall and into his grandfather's study. As he had anticipated, the room was as hot and airless as the inside of a crucible. The emaciated form of Robert Shiloh sat huddled in an armchair next to the fire. He was smoking a small cigar and clutching a glass of bourbon in one claw-like hand. Thin strands of stringy white hair hung from the back of his liver-spotted pate.

"Hi, Gramps," Edgar said.

The old man slowly turned to look at him. "Hello, dummy," he rasped. "You hung up on me today."

Edgar walked into the room and sat down beside the Bruce. "Yes, I did."

Gramps took a sip of his drink. "Ah, hell," he said, "I can't say I blame you. Tell you what, I'll forget it if you will."

"It's a deal."

"Good," said the Bruce. "But I still think you deserve an ass-kicking." He punctuated the statement with a papery chuckle that transformed itself into a vicious cough. It shook him with such ferocity that he lost his grip on the glass, but Edgar reached out and caught it before it struck the carpet. A few drops of the liquor splashed onto his sleeve, but most of it stayed in the tumbler.

"Fast hands," the Bruce gasped as the cough subsided. "Just like I used to have."

"Never as fast as you," Edgar said.

"Oh, spare me the bullshit. Look at you, not even twenty-five and you're already one of the biggest men in town. When I was your age, I was still breaking legs for Swede Jorgenson's father, the old bastard. I was fifty years old before I ran the docks. By the time you hit that age…Hell, boy, I bet you'll be running every racket in the country."

The old man sounded more jealous than proud, but Edgar was still genuinely moved. "You've never said anything like this to me before," he said.

"I know, I know. I'm pretty hard on you, Eddie, but it's for your own good. I'm just trying to toughen you up, make you strong. I screwed it up with your father…"

Edgar was shaking his head. "Gramps, please."

"I let your grandma spoil him," continued the Bruce, "and he turned out to be a worthless drunk." He clenched his fists. "I told her she was going to ruin him! I wish she'd lived to see what came of all that goddam coddling."

"Dad was weak," Edgar said sharply. "But I'm not. You'll see. Everybody will see."

"Maybe they will, at that," said the old man. "Now, what are we going to do about this guy, this Bonehead or whatever the hell his name is?"

"I'm going to get rid of him."

"How?"

"Turn on the radio tomorrow at noon. Brother Bones is going to find out what happens when you trifle with a Shiloh."

"All right," Gramps said. "I'll be looking forward to it."

Edgar smiled. A vote of confidence from Gramps! He couldn't remember when he had been so happy.

"So, why are you this late getting home?" asked the Bruce.

"I was busy at the office."

The old man grinned and patted Edgar on the arm. "Ha. Busy with that secretary, I'll bet."

"Maybe."

"If I was twenty years younger, I'd show you how to handle her."

"Then you may get your chance by the end of the week."

The Bruce's watery eyes bulged in their sockets. "Are you saying what I think…?"

"He called me this morning. He said we could do it in three days. He gave me his word."

Gramps turned to the fireplace, and took a deep, rattling breath. "Do you really think he can make it work?" he whispered.

"He's done it before."

The old man cringed. "That was different."

"The principle is the same. It'll work. I know it will."

"Have you actually seen it?"

"Seen what?"

"Don't be a smart-ass. You know what I'm talking about."

Edgar smiled. "I went by there earlier this evening. He showed me everything. It's incredible. Do you want to see for yourself? I could take you. We could go right now."

The Bruce stared into the fire. "I don't think so."

"Why not?"

"I'm…afraid to look at it. I somehow feel like, if I see it before the operation, it'll jinx the whole thing. Stupid, I know, but there it is."

Edgar placed a hand on the old man's shoulder. "It's all right. I understand."

Gramps gave him a sly smile. "Say, when it's all over, do you promise to let me have a turn with that Mrs. Timms?"

"I'll make her give you as many turns as you want."

The Bruce's yellow teeth gleamed in the firelight.

DAY TWO

It was just after midnight when Bobby worked up the nerve to knock on Bones' door.

"Bones," he said, "can I come in? I want to talk to you about something before I go to work."

Silence.

"Bones?"

Bobby sighed. After a minute or so, he gave up and walked over to his small kitchenette. He ran some water for coffee. After he lit the burner and placed the kettle on the stove, he turned and uttered a strangled cry at the sight of Brother Bones sitting at the table.

"Dammit, Bones! You scared the hell out of me!"

Was there a faint light of amusement in those black onyx eyes? Bobby thought there might be.

"What do you want?" Bones asked.

"Don't you ever take that mask off anymore?"

"Sometimes. When I'm alone. Is that what you wanted to talk about?"

"Oh, come on. You know better than that. Listen, you're not gonna believe this, but I was talking to Preston Elliot last night and –"

"Who is Preston Elliot?"

"You don't know who…?" Bobby shook his head. "Of course not. Why would you? Jeez, this is gonna take a while."

The kettle began to whistle. Bobby took it from the stove and prepared his coffee. He did not offer any to his roommate. To the best of Bobby's knowledge, Bones never ate or drank anything. He didn't even breathe, unless he needed the air to speak.

"I'm waiting," Bones said, using some air.

Bobby told him about Preston Elliot's new radio show.

"As you can see," Bobby said, "they've gotten a few of their details wrong. Well, except for the part about the 'lavish style' that you keep your sidekicks in. That's pretty much on the money. I mean, just look at this place."

Bones did not reply.

"Well?" Bobby said.

"Well, what?"

"Don't you have anything to say about what I just told you?"

"No."

"It doesn't bother you at all?"

"There are no innocents harmed by it, so it doesn't concern me. I couldn't care less."

"But that's not the point."

"What is the point?"

Bobby groaned. "Bones, they're making you into a shill for soda pop. It's an insult! Doesn't that make you…I mean…Dammit, Bones, it's beneath your dignity!"

Bones made the sound that he used for a chuckle. "You're offended on my behalf," he said.

"Well, yeah. I guess I am."

There was a moment of silence. Bones tilted his head slightly. He reached into his coat and pulled one of his silver-plated automatics. He laid it on the table.

"What is that?" he asked Bobby.

"It's a gun, Bones."

"Yes. Does it have dignity?"

Bobby frowned. "It's a weapon, Bones. It doesn't have feelings."

Bones nodded. "I am a weapon," he said. "There is a power that aims and fires me just as I aim and fire that pistol. That is my purpose. That is all that I am. I understand it and accept it. You should, too."

Bobby rose from the table. He washed his mug out at the sink and stepped over to the door. "So, you're just a talking gun, huh?" he said, reaching for his coat. "What does that make me?"

Bones said nothing.

"Yeah, that's what I figured."

Bobby opened the door, stepped out, then paused on the stoop. He turned to face Bones. "You know," he said, "I've always been grateful to you for saving my life. Even when I was scared to death of you, I was grateful. I just wanted to say that."

Bones said nothing.

"Thank you," Bobby said, and he closed the door.

Just after dawn, many hundreds of miles from Bobby Crandall's cold water flat, there was a fisherman on the road. He was driving a sporty little two-door convertible with the top down, so that he could better enjoy the coastal breeze. He was a handsome, square-jawed blonde in his early thirties, tanned and athletic, with light brown eyes and a winning smile.

He was very proud of the smile. It was his most effective lure. He practiced it constantly, and he knew exactly how to use it to flash everything from shy innocence to sly mischief. He could easily shift this protean smile into a charming grin. It was a beautiful grin. He'd had a lot of work done on his teeth, and they were all as straight and white as piano keys.

Over the years, a great many catches had been hooked by the smile, netted by the grin, and then pulled into a hostile place where they could no longer breathe. Shocked and terrified, they would twist and flail about, until they were finally bludgeoned and gutted by the laughing fisherman.

Like all sportsmen, he kept trophies. In the trunk of his car was a locked box filled with shiny baubles; pendants, earrings, wedding bands, and the like. It was foolish, he knew, to keep these things so close, but he couldn't help himself. He was tethered to the box in ways that even he couldn't fully understand. Where he went, the box went. Anything else would have been unthinkable.

Also in the trunk was a duffle bag filled with rope and duct tape and a selection of items purchased from several discreet mail-order companies. Like the box, the bag was always close at hand. One could never tell when these things might come in handy.

Like now, for example.

The catch was jogging down the side of the road. This, to the fisherman, was an intriguing novelty. He often ran for exercise himself, but he had never encountered it in a catch. They usually liked to play golf or tennis.

The fisherman licked his lips. This one was a prize. She was a lovely, leggy thing with a figure that even her loose-fitting exercise clothes couldn't diminish. Her long black hair was tied back in a ponytail, and the fisherman was seized by a compulsive need to wind his fingers through it and pull.

He took in all these details at a glance, then accelerated around a curve, drove another fifty yards or so, and pulled the car over. To his left was a steep, rocky incline, and to his right was an equally steep drop into the Pacific. It was a good place to limit someone's choices. He briefly considered a variety of strategies for going after the catch, but ultimately decided on the direct approach. This stretch of road was quiet in the morning, but far from abandoned. There wasn't any time for the niceties. He needed to get her close, and then bundled into the trunk as quickly as possible.

He reached under his seat and grabbed a small-caliber automatic. Watching his rearview mirror for the approach of the catch, he removed a roadmap from the glove compartment and stepped out of the car. He tucked the pistol into his waistband at the small of his back, lifted the map to conceal his features, and turned to face his prey.

The catch came jogging around the curve.

The fisherman mentally reviewed his collection of smiles. He selected *boyish,* and plastered it on his face. He listened for the approaching footfalls. When the catch was almost beside the car, he would lower the map in surprise. *Oh, hi! Gosh, I can't believe this, but I think I'm lost. Could you come here for a second? I sure could use a second pair of eyes…*

He stared at the map and waited. A minute passed, then two, but the catch did not come running by. He chanced a peek over the map, and his brow furrowed in confusion.

She was standing about a hundred feet away, staring at him.

He reached into his stash and grabbed *relieved, slightly embarrassed.* He lowered the map completely and said, "Hello, there. I'm sorry if I startled you. I'm just trying to figure out where I'm at."

The catch did not move, did not speak.

The fisherman shifted into *puzzled, a little hurt.* "There's no need to be unfriendly," he said. "Say, are you staying at that lighthouse I passed a couple miles back, the one they converted into a bed and breakfast? That's a nice place, isn't it?"

The catch started to jog toward him.

The fisherman's face lit up with *pleasantly surprised.* He started walking to meet the girl. The way she was going, it looked like she might run right into his arms.

She sped up.

Something was wrong. The fisherman's smile cracked and fell off his face.

Now she was running at full speed, closing hard and fast. She flicked her wrist, and a small, wickedly curved knife appeared in her right hand. It was a skinner. The fisherman owned one just like it.

He dropped the map and went for his pistol. He couldn't bring it to bear before she was on him. She leapt through the air and brought the knife down on his right shoulder, driving the steel straight into the nerve cluster known as the Brachial Plexus. The fisherman, knowing a few things about anatomy, understood exactly what was happening when his arm went numb and his pistol fell to the pavement. He had a second to marvel at the clinical accuracy of the catch's attack. Then she tore out the knife and laid open his cheek on the backstroke, exposing his perfect teeth.

Then she began to cut him in earnest.

The fisherman felt as if he had walked into a tornado filled with razors. Screaming, blinded with blood and pain, he ran for his car. Over his cries he could hear the knife singing through the air at his back, ripping his Arrow shirt and the flesh beneath it into a mass of red ribbons.

He hit the door of the car so hard that for a moment he was bent double. Before he could right himself, a hand closed around his left ankle, lifted it, and there was an electric burst of agony as his Achilles tendon was severed. The process was swiftly repeated with the right foot. Then he was roughly flipped into the roadster, his now useless feet flopping against the dash as he tumbled over.

The door was opened, and the fisherman's head fell back out of the car. He looked skyward at the face of the catch. She stared down at him with empty amethyst eyes.

"How…how did you know?" he gasped.

"You were holding the map upside-down," she said.

He groaned, and not just from the pain.

"Yeah," said the catch. "I decided to push you a little, just to see what you would do."

"You…pulled…a knife…"

"And you went for a gun. Bad move. So, what's your game, anyway? Were you planning to kill me?"

He managed a feeble laugh. "Eventually."

She smiled at him. He was surprised to see that it was *wry and ironic*; one from his very own repertoire.

"Well, it's been fun," she said, "but now I have to show you the door."

She slammed the car door on his head.

Then she did it again, and again, and again…

Dr. Samuel Marax gazed out at the Pacific from the gallery of the lighthouse tower. The rhythmic crashing of waves against the rocks mingled with the sound of the salt-laden wind to create a gentle roaring in his ears. He closed his eyes, and for a moment he had the sense that he was airborne; standing, perhaps, at the prow of some cyclopean airship, navigating the skies over a world of endless sea.

Oh, how Catherine would have loved this, he thought.

A shadow appeared on his imaginary skyline. He saw it only in vague outline, but he knew it immediately for what it was.

His eyes snapped open, and his hands clutched the iron rail.

You don't have to remind me. You don't. Thinking of her only strengthens my resolve. You have no reason to doubt my commitment…

Someone was ascending the stairs. Marax was annoyed. He had told the innkeepers—a dotty pair of senescent sisters—that he wanted some time alone. Why couldn't people comply with even the simplest requests?

Marax turned and scowled at the glass door to the gallery. He was surprised to see his assistant, Erika, appear at the top of the stairwell. He was even more surprised to see that she was covered in blood.

"Have you been injured?" he asked as she joined him on the platform.

"No, sir," Erika replied. "I had to kill someone while I was out on my morning run."

Marax frowned. "Details, please."

Erika related her encounter with the fisherman. Her account was succinct but thorough. When she finished, Marax gave a satisfied nod. "The fellow got exactly what he deserved," he said. "Any witnesses?"

"No, but I had to drive back here in his car. It was a risky move, but less dangerous than a two-mile run in this condition."

"The body?"

"Stuffed in the trunk. But I'm afraid we have another problem."

Marax sighed. "Don't tell me. When you came back, you were seen by the innkeepers."

Erika nodded. "I tried to slip by them, but…"

The Doctor's mouth quirked at the thought of how the old maids must have reacted to the sight of the blood-soaked Erika. "Where are they now?"

"I locked them both in the fruit cellar. Do you want me to kill them?"

Marax thought it over. "No," he finally said. "Leave them to providence. Get yourself cleaned up and then pack our things. We're going."

"You don't want to take any other precautions?"

Marax shook his head. "With any luck, the sisters won't be found for a few more days, and by then it won't matter anymore."

"Yes, sir," Erika said, and she disappeared down the stairs.

Marax kept his eyes on the horizon. The dark shape, no longer only in his imagination, swooped in lazy circles through the azure sky.

Soon, my friend, thought Marax.

Yes, replied the darkness. *Soon.*

Krause waited until the twins were gone before lighting his first cigarette of the day. It was a small courtesy—inconsequential, really—but one should be gallant at every opportunity. The girls would be far more appreciative of the bonus he had slipped into their purses while they slept. They had certainly earned it. Such energy and invention! He grinned at the memory. Perhaps there would be time to seek them out again before he had to leave the city.

He called room service to order breakfast, and just as he hung up, the phone rang. He answered, and was pleased to hear a familiar English accent.

"Good morning, Krause."

"Harrow! How are you, my friend? Are you in Cape Noir?"

"Not yet," replied Sterling Harrow. "I expect to be there tomorrow. Have you heard from any of the others?"

"No, but something extraordinary has happened that I really must share with you."

"Yes?"

Krause told Harrow about the flash of Insight. "Whoever this fellow is," Krause said, "he's being very parsimonious in the use of his power. I haven't felt anything since yesterday."

"You're certain it wasn't one of the brethren?" asked Harrow.

"I'm positive. I was wondering if perhaps you could…"

"Could what?"

"Use some of your special skills to track him down."

"What special skills?"

Krause smiled. "Don't be coy, Sterling. I know you've been using the Insight to master certain…abilities."

There was a long silence. "When did you discover this?"

"Two years ago."

"Ah, you mean that night when –"

"Yes, in London."

"I didn't think anyone noticed."

"No one did. Except me."

"Have you told any of the others?"

"About you dabbling in the Dark Arts? I have not. You would be cast out of the Order, and I can't be responsible for such a thing. The guilt would destroy me."

"That's very witty, Gerhard. Let me assure you, the guilt would be the least of your worries. However, I do appreciate your...discretion. I am in your debt."

"We can discuss that another time. Now, will you help me find this stranger?"

Harrow said that he would. Krause bade him good day and hung up. He stepped over to the radio and switched it on. He was surprised to hear the soothing sounds of Bach's *Bourrée in E minor* issue from the speaker. It seemed that the local station was not entirely given over to vulgar entertainments. There was a knock at the door.

"Yes?"

"Room service," said a falsetto voice.

Krause was pleased. He always appreciated prompt service. He opened the door and made a single, sharp intake of breath at the sight that greeted him.

The tall, muscular man behind the food cart was not a bellhop. His face, scarred but handsome, wore a smile as cold as a mid-winter moon. He was aiming a Mauser at Krause's stomach.

"*Guten Morgen*, Krause," said the man, not in a falsetto.

"Hello, Zorn," Krause said. "I didn't know you worked at this hotel."

Zorn grinned. "The young lady who was delivering this met with a fatal accident."

Krause nodded. When the accident was Josef Zorn, the killer known as the Hessian, the result was usually fatal.

Zorn gestured with the pistol. "Aren't you going to invite me in?"

Krause backed up enough to allow Zorn into the room.

"Go sit at the table," Zorn said. "You should try the Eggs Benedict. They're quite good."

Krause silently obeyed. The Hessian gave a slight bow and set out the food. Krause made a production out of arranging his napkin, pouring the coffee, preparing the toast...all the while sending out frantic calls for help to the brethren. He received no answer. They were still too far away.

"What are you thinking about, Krause?"

Hear me, my brothers! I am in deadly danger! Help me! Help me! HELP ME!

"I was just wondering if you would like to join me," Krause said.

☠ ☠ ☠

In the modest room where he lived at the back of the Antiquarian Book Shoppe, Arthur Sinclair was enjoying his orange juice and working on the crossword in the morning Tribune.

"*Wyrm*," he muttered. "Six letters." He thoughtfully chewed the pencil. "Wyrm? Oh, of course, it's—"

HELP ME!

Sinclair fell from his chair. His glass tumbled to the floor and shattered, covering him with juice.

HELP ME! THE HESSIAN IS HERE! HE HAS COME TO KILL ME!

"Good Lord!" Sinclair said. "What on Earth...?"

WHO IS THAT? SOMEONE IS THERE, I CAN SENSE IT!

Sinclair cried out in pain. "Stop it," he gasped. "Please, you're going to split my skull."

I am sorry. Can you still hear me? Please answer!

"I can hear you," Sinclair said. He tried to stand up, but couldn't. His legs felt as if they were made of rubber.

You are the man in the bookshop, yes?

"I suppose so," Sinclair said. "Who are you? How did you get inside my head?"

I am communicating with you through the Insight.

"What? That's impossible! I'm the only person who knows how to use—"

Stop babbling! My life is in danger! You must help me! Call the police and tell them they must come to...come to...they must...

"What? What do you want me to tell them?"

Drugged...he drugged...coffee...

"Concentrate," Sinclair said. "Where are you? Give me a name! Part of a name! Anything!"

I...can't...I...

"Please! I want to help you!"

Oh...God...

"Please," whispered Sinclair. The only reply was a faint buzz which slowly dwindled into silence.

Krause was uncomfortably numb. He felt as if he were fluttering about inside of his own body, like a firefly trapped in a jar.

"I see the drug has taken effect," said the Hessian. "You should have another few moments of consciousness, then a deep and restful sleep."

"Please…" Krause's voice was a barely audible exhalation.

"Tut, tut," chided Zorn. "You brought this on yourself. You and your endless womanizing! You should have known that Graf Von Stolberg would never forgive you for dallying with his wife. She has already been chastised. Now it is your turn."

"No…"

"Yes," said Zorn. "The Graf has specified that your death be slow and painful. I will make preparations while you doze. When you awaken, I will fulfill the terms of the contract."

"No…"

"Yes," said Zorn. "And don't bother to hope for any last-minute escapes. Your days of fast talk and cunning schemes have come to a close, *mein Freund*. Believe me when I say that, for next few hours, you won't be able to concentrate on anything but your own agony."

"No…"

"Yes," said Zorn. "Stop fighting it, Krause. Go to sleep. Enjoy your final moments of peace in this world. When you open your eyes, the hell will begin."

The Hessian reached into a cabinet at the bottom of the food cart and produced a black medical bag. Krause, his heart brimming with horror, closed his eyes.

The strains of Bach's melody followed him into the abyss.

Sinclair's hands were shaking. He cut his fingers twice on the broken glass before he could get it all cleaned up. He stepped into the bathroom to clean and dress the small wounds. He glanced at himself in the mirror, and was startled to see that his nose had been bleeding.

"What just happened?" he asked himself.

He said he was using the Insight…

"Impossible," Sinclair said. "I'm the only person who knows about the Insight. Mr. Mendoza would never have lied to me about a thing like that."

But what if he did?

"He didn't."

"WHAT JUST HAPPENED?"

Okay, what if he was wrong? What if there are others he didn't know about?

The brass bell rang.

"Sinclair? Where are you, pal?"

April! What is she doing here this early?

"Sinclair?"

"I'll be there in a moment," Sinclair called out. He reached for a washcloth and began to vigorously scrub the blood from his face.

"So!" exclaimed Brother Bones. "That arch-fiend thinks he can escape me in his zeppelin, does he? Gus!"

"Right here, Boss!"

"Go to the hangar and prepare the Wing-Bone! We shall give chase!"

"Sure t'ing, Boss!"

Bones fell silent. He glowered at Gus.

"Uh, is something wrong, Boss?"

"Why did you do that? I told you not to do that."

"Do what?"

"Say *t'ing* instead of *thing*. It makes you sound like a moron."

"I'm very sorry Preston," said Steve Traynor, not sounding very sorry. "It just feels natural for Gus to speak that way. Listen, why don't you let me do it my way for a full rehearsal, just once. I think that you'll agree with me when you've heard—"

"Dammit, Steve! I created the character! I wrote the script! Don't try to tell me about—"

Preston Elliot clenched his teeth, biting off the words. *Actors!*

They were rehearsing in WXYZ's new fifth-floor studio. It was designed to Elliot's specifications, and he had personally selected the room's state of the art equipment. He had also selected the talent, so he had no one but himself to blame for that.

Elliot was distracted a flicker of motion at the corner of his eye. He turned and saw one of the engineers waving at him from behind the soundproof glass partition. Elliot nodded, and there was a click on the intercom.

"Sorry to interrupt Mr. Elliot, but Mr. Fraley asked me to remind you of your appointment."

Elliot checked his watch. "Okay, everyone, listen up. I have to go to a meeting. I'll be gone for about an hour. Fred, you stand in for me. If anyone else has random urges to improvise, please get them out of your system before I return."

Elliot stepped into the hall. He was joined by a balding, rotund man chewing an unlit cigar. "Preston, do we really have time for this?" Bill Fraley asked. "I appreciate what you're trying to do, but there are only so many hours in the day and I don't think that– "

"Bill," Preston said.

"Yeah?"

"How did you get started in this business?"

"I worked in the mailroom. You know that."

"Yes, and I used to be a lowly technician. In fact, I helped put the transmitter on the roof of this very building. Have I ever mentioned that?"

Bill rolled his eyes. Preston never got tired of boasting about his humble beginnings.

"And look at us today," Elliot continued, "a pair of Horatio Alger characters come to life. You're the station manager, and I'm the idol of millions. But we had a little help getting here, didn't we?"

"You're talking about Mr. Lofficier," Bill said.

"Yes, I am."

Bill nodded. His predecessor, John Lofficier, was a radio legend. The man had a preternatural knack for spotting talent in the unlikeliest of places, and he had given more than a few people chances they otherwise never would have had.

"It's a way to honor his memory," Elliot said. "That's why I make time for this every week. Do you understand?"

"You really think one of these kids is going to be the next Preston Elliot?"

"I hope they're aiming higher than being the next Bill Fraley."

"Ha-ha. Very funny."

They entered a sunlit meeting room bisected by a long conference table. In the center of the table was an ice chest filled with bottles of TenaciTea. Both men ignored it and went for the coffee percolating in the corner.

"So, who's on the agenda?" Elliot asked.

"A young man named Milton Pender," Bill said. "He's got an idea for something called 'The Black Haze'."

"Sounds interesting. Let's hear what he's got to say."

April had accepted Sinclair's offer for a glass of juice. "This is really good," she said.

"Fresh squeezed," said Sinclair. "It's my only indulgence."

"Really? Maybe you should get out a little more."

That stung. Sinclair changed the subject. "I wasn't expecting you for another few hours."

"I couldn't wait that long. I let you put me off yesterday, but now I want to hear it all. C'mon Sinclair! Spill it! Tell me how you read that guy's mind."

Sinclair chewed his lower lip. He knew he shouldn't but…God, she was beautiful! When was the last time a beautiful woman had been interested in anything he had to say? Would it really be so bad to share it with her? Mr. Mendoza had always said to be discreet, but he never actually, specifically, categorically forbade…

April affected an exaggerated frown. "If you don't tell me, I'm going to be *awful* disappointed."

Sinclair stepped over to the door, locked it, and turned the OPEN sign to CLOSED.

"This is going to take a little while," he said.

"Come in, Mr. Pender," Bill said. "Let me introduce you to—"

"Preston Elliot!" Pender said as he shouldered past Bill. "This is such an honor! You're one of my heroes!"

The pudgy kid grabbed Elliot's hand and shook it like he was pumping for oil. Bill wasn't impressed. It was a cool morning, but the boy's shirt was already wet with perspiration. Bill could only imagine how moist his handshake must be.

"Would you like a cup of coffee?" Elliot asked, pulling his hand away and discreetly wiping it on his pants.

Pender's red-rimmed eyes fell on the ice-chest. "Thanks, but I'd rather have a TenaciTea. Do you mind?"

Bill and Elliot exchanged a look. "Help yourself," Bill said.

The kid reached for a bottle, twisted off the cap, and drank half of it in a single draught. "Thanks a lot," he said. "I didn't realize I was so thirsty."

Elliot gave the kid an encouraging smile. "You're just nervous," he said. "Why don't we sit down and you can tell us about your idea."

"Okay! Sure! I'll be glad to –" Pender interrupted himself with a noisy and prolonged belch. His face went crimson. "I'm…excuse me."

"Think nothing of it," Elliot said. "Let's hear your pitch."

"You call it the Insight?" April asked.

"Yes," replied Sinclair. They were sitting at the chess table. The pieces were in place, but neither of them were interested in playing.

"Have you always had it?"

"No. It was…I guess you'd say *bequeathed* to me by Mr. Mendoza. He literally passed it to me on his death-bed."

"Who was Mr. Mendoza?"

"The original owner of this bookshop. He took me in off the streets when I was just a boy and practically adopted me. When I turned eighteen, he told me about the Insight and started preparing me for the day when I would wield it."

"Wield it how?"

"As a member of the Order."

"Jeez, Sinclair, are you going to make me pull this out of you one little piece at a time? What kind of Order?"

Sinclair involuntarily straightened in his chair. "I am the only surviving member of the Order of the Aspen Lance."

April's eyes widened. "That sounds pretty impressive. Are you some kind of a monk, or something?"

"More like a warrior," Sinclair said, and immediately regretted it. He had regarded himself as such for many years, but never actually put it into words. Now, saying it aloud, he cringed at how pompous it sounded. He half-expected April to laugh at him, but she merely nodded.

"If you're a warrior," she said, "then you must be fighting for something. Or against something…" The question was there in her voice.

Sinclair took a deep breath. "As a Lancer," he said, "my sacred trust is to defend the world from the Dragon."

She did smile a little at that one. "You mean like Saint George?"

"No. Saint George fought a dragon. I have to fight *the Dragon*."

Pender couldn't stay seated. He was pacing back and forth in front of Bill and Elliot, waving his arms in broad, dramatic gestures. "Crime is a weed," he said. "It chokes the garden of justice. It winds itself around the hearts of men and feeds on the evil that lurks there." He paused. Elliot nodded at him. He continued. "There is one man who can pull that weed. One gardener who can rescue the flowers of righteousness. He is the man known as…*the Black Haze!*"

Bill glanced at the sheaf of papers the young man had handed him. "So this guy's a vigilante?" he said. He gave a sideways glance to Elliot, who ignored him.

"He is a creature of Darkness, but he serves the Light," said Pender. Bill could hear the capitals. "By day he is a dashing millionaire named Haywood Holt. But when the sun sets, he straps on his twin silver-plated automatics and becomes –"

"A black-clad avenger who strikes terror into the hearts of criminals," finished Elliot. His eyes were closed and he was pinching the bridge of his nose.

"Exactly!" Pender said. "Have you…" He trailed off as he took note of Elliot's expression. "Is something wrong?"

Elliot opened his eyes. "Do you listen to WXYZ very much, Mr. Pender?"

"Of course! Well, only in the afternoons. I'm a bellhop at the Chandler Arms, so I don't get to tune in much in the evenings. I'm sorry if…Have I said something…?"

"It's all right, son. I guess you haven't heard the ads."

Pender was sweating more than ever. "I don't understand."

Bill spoke up. "Listen, kid, we're already doing something like this. We're broadcasting a live premiere in four days. You should study your market more if you want to make it in this business."

Elliot gave Bill a cutting look. "And someone should vet these proposals better before inviting the writers in for a meeting," he said.

"Does this mean you're not interested?" Pender said. His bloodshot eyes were glistening. He would have looked more hopeful if he was headed for the electric chair.

"Not in this particular idea," Elliot said. "However, I want to say that some of the things you've written here are…"

Pender turned and walked out the door.

Bill got up and went after him. He reached the door in time to see that Pender's walk had accelerated to a run, and Bill caught a final, fleeting glimpse of the kid as he rounded a corner at the end of the hall.

Bill turned to Elliot. "Do you think I should call security?"

Elliot was looking at the papers Pender had left behind. "No," he said.

"What a nut," Bill grumbled.

"He was just scared," Elliot said. He gestured toward the ice chest. "And I think he's been hitting too much of that poison. Did you see his eyes?"

"Aw, for Pete's sake, Preston. It's just a soft drink."

Elliot didn't respond. He continued to sift through the papers. "You know," he said after a moment, "I can't shake the feeling that the kid had talent. I wish he would have stayed and let me talk to him."

"Well, he didn't. Maybe the next one will be better. I'm headed back to my office unless there's something else…"

Elliot stared at Pender's ill-fated proposal as if it were a riddle he needed to solve. "It winds itself around the hearts of men," he murmured, "and feeds on the evil that lurks there."

Bill gave him a few more seconds, then shook his head and walked away.

Elliot took a pen from his pocket and tapped it on the table. After a moment, he removed the cap and wrote something in the margin of the first page:

Who knows what evil lurks in the hearts of men?

He stared at the phrase. He said it aloud, his voice registering just above a whisper. He got up from the table and stepped over to the window.

"That boy had potential," he said to himself. "I hope he doesn't give up."

He stayed there for a few minutes more, then turned to go back to the studio. On his way out the door, he dropped *The Black Haze* into the trash.

Milton couldn't stop running. He earned a lot of hostile looks from irate pedestrians who barely avoided colliding with his ample frame.

They hated me!

He would have run to the other side of the world if he could, but his body only carried him three blocks before it gave out. He staggered into an alley, braced himself on the wall, and threw up.

I made a fool of myself and they hated me!

He retched until his stomach was empty, then his dry heaves transformed into sobs. He trembled from head to toe, and he would have collapsed into the filth if not for the support of the wall.

"Stupid," he gasped. "Stupid. Stupid. *Stupid!*"

"Hey, Pender! Is that you?"

Milton's head snapped around. At the mouth of the alley was a diminutive man wearing a wrinkled suit and a gray homburg. It was Mr. Gordon, Milton's boss from the Chandler Arms.

"Sir?" Milton said in a tremulous voice. He could barely credit his eyes. What malicious whim of Fate had brought the man to this particular place at this exact moment? Milton felt like throwing up all over again.

"What the hell's wrong with you, kid? Are you drunk?"

"No! No, sir. I'm just...I'm not feeling well."

"Well, get over it. You're supposed to be on the job in a few hours, and I damned well expect you to be on time."

"Yes, sir. Whatever you say."

Gordon stepped a little closer and looked up at Milton. "Jeez, kid," he said. "You really do look like crap." His eyes narrowed. "Are you sure you haven't been into the booze?"

"No, sir. I swear it."

Gordon shook his head. He looked at his watch. "Listen, Pender. I think you should grab something to eat before your shift starts. Do you have any money?"

"Thank you, Mr. Gordon, but I'm not very hungry."

"You sure about that? I'm not a total Scrooge, y'know. I'm willing to help you out if you're in a pinch."

Milton thought about it. He wiped his mouth with the back of his sleeve. "Well," he said, "if you don't mind, I think I would love to have a TenaciTea."

"In the year 1134," said Sinclair, "in the back country of Spain, the Dragon appeared and began slaughtering people and livestock. It rampaged all over La Mancha, until it was challenged by a brave *caballero* named Don Julio Jiménez Luquero."

April grinned. She was having fun. "Was he a *parfit gentil knight*?" she asked.

"What? Oh, you mean like in Chaucer? I don't know. *Parfit* maybe. I'm not so sure about *gentil*. Don Julio charged the Dragon and ran him through with an aspen lance. The Dragon, wounded but not dead, vowed vengeance on Don Julio and disappeared into a puff of smoke."

"He 'vowed vengeance'? He could talk?"

Sinclair smiled. "Dragons can talk in all the old stories, can't they?"

"Yeah, but those are just stories. According to you, this dragon was real."

"That's right."

"So what does any of this have to do with you?"

"Don Julio took the threat of the Dragon seriously. He devoted the rest of his life to preparing for the monster's return. He lived as a hermit; secluding himself with ancient texts, meditating, consulting with wise men from around the world. At some point, no one knows exactly when, he stumbled upon the secret of the Insight."

"Ah," said April, "now we're getting somewhere!"

Sinclair nodded. "Don Julio felt that the power of the Insight would be an invaluable weapon in the struggle against the Dragon, should he ever reappear. After mastering the ability himself, the Don selected a single acolyte, and the Order of the Aspen Lance was born.

"For eight hundred years, every generation has been watched over by a lone Aspen Lancer, who, at his passing, grants the Insight to a successor who takes up the task of protecting humanity from the Dragon."

April laughed aloud. Sinclair was offended, but only a little. There was something so warm and good-natured about it that he couldn't bring himself to be truly angry.

"That's a great story," she said at last. "How much of it do you think is true?"

"All of it, of course."

April smiled and regarded Sinclair with a look that seemed to say, *There you go again, you rascal.*

"Here," Sinclair said, "let me show you something." He reached inside his collar and pulled up the pendant concealed beneath his shirt. "The Insight isn't the only thing Mr. Mendoza gave me."

April squinted. "What's that supposed to be? It looks like a wood shaving."

"You might call it my badge of office," Sinclair said. "It is an authentic piece of Don Julio's aspen lance."

April lifted her brows. "That's pretty medieval, Sinclair. Do you have a piece of the True Cross to go with it?"

Sinclair was annoyed. "Why do you keep making jokes? You've seen what the Insight can do. If you accept the reality of my power, why do you scoff at everything else I tell you?"

April waved a hand "It's too much like a fairy tale, Sinclair. But I'd like for it to be true. I really would. The world is such an awful, ugly place. It would be wonderful to believe that there really was a time when honest-to-God noble knights fought talking dragons."

"Then believe it! Do you really think I would just make all of this up?"

April shook her head. "Of course not. I know you're not lying. I just think that you're wrong. There's a difference. Don't take it personal."

Sinclair did take it personal. He felt hurt, and he was shaken by this casual dismissal of his most fundamental beliefs. On the other hand, what had he really expected? Doe-eyed hero-worship and a request to learn at his feet? *Oh, Sinclair, it's all so glamorous! Will you teach me the sacred mysteries?*

"Why are you smiling?" April asked.

"I thought of something ridiculous," Sinclair replied. "I do that sometimes."

"I'm glad you're not upset. That was pretty tactless, some of those things I just said. I didn't mean to be so blunt."

Sinclair rose to his feet. He was grateful that she cared about his feelings, but he was ready for April to go. "Don't worry about it. I guess you should be getting to class, now."

April stayed in her seat. "I've still got some time."

"Is there something else you wanted to ask?"

April gently tugged at her left ear. It was a familiar mannerism. Sinclair had often watched her do it as she contemplated a chess move. "Do you... Do you have to be touching someone to see their thoughts?"

Sinclair eyed her warily. "Yes."

"Is there anything else you can do? Can you see the future?"

"I've never had a clear vision of something that was going to happen, if that's what you mean. But I have had feelings, flashes of intuition. There was the week before the crash in '29, for example. I knew that something terrible was going to happen that Thursday, but I wasn't sure what."

"Have you had any feelings like that lately?"

Sinclair thought of the voice crying for help, but elected not to mention it. "I have nightmares all the time," he said. "I think that's part of the price one has to pay for the Insight. It comes with a lifetime of the Dragon haunting your dreams."

"Hmm. Could you use it to pick numbers at roulette, or something like that?"

"I wouldn't if I could."

"You wouldn't? Come on!"

"I would never use the Insight for such a base purpose. It would be wrong."

April stared at him, whether in admiration or incredulity, he couldn't be sure. "You really mean it," she said.

"Yes, I do."

"Ha! Sinclair, you're one in a million."

"Thanks, I guess."

She stood up and held out her hand. "Will you do it to me? Like you did with that man?"

Sinclair was taken aback. He stared at the long, delicate fingers. What would it be like to touch them? To travel through them into the kaleidoscope of her dreams and memories?

"Please," she said. "I just want to know how it feels."

So do I, thought Sinclair.

He raised his hand…and lowered it with a sigh.

"April," he said, "You really don't know what you're asking. It's not like getting your palm read or your fortune told. You would be letting me see your most intimate –"

April reached forward and took his hand.

The Hessian paused in his labors to regard the flayed and mutilated thing that had been Gerhard Krause. The Graf would be well-pleased. Though Zorn had taken no particular pleasure in the work, he had made an excellent job of it. He took out a camera to make some pictures for Von Stolberg's scrapbook. The bulb flashed. A gurgling sound issued from Krause's lipless mouth, and tiny red bubbles appeared between his broken teeth.

Zorn shook his head. "Still clinging to life, eh?" he murmured. He considered granting the fellow a *coup de grace*, but decided against it. Such a mercy would be in violation of the spirit of his contract. No, the man would just have to suffer.

The Hessian divested himself of his blood-soaked clothes and stepped out of the bedroom into the parlor area of the suite. It was a very impressive room. If he ever returned to Cape Noire, he would make a point of requesting it.

Behind him, Krause moaned.

"Oh, do be quiet," Zorn said. "I am going to get cleaned up now. I advise you to expire as soon as possible. I plan to empty a bottle of acid on you before I leave, and I think you would like to be dead for that. I certainly would, if I were you."

Krause moaned again. The Hessian rolled his eyes, turned up the radio, and headed for the bathroom.

See the girl. Lean and strong and laughing. She runs along a weathered wooden fence, calling to the lowing cattle. Her corn silk hair billows on a warm summer breeze, the air redolent with the scent of freshly-turned earth. Sinclair is beside her, with her, inside her. He feels her inexpressible joy and energy and love of simply being alive and—

Home. Oh, it's so wonderful. I want to stay here forever. I want—

See the man. Denim-clad and stern of countenance. His eyes are shadowed beneath the brim of an old straw hat. He lifts the hat ever so slightly and his eyes are blue like the girl's. His grim face breaks into a smile like the sun and he opens his arms wide and Sinclair knows that this man is—

Daddy! What are you doing here? Oh, Daddy they told me you were—

See the house. Dark and cold and empty. There is a wreath on the door. A woman sits alone on the edge of the porch. Her hands cover her face. Her body trembles and—

Mama please stop crying. What they said was a lie! Daddy's the strongest man in the world! He can't be—

See the grave. Carefully tended. The years pass by but the flowers are always—

Mama, please don't say I have to go there! I don't need to go to college! I've had enough school! I know it's what Daddy wanted but he's not here and you need—

See the bus. Rusting and rumbling and stinking with exhaust. The doors swing wide to admit the souls bound for Perdition. The girl with the corn-silk hair is among them. Tears flow from the pale blue eyes and—

I don't want to go to Cape Noire. Why can't I just stay home?

See the driver. Pale and devilish and hollow-eyed. "Are you going to get on or not, kid? I don't have all day. We can't keep the Dragon waiting. The Dragon is coming. The Dragon is –"

Dragon? Is that you, Sinclair? I hate this! I hate it! Get out of my head!

See the red horror. Slashed and butchered and burned. "Oh dear God, I can't bear this pain! Why won't he just kill me and be done –"

You're not Sinclair! Who are you? Get out of my head!

"Christ in Heaven free me from this agony I'm begging –"

GET OUT OF MY HEAD!

She wrenched her hand from his and glared at him, her eyes blazing with rage and pain. "Who was that man?" she shouted. "Did you see that man? He was covered in blood!"

"Yes, I saw him, but I don't—"

"It was horrible! Why would you make me look at something like that? Why?"

"I didn't. I promise you that I—"

"And my father! Oh, how could you…You shouldn't have…Those things were private!"

"I don't choose what to see," he said. "I tried to warn you."

"Shut up! Shut your stupid mouth!"

"April, please."

"I said to shut…shut…" She collapsed into the chair, weeping. She seemed to grow smaller and younger in the grip of her grief, as if she were becoming once more the girl who ran by the fence, the girl who thought Daddy was the strongest man in the world.

Sinclair wanted to comfort her, but he didn't have the words. Without thinking, he extended his hand.

April caught the movement and recoiled with such ferocity that she fell from the chair. "Don't touch me! Don't you dare!"

"April, no! I wasn't going to…I wouldn't have…"

"Stay away from me!"

Sinclair stood silent and motionless as she ran out the door.

Zorn, refreshed and revitalized by his ablutions, hummed along with the radio as he poured himself a snifter of Krause's brandy. The liquor was of the highest quality, and it would be criminal to let it go to waste. To think, this prize was probably destined for the clutches of some sticky-fingered plebe who would quaff it like a cheap sherry! The world groaned under the weight of such fools. Their abundance served as a living rebuke to Darwin's theories.

The music ended and some twit began to prattle about a special announcement from the makers of tenacity. Zorn looked at the radio. The makers of *tenacity*? Had American industry advanced so far that a quality of being could be manufactured and sold? If so, Krause must have purchased a case or two. How else to account for his persistent respiration after the punishment he had endured?

Curious, the Hessian settled into a chair and listened to the broadcast.

"Good afternoon, listeners. I'm Edgar Shiloh, president of the Shiloh Bottling Company, proud maker of TenaciTea, the drink that helps you hang in there! As you are no doubt aware, in just four days my company will sponsor the world premiere of 'The TenaciTea Midnight Mystery Show,' featuring the exploits of the mysterious crime-fighter known only as *Brother Bones!*

"Who is this strange and dangerous avenger that stalks the Cape Noire night? In our thrilling program, he is Thomas Bonaparte, a dashing millionaire aviator and adventurer. There is, however, *another* Brother Bones who has a life far beyond the confines of our exciting new drama. He lives in the myths and legends and, some believe, the violent reality of our very own crime-ridden streets. That's right, dear listeners. There are those who say that Brother Bones is no imaginary character! There are those who say that he is a living, breathing engine of destruction which, to your sorrow, you may actually encounter in some dark alley on some lonely night!

"Are the legends true? Is there really a Brother Bones? I think it's time we answered that question once and for all! I am personally offering a reward of fifty thousand dollars to anyone who can bring me Brother Bones, dead or alive! I say again, *fifty thousand dollars.* Cash, of course."

The voice from the radio droned on for a few more minutes about *solving one of the great mysteries of our times* and other, similar nonsense before finally giving the relevant contact information. Zorn scribbled it down. He was already thinking of how he would spend the money.

Edgar Shiloh had barely stepped away from the microphone when he was accosted by a distraught Bill Fraley. "What the hell was all that about, Edgar? 'Bring him to me, dead or alive.' Are you nuts? This isn't the Wild West! You could get somebody killed with a stunt like that! Worse, you get this station sued!"

Edgar smiled and gave the man a pat on the shoulder. "Relax, Bill. It's only a harmless gimmick. It's like offering a reward for the Abominable Snowman, or the Loch Ness Monster. I'll bet I just got us a few thousand more listeners for the premiere."

Bill frowned so that the cigar in his mouth pointed at the floor. "Yeah, sure. And what if some poor dope gets shot cause some other poor dope mistakes him for Brother Bones?"

Edgar waved it away. "Oh, don't be such a nancy-boy. The man walks around wearing a skull mask, for God's sake. Do you know a lot of people who do that? I don't. The real Brother Bones, if he exists, is the only one with anything to worry about."

"Really? And what if somebody actually brings him to you? Then what?"

Edgar grinned. "I'll give you his mask as a memento."

"You wouldn't want to keep it?"

"No. I just want his head."

About four hours after Edgar Shiloh's announcement, Milton Pender stepped through the employee's entrance of the Chandler Arms. He was on time. His uniform was clean, and his shoes were shined. Mr. Gordon gave him an approving glance. "You doing better, kid?" the man asked.

"Yes, sir. Thank you, sir."

"I dunno. You still look a little green around the gills."

Milton wasn't sure what to say. He cleared his throat.

Gordon shook his head. "Forget it. Come over here. I got a little job for you."

Milton stepped over to his boss's desk and was handed a master key. "Go check on the guy in the Presidential Suite. A couple of his neighbors have been complaining about the radio and they say there's a bad smell."

"A smell?"

"Don't ask me. Maybe he's cooking something in his room. Who knows with these damn foreigners? Anyway, he won't answer his phone and I just want to make sure he's not up to something fishy."

"Okay. You want me to get Mr. Newton to go with me?"

"The house dick? Nah. We don't want the guy to feel like he's getting raided. He is a guest, after all. Just let me know if something doesn't feel right and I'll take care of the rest. By the way, have you seen Martha around?"

"Not since yesterday."

"Hm. She apparently skedaddled this morning after delivering the guy his breakfast. He probably tried to get in her pants and she took off running. If that's what happened, she should have said something to me. I would have kicked his ass out of the hotel. Instead, I'm going to have to fire her for leaving her post." He shook his head. "Why is everybody so stupid?"

Milton shuffled his feet. "I don't know, sir."

"Yeah, well, I wouldn't expect you to. Get on up there. Give me call if you find anything I should know about."

Milton nodded and headed for the Presidential Suite.

Sinclair sat in his office and gazed pensively at the empty chair on the other side of the chess board. Would she ever sit there again?

Shut up! Shut your stupid mouth!

He clenched his teeth and resisted the urge to sweep the chessmen into the floor. Why had she been so damned unfair?

Don't touch me! Don't you dare!

"Why wouldn't you listen?" he muttered, unaware he had spoken aloud.

Did you see that man? He was covered in blood!

Sinclair picked up a knight and idly turned it in his hand. He had seen the man. At first, he had thought the vision was some repressed memory of April's, but now another idea entered his mind.

"The stranger with the Insight," Sinclair said.

He closed his eyes and concentrated, trying to remember every word the man had communicated earlier that day. He said that his life was in danger, that he was being threatened by someone called…the Horseman? No. *Hessian*, that was it. But why had he appeared in April's mind? It just didn't make –

Sinclair opened his eyes. "He was there because *I* was there. Our minds were touching because I was using the Insight. But the way he looked…"

Oh dear God I can't bear this pain!

Sinclair stood up and began to pace the floor. He was overcome by the dreadful feeling that he had completely ignored a desperate cry for help.

He just hadn't been thinking straight. It was all April's fault! If she hadn't been so childish...

"Don't be an ass," he whispered. "She *is* a child. What's your excuse?"

He decided he didn't have one and dropped it. There were bigger things to consider. If he was right, a man's life was at stake. Was it too late to help him? Maybe not.

He sat down on the floor and assumed the lotus position. This was his custom whenever he was meditating, and it felt appropriate for what he was about to try. He closed his eyes, turned his gaze inward, and made a swift descent into the center of his being. There, floating amid the constellations that made up his inner world, Sinclair could see the valise that held the Insight.

He chuckled to himself. He had no idea why he had always imagined the power as being contained in a case of leather and gold, but he did. He willed the valise to open, and the golden light of the Insight came blazing forth. Ordinarily, he would now seize it and direct it—*lasso the lightning*, as Mr. Mendoza used to say—but instead he just let it burn onward and upward, shining from his spirit like a searchlight into a dark and empty sky.

The question now was, would anyone see it? And if so, how would they respond?

Sinclair basked in the chill glow of the Insight, and waited.

Milton could hear the radio inside the room. It was very loud. He was not surprised the other guests had been complaining. They were right about the smell, too. It was faint, but utterly repellent; the stench of freshly spilled offal.

Milton was nervous. What in the world was going on in there? Was the guy butchering a cow? He had seemed like such a nice fellow the day before. Good tipper, too.

"Hello?" Milton said, knocking on the door. "Anyone in there?"

A commercial for TenaciTea came on the radio. Milton swallowed. He sure could use a swig right now. He waited another moment or two, then decided it was pointless to put it off any longer. He inserted the key, turned it, and opened the door.

Sinclair heard something, a tinny, distant echo of…music?

It's the taste that gives you hope…When you're at the end of your rope…
It was a jingle. Sinclair recognized it. It was an ad for a drink called—
TenaciTea…Helps you hang in there!

"Hello?" Sinclair said, both aloud and in his mind. "Can anyone hear me?"

The smell was much worse inside the room. Milton gagged. God, it was disgusting! He headed straight for the phone to call Gordon. He had to notify the man and then get out of here. He dialed the number and a moment later Gordon's voice was in his ear. "Is that you Milton? What did…? Are you…? Dammit, Milton, will you turn off that friggin' radio! I can't hear a damn word you're saying!"

Milton sat down the phone and went to obey. His path was blocked by a stainless steel food cart that was in the center of the room. What was that doing in here? Wait, didn't Gordon say something about that? Something about a breakfast delivery that Martha had made?

He tried to push the cart, but it would barely move. *Golly, what's inside this thing?* Frustrated and annoyed, he eased around to the other side of the cart and opened the doors to the cabinet that made up its lower half.

Doc Micah's Chill Tonic is guaranteed to relieve all the symptoms…

Sinclair shook his head. Was he actually picking up a radio signal? How bizarre. He had heard of people hearing music through the fillings in their teeth, but he wouldn't have expected—

The music was overwhelmed by something else. Sinclair's pulse began to race.

He could hear someone screaming.

Martha had been stuffed into the tiny cabinet like a bundle of dirty linen. Broken bones protruded from her torn flesh, and her lifeless eyes stared at Milton with glassine indifference.

The horror of it struck Milton like a sledgehammer. He screamed like a frightened child until his lungs were empty, then he filled them again with great gulps of the noxious air that filled the room. He scrambled to his feet and was about to go for the door, when he caught sight of something in the shadows of the adjoining room. Something was stretched out on the bed. Something large and wet and glistening.

Every atom of his being was roaring at him to run like hell, but he did not. Something had taken hold of him. He was transfixed by the sight of the thing in the shadows. What was it? He had to see. He had to know. Maybe then he would run.

The screaming stopped.
Sinclair held his breath.
The makers of Snowdrift Soap are proud to announce…

Milton had left behind fear and disgust for a state of appalled fascination…and excitement. Something unbelievably terrible had happened in this room and he, Milton Pender, was the first one on the scene! This was his chance—perhaps the only chance he would ever have—to be a man of consequence. If he could just control his feelings, just ignore the horror, he might be able to discover some vital clue that he could present to the police with a dramatic flourish. He could be a hero. Just like the Black Haze.

He flipped the light switch in the bedroom and beheld a medical experiment gone awry. At least, that was his initial impression. He did not cry out at the sight, nor did his gorge rise. He was a detective now, an investigator. He stepped closer.

And the thing on the bed sat up.

FOR THE LOVE OF GOD PLEASE KILL ME!
The thought exploded like a grenade in the center of Sinclair's skull.
KILL ME! KILL ME! KILLMEKILLMEKILLMEKILLLLMMMMEEE-EEEE!!!

Moist red hands closed around Milton's head, and a fetid howl of agony came shrieking into his face. The façade of cool detachment he had put on was blown away, and he chorused the cries of the dying thing.

Then he felt the power. It came from the mangled hands like a jagged blast of lightning that coursed through Milton's mind and body. A cyclone of ice and fire began to spin at the center of his being and sweep through his thoughts, his emotions, his sense of self....

IM DYING I CAN FEEL IT OH THANK CHRIST!

The thought belonged to the red thing, but Milton felt it, too. He lifted his hands and tried to push the thing away, for fear that it would carry him with it into oblivion, but something kept him from breaking the connection. Something inside him wanted to keep the cyclone going for as long as possible. It was terrifying, but it was also—

Ecstasy.

Sinclair was at the center of a driving storm of power. No, he *was* the storm, raging across a dark and unknown sky.

He threw back his head and laughed with the sheer exhilaration of it. He had felt this sensation only once before. It had been on the night when Mr. Mendoza died. The night when the old man took Sinclair's hand and passed him the gift of—

"The Insight," Milton whispered as the thing released him, and he fell to the floor in a boneless heap.

"Yes," Sinclair said, "the Insight," and his vision went black as he slipped into unconsciousness.

And now, back to our program…

Night embraced the city like the welcome return of an accommodating lover. There was a subtle change in the mood and energy of the people who crowded the Cape Noire streets. Their restless energies seemed to rise as they shifted from diurnal to nocturnal pursuits.

Dr. Marax regarded them from the back seat of his gray Pierce-Arrow. Erika, clad in the chauffeur's uniform that was her normal attire, was leisurely driving him around the city. They had arrived in town just as the sun was sinking below the horizon, and for the last hour they had cruised aimlessly through the urban labyrinth, never exchanging a word.

"It hasn't changed at all," Erika finally murmured.

Marax looked at her eyes in the rear-view mirror. They were heavy with a sort of sick and dreadful heartache. He wasn't surprised. This city had violated her in every possible way.

"*We* will change it," he said.

The dread took flight, and was replaced by grim resolution. "Yes, sir. We certainly will."

Marax glanced down at the instrument of change. It lay on the seat beside him. A casual observer would have identified it as a music box. Marax himself thought of it as such, though he knew it to be something far more complex, and infinitely more dangerous.

The box was filled with hundreds of small and delicate interlocking components, each individually crafted to exacting specifications by artisans from around the world. None of those worthy craftsmen had ever beheld the complete design. That privilege was reserved for Dr. Marax.

The schematic was stored in a metallic tube nestled in the bottom of the Doctor's suitcase. It was printed on a weathered scroll that was always strangely warm to the touch, and could not be studied for long without causing blinding headaches. If one were willing to brave the pain and conduct a close comparison of the design to the completed box, an interesting discovery would be made: The music box was not truly complete. There was a single component missing, one final piece to the intricate puzzle. A piece that would be found in this city.

The Doctor caressed the surface of the box and returned his gaze to the humanity that surrounded him. How like insects they were! Ants moving with mindless urgency along the streets and sidewalks. He sneered as he observed them. He savored his contempt like a fine wine.

Then something else, something unseen by all save Marax, came drifting slowly into view. It floated alongside the car, its intangible form passing effortlessly through all obstructions as it kept pace with the vehicle. Although it did not ride on currents of air, it moved its leathery wings in a measured beat, and turned its tail as if using it for a rudder. Ebon-hued scales rippled along its massive, muscular form, and gleaming talons compulsively closed and opened around the heads of oblivious passerby. It turned its head toward the Doctor, and regarded him with burning yellow eyes.

Marax smiled and gave it a friendly wave.

The thing bared its fangs in a reptilian grin.

The Dragon had come to Cape Noire.

DAY THREE

"Can you fellows tell me about Brother Bones?"

Mick, Benny, and Pete looked up from their drinks. They had been occupying a corner table of the Gridiron Saloon for hours, commiserating in their misery. They gazed at the questioner with a bleary-eyed mixture of curiosity and annoyance. He was big, broad-shouldered, and dressed in a spotless white suit. He stood ramrod-straight, and his stone gray eyes seemed to be viewing them from a great height, much as a hawk might view mice that scurry among the rushes.

"Who the hell are you?" Mick asked. Or at least tried to. It came out all mushy—*whodehelryou*—and Mick was embarrassed because he was just sober enough to realize how drunk he sounded.

"I am someone who is willing to pay for information," the big man said.

"About Brother Bones?" Benny asked. He unconsciously reached up and touched the shiner that had nearly closed his right eye.

"Yes. I have been given to understand that you three gentlemen recently encountered the man. Is that true?"

"Who told you that?" Mick asked, carefully enunciating each word.

The big man cocked a thumb at the bar. Mick turned to see Butch Hammer, the Gridiron's owner and operator, flash him a mischievous grin. *What a jerk*, Mick thought. Then he saw that Pete, always ready to tell a story, was gesturing to an empty chair.

"Why don't you have a seat, Mister…?"

"Zorn."

"That's a German name, isn't it?" Pete asked. "I thought I recognized that accent."

"You've been to my country?"

"Nah, but I met a few of you guys in France. Shot a few, too."

"I met some Americans the same way. I would wave to them from my *Fokker* as I watched them fall to the ground in flames."

Pete and Zorn eyed each other for a few seconds, then the German broke into a smile. "Ah, but the Great War was a long time ago, yes? And tonight we meet as men should meet, not as enemies but as friends over a glass."

After a brief moment, Pete returned the smile. "Sure," he said. "Why not? Next round's on you?"

"Certainly."

Pete turned to Mick. "Any objections?"

Mick looked at his watch. Only ten past midnight. Plenty of time before Butch shut the place down. "Let's hear it, Pete."

Pete leaned forward. "Okay, Mr. Zorn, let me tell you a story. Once upon a time, there were two brothers…"

Father Dennis O'Malley was nodding over a passage of St. Augustine when he heard someone tapping at the door. He dog-eared the book, forced himself to his feet, and crossed to the window. Peeking through the curtain, he smiled with pleasant surprise at the sight of the man on the stoop.

O'Malley unbolted the door and said, "Dan Rains, as I live and breathe! How are you m'lad?"

Dan gave him the ghost of a smile. "Sorry to bother you. I saw your light on and I thought…"

"No apologies necessary, Dan. Come on in. Would you like a nip, or are you on duty?"

"I'm not on duty," Dan said, removing his hat as he crossed the threshold. "And I would absolutely love a nip."

The priest gestured to a large, overstuffed chair and Dan sank into it with a weary sigh.

"What's on your mind, Dan?" O'Malley asked as he splashed some Irish whiskey into a pair of tumblers. "And don't try to tell me you just popped in for a friendly chat, not at this time of night."

"I needed someone to talk to," Dan said.

O'Malley passed Dan a glass. "I'm a little surprised to hear that. You've never been one to share your troubles." He paused, then hastily added, "I'm not saying you shouldn't, mind you. I'm just saying that—"

"It's okay," Dan said. "I understand what you meant. You're right, I don't like to flap my gums about stuff, but sometimes…"

"Yes?"

Dan swallowed some whiskey. "I saw something tonight," he said. "The worst thing I've ever seen, and that's really saying something."

"A crime scene?"

Dan gave a bitter laugh. "Oh, it was a crime scene, all right."

"I NEEDED SOMEONE TO TALK TO."

O'Malley refilled Dan's glass and waited for him to continue. After a few moments, he did. Later, after the tale was told and the bottle was more than half empty, the priest wondered how many nights he would dream of the two dead bodies at the Chandler Arms. "The man who was tortured," he said, "do you know his name?"

"He was registered as Gerhard Krause. The girl's name was Martha Sawyer."

"I will pray for them."

Dan's eyes flashed. "Oh, yeah? That'll help a lot! If you want to pray for something, why don't you—" He broke off and averted his gaze. "Sorry," he said. "I didn't mean to take that tone. That was the booze talking."

"No need to apologize," O'Malley said. "No need at all."

Dan looked up. "I know someone you should pray for. There was a kid, a bellhop, he was the one who found them. He was really shook up. His name was Pender."

"I will remember him. Do you think he would like someone to talk to? I can recommend some people who specialize in that sort of thing."

"I'll mention it to him. I'm sure I'll be seeing him again. You know, there was something about that kid…"

"Yes?"

Dan started to reach for the bottle, but changed his mind. Then he changed it again, and poured another dram. "At the start of the interview, I shook hands with him and…something happened."

"What kind of something?"

"It was like getting an electric shock, but without the pain. I had this weird sense of something passing through my body. No, not my body, my *mind*."

"You make it sound like a mystical experience."

"Well, that's how it felt. It only lasted for a second or two, but it was like someone opened up my skull and took a peek at everything that was in there, then slammed it shut before they could get caught snooping. Doesn't that sound crazy?"

"It's not the craziest thing I've ever heard."

"That's good to know." Dan closed his eyes. He was tired and tipsy and dreaded having to get out of the chair. "I can't stop thinking about what that Krause guy must have gone through. And that girl. She was so young. Whoever did this, he must be trying for the Devil's throne in Hell."

O'Malley, no less tipsy, shook his head. "The Devil isn't in Hell," he said. "He's never been there, and has no desire to go."

"Really? I thought he ran the place. Doesn't it say in the Bible that he'd rather reign in Hell than serve in Heaven?"

"No, no, not the Bible. You're thinking of *Paradise Lost*. When Lucifer was exiled from Heaven, he and his minions weren't sent to the infernal regions. They landed here."

"In Cape Noire? That explains a lot."

O'Malley chuckled. "Not *here* specifically. This world. Our world. They're all around us. You know those cartoons with the little demon sitting on the man's shoulder, whispering temptations into his ear? There's a certain amount of truth in that."

Dan scratched at his shoulder. "So they're stuck here with us, huh?"

The priest nodded. "Until the end of days."

"Poor devils," Dan said, and both men laughed.

In a dingy third-floor walkup a few blocks from the city morgue, Milton Pender lay staring at the cracks in the ceiling. He felt sick and exhausted. He didn't even want a TenaciTea.

Maybe I should have gone to the hospital, he thought. *That cop told me I should. He was trying to look out for me. He was a good guy. He really cared.*

Milton frowned. Why was he so sure of that?

Because I know him.

But that didn't make any sense. After all, he had only just met the man.

But I know him! I knew him from the moment I shook his hand…

"Hello, son," the cop had said. "You've had one helluva shock tonight. I'm sorry you had to see all this. Sit down over here and let's talk." He extended a hand. "I'm Lieutenant Rains, but you can just call me Dan."

Milton took the hand, and in the space between two seconds he traveled every highway and byway of Dan Rains's soul. It was a journey through another man's lifetime on the back of a bolt of lightning.

Rains winced and snatched his hand away as if he had touched a hot coal. "What the..?" He blinked at Milton, then shook it off, apparently dismissing the feeling as some fleeting bit of strangeness, best ignored and forgotten.

Milton played along. He had a feeling that it would be in his interest not to acknowledge that anything out of the ordinary had just happened. He pulled it off, too, but it wasn't easy.

I could have just told him the truth.

Milton shook his head. Rains might have been a stand-up guy, but that didn't mean he wouldn't have thought Milton was crazy.

Maybe I am crazy.

"No, I'm not," Milton whispered. "That man who died, Mr. Krause, he did something to me. I can read minds. Maybe even more."

How much more? Milton was eager to find out, but not at that moment. He was just too tired. He needed sleep. Later, after he was rested and refreshed, he would go somewhere, conduct some experiments, test his limits…

The limits of my power, he thought, and he slipped into a restless, fitful sleep.

Sinclair slipped out of a restless, fitful sleep, and immediately wished he could slip back in. He was still on the cold, hard floor where he had been knocked flat by the Insight. His muscles ached, his head was pounding, and his spine felt like a mangled rod of rusted iron. Also, he badly needed to go to the bathroom. It was this last that forced him to his feet, in spite of the vociferous protests from every part of his body. The room was dark, but he didn't bother to turn on a lamp. He knew where the toilet was.

A few minutes later, he staggered out of the lavatory and collapsed into his small bunk. His head had cleared a little, and he was beginning to apply his mind to puzzling out exactly what had happened to him. It was such an interesting problem that he almost didn't notice the ghost standing at the foot of his bed.

The ghost was easy to miss. It was more of an impression than a person, like the afterglow of an abruptly extinguished light. For a moment, Sinclair thought he was hallucinating. He stared at the ghost, wondering if it would fade away. It didn't. The wan, insubstantial features remained fixed in place. The eyes, twin pools of nothingness, gazed down at Sinclair.

"Are you the man who asked me for help?" Sinclair asked.

The spectre gave a single nod.

Sinclair was more remorseful than frightened. "Please forgive me."

You have done me no wrong.

The whisper seemed to come from every corner of the room, but Sinclair knew he wasn't hearing it with his ears.

"Why have you come here? Do you want me to help the police catch the man who killed you? If you can tell me his name…"

The ghost was shaking his head. *Not important. The Dragon. The Dragon is here.*

"Here? In Cape Noire?"

You have the Insight. The visions should have warned you.

"I've had nightmares about him for most of my life. Is that what you mean?"

I don't know. You are not like me. Or the others.

"Others?"

The brethren. My fellow Lancers.

Sinclair's chest tightened. He was having trouble breathing.

They will seek you out. Join them. Take my place. Your skills will be needed.

"I thought…I thought that I was the only one."

You were wrong.

Sinclair was struck by a sudden grief for Mr. Mendoza. He had often missed the old man over the years, but never more than at this moment. He wanted so badly to speak with him, to share with him these amazing events.

To ask him if he had deliberately lied.

The ghost broke into Sinclair's melancholy ruminations. *Our minds were joined when I died. Were you in the room with me?*

"No."

Then there was someone else. It is very hard to remember. I was in so much pain. The ghost lowered his head, as if in contrition. *I have to go now. Something is calling to me. Something that will not be denied.*

"What is it?"

I'm not sure, but I am afraid of it. I think it might be…judgment.

The ghost disappeared.

Sinclair lay back and stared into the darkness. He was certain that he would not sleep, but in less than ten minutes he was in the arms of Morpheus, dreaming of a grinning black leviathan, and a Cape Noire engulfed in flames.

"…and that's the tale of Brother Bones," Pete said.

"Fascinating," said the big German. "A remarkable story, remarkably well-told. You should write it as a poem and set it to music."

Pete responded with a smile that didn't touch his eyes. He suspected that he was being made fun of, but he wasn't completely sure. Even if he had been sober, which he wasn't, Pete would have found Zorn a hard guy to read. As it was, he had picked up the clear impression that something about the man was…wrong.

At first, Pete had dismissed the feeling as his natural aversion to Huns, but he had gradually come to the realization that there was more to it than that, something deeper than a learned prejudice. Something instinctive.

"Last call, boys," Butch yelled from the bar.

Zorn gestured for a final round, then added, "Just for myself and my friend." There was no need to extend any courtesy to Mick and Benny. They had both collapsed into drunken stupor, their heads lolling heavily on their shoulders. After the drinks had been delivered, Zorn raised his glass. "To Brother Bones," he said.

Pete shook his head. "I don't think so."

"As you wish," said the German. He downed his drink to the Undead Avenger and set his glass on the table. "May I ask a final question before we part company?"

"Go ahead."

"How can I meet him?"

"Brother Bones? You don't. He meets you. Then you never meet anyone again."

"Tut, tut. You know that isn't true. You and your friends are living proof."

"Yeah, but we're the exceptions. We're just errand boys who were in the wrong place at the wrong time."

"Just so, and Brother Bones does not waste his efforts on third-tier factotums. He will, however, make time for a murderer, yes?"

Pete stared at the German. Through the fog of his inebriation, he had a moment of clarity, and he realized exactly what kind of man he was talking to.

"Well?" said Zorn.

"He'd make time for you," Pete said.

Zorn grinned. "I thought so. Do you know anyone who could get a message to him for me?"

Mick, to Pete's consternation, chose this moment to rouse himself. "Sally Paige could do it," he mumbled.

Pete winced. Zorn noted the reaction, and a hungry light came into his eyes. "Who is she?" the German asked.

"Nobody," Pete said. "Don't pay him any mind. He's drunk off his ass."

Mick was too plastered to follow Pete's lead. "Sally knows everybody," he said.

"She doesn't know me," Zorn said, "but I would like to know her. I ask again, who is Sally Paige?"

"Reporter for the Tribune," Mick said. "One juicy tomato. Ain't that right, Pete?"

Zorn raised his eyebrows. "Is that right, Pete?"

Pete swallowed. "Yeah, that's right."

Zorn stood up and slid his chair under the table. "Gentlemen," he announced, "you have been both entertaining and informative. As a gesture of my appreciation, I am never going to speak to any of you again."

"Whuzzat s'pose to mean?" Mick slurred to Zorn's back as the man walked away.

"It means he's going to let us live." Pete said.

The police had not left anyone to guard the crime scene. Sterling Harrow was grateful for that. It simplified matters. He wandered to and fro through the darkened rooms where Gerhard Krause had lost his life, considering with clinical interest the psychic pain which still sang within the walls.

Serves you right, Gerhard, Harrow thought with satisfaction. *You always were a reckless idiot. If this assassin hadn't done for you, I probably would have killed you myself.*

He could still hear the smirk in Krause's voice when the cheeky little prat had revealed he was aware of Harrow's experiments in the Dark Arts. What had he been planning, anyway? Blackmail? Possibly. All of the brethren were fond of the good life, but Krause had been profligate even by Lancer standards. It would have been just like him to cast a covetous eye on Harrow's fortune.

Well, it hardly matters now, does it? He's been more than adequately punished for his insolence, considering what happened in that bedroom...

Harrow had been unable to spend more than a few minutes in that area of the suite. It was too much, even for a heart as jaded as his. The echoes of agony reverberated there like a soul-rending chorale for the damned. Harrow had forced himself to listen closely to this hellish music, then withdrew before it became more than he could bear. After he had returned to the parlor and rested a moment, he mentally replayed the cacophony. He parsed every passage, examined every note, and gleaned all the enlightenment he could from what he found. And he discovered something that alarmed him.

"Krause passed his power to an outsider," he murmured.

"Do you know who it was?" someone asked from the door.

Harrow recognized the voice, and smoothly concealed his surprise. "No, Leandro, I'm afraid I don't" he said. He slowly turned to face his fellow Lancer. "Have you been lurking there long?"

"Not long at all," said the handsome Spaniard. "Do you mind if I turn on a light?"

"Go right ahead."

Leandro flipped a switch. Harrow noted, not for the first time, that the man was surely coloring his hair. He was Harrow's senior by at least twenty years, but his wavy locks were as black as the Cape Noire night. Harrow, having gone gray when he was still in his thirties, was sensitive to such things. Clutched in Leandro's right hand was a black walking stick; an accessory not dissimilar from the one that had belonged to Gerhard Krause. Harrow was carrying one as well.

"When did you arrive in the city?" Harrow asked.

"Only a little while ago. I sensed the aftershocks of Gerhard's passing as soon as I got here. I didn't sense your presence, though…"

Harrow deflected the implied question with one of his own. "Tell me, why do you think Krause passed the Insight to someone who wasn't a trained apprentice?"

"Isn't it obvious?"

"Not to me."

"He had gone mad from the pain, of course. In any event, we should find this person, and quickly. The visions are escalating in force and intensity. The Enemy will manifest himself soon. We have to be ready."

"I agree, but there is something else we have to consider."

"Yes?"

"There is a rogue Lancer in Cape Noire."

"What? Don't be absurd!"

"It's true. A stranger was touching Krause's mind when he died. Krause thought of him as 'the Shopkeeper,' something to do with books."

"Books…" For a moment, Leandro's gaze seemed to turn inward.

"Does that mean something to you?"

"No," Leandro said. "Nothing at all. Are you sure of this?"

"Go in there," Harrow pointed his stick at the bedroom, "and fully open yourself to the Insight. You will see."

Leandro followed Harrow's instructions. When he emerged from the room a few minutes later, his bronze skin had slightly paled and his face was covered by a sheen of sweat. "I am sorry I doubted you, *mi amigo*."

"I accept your apology. Tell me, have you spoken to any of the others since you arrived?"

"Oleg and François should be here before noon. The others will arrive a few hours later. They're all staying here or at the Falmouth Inn."

"I'm at the Falmouth as well. There is a conference room there which will accommodate all of us comfortably. I suggest we meet there at ten this evening."

"That is a good idea. I will inform the others." Leandro stifled a yawn and examined his fingernails. "In the meantime, I think I will try to locate this…'Shopkeeper.' Do you have any objections?"

Harrow thought the Spaniard was being just a little too casual about his interest in the mystery Lancer. *What are you not telling me, Leandro?*

He considered pushing the issue, then decided he really didn't care. He had his own agenda to pursue. "No objections at all," he said. "I'm sure we would all be interested in meeting him. While you're taking care of that, I'll be hunting for inheritor of Krause's Insight. We'll both work better if we're alone, don't you agree?"

"Completely," Leandro said. "Until this evening, then."

"Yes. Until this evening."

"We're here, sir," Erika said as she parked at the curb.

Dr. Marax surveyed the dilapidated brownstone with a dubious eye. It didn't look much like the workshop of a brilliant scientist. "Are you sure this is the right address?"

"It's the right address, sir."

Marax grunted. He checked his pocket watch. "Not quite time," he muttered. "Maybe he'll see us early." He picked up a briefcase from the floor of the car. "We have his money, after all."

Erika got out and opened the door for the Doctor. She escorted him up the seven steps to the building's front entrance, a single wooden door covered with faded and peeling paint. Beside the door was a small metal sign that read, 909 OLD TOWN WAY, and beneath that, SHILOH PROPERTIES LTD.

Erika knocked at the door, and a moment later it was opened by a well-dressed giant—seven feet tall if he was an inch—with an elongated, misshapen face. His appearance was so startling that Erika took an involuntary step backward.

The giant looked down at her, then over her head at Marax. "Can I help you?" he inquired in a deep, soft voice.

"I have an appointment with the Professor."

"And you are?"

"Dr. Samuel Marax."

"You're early."

"Only by a few minutes."

The giant turned his large, wet eyes to Erika. "And who might you be, little one?"

Marax stepped forward before Erika could speak. "She is my personal assistant."

"Hello, personal assistant" said the giant. His thick lips parted in a wry smile. "My name is Waldo. I'm sorry if my appearance frightens you."

"Nothing frightens me," Erika said firmly.

Waldo grunted. "Really? I wonder what that would be like, to never be frightened."

Erika's eyes narrowed, but she said nothing.

The giant turned and gestured for them to follow. "Come with me. I'll let the Professor know you've arrived."

Waldo led them down a short hall into a sparsely appointed office. The minimal furnishings were tasteful, but cold and utilitarian. It was all hard wood and bare walls and emptiness so complete that even the dust motes must have felt lonely.

Waldo sat behind one of two large desks, lifted a phone, and dialed. After a moment, he said, "Professor, your appointment is here," and hung up. He gestured to a pair of red leather chairs in front of the other desk, which stood several feet away at a right angle to his own. "He'll be down shortly. Please, make yourselves comfortable."

Marax complied, but Erika remained on her feet, just within arm's reach of the Doctor. She gave Waldo a challenging look, but the giant ignored her and began sifting through some mail on his desk.

"The Professor doesn't have much of a taste for luxury," Marax observed.

"He lives for his work," Waldo replied.

"That's commendable. May I ask you a personal question?"

Waldo stopped shuffling the letters. "Yes?"

"Do you suffer from acromegaly?"

Waldo's brows lifted a little. "You're familiar with my condition?"

"I've never treated it, but I recognize the symptoms."

Waldo resumed his perusal of the morning deliveries. "A disorder of the pituitary gland," he said. "The Professor thinks he can reverse the effects. Maybe he'll find the time to work on it, one of these days." His eyes shifted to Erika. "I wasn't always like this, you know. Believe it or not, I was voted the handsomest boy in my senior class."

He was clearly hoping for some sort of response, so she gave him one. "That must have been a long time ago."

"It seems like a hundred years," Waldo said.

Erika heard the unmistakable clank and rumble of a descending elevator. Waldo rose from his desk and opened a door in the far left corner of the office. A moment later, a lean, compact specimen with unkempt gray hair and wildly bushy eyebrows stepped smartly into the room. He wore a white lab coat over a pinstripe suit, and Erika thought he looked like a lawyer disguised as Einstein for an office Halloween party. He gave a short bow to Marax and Erika, then seated himself behind the desk.

"Good morning," he said in a clipped, mechanical voice. "I am, as you have no doubt surmised, Professor Bugosi. It is a pleasure to meet you, Dr. Marax." He gave Erika an appraising glance. "Is this young lady your daughter?"

The Doctor stiffened. "Erika is my assistant."

"Ah," said Bugosi. "I hope she is more efficient than mine. Waldo is a complete dolt. Isn't that right, Waldo?"

The giant's face reddened. "Professor, I'm not sure I understand—"

"Waldo is such an incompetent," Bugosi continued, "that he disturbs me in my lab at eight fifty-four with the useless information that my nine o'clock appointment has arrived, thus shattering my concentration and making me lose six valuable minutes which I will never recover. This is the action of a dolt, is it not?"

Waldo looked down at his desk and mumbled something incomprehensible.

The Professor cupped a hand to his ear. "What was that?"

"Yes, Professor. It's the action of a dolt."

Erika looked at the floor, averting her eyes from the giant's humiliation. For a moment, she felt a flicker of pity, and this puzzled her. She thought that particular sentiment had been hammered out of her years ago. The blows of the smith that forged her had been many and hard, and the weapon she had become was as tough as Toledo steel. From where, then, came this faint glimmer of feeling? She frowned and pushed the question aside.

"If you don't mind, Professor," Marax said, "I'm not here to compare the merits of our employees." He lifted the briefcase. "I have the sum we agreed upon. May I please see the item?"

"It's locked in the safe behind Waldo's desk."

"I didn't ask where it was. I asked if I could see it."

The Professor leaned back and laced his fingers over his middle. "In due time," he said. "I would like to ask you a few questions, if I may, before we conclude our deal."

Erika looked to Marax for a signal. She could slit the Professor's throat before Waldo was half out of his chair. The giant would be a little more problematic, but Erika would start by taking out his eyes. After that, he wouldn't be much trouble at all.

"What kind of questions?" Marax asked. He stroked his moustache, and Erika stood pat. The Doctor didn't want her to do anything. Yet.

"Doctor Marax, I have created many things for many people, but I have never worked on anything quite like this device. Can you please explain to me exactly what it does?"

"I cannot."

"You cannot or will not?"

"The latter."

"Oh, come now," Bugosi said mildly. "Don't be churlish. You know my reputation. I am the very soul of discretion."

"Your reputation," Marax said, "is that of a professional who knows how to mind his own business."

"It is precisely *because* I am a professional that I am *making* this my business. You sent me a schematic that I was unable to examine for more than a few minutes without developing a paralyzing migraine. How did it do that? I do not know, but I would like to."

Bugosi paused to give Marax a chance to respond. He didn't.

"From this pain-inducing diagram," Bugosi continued, "I fashioned an object that is continuously recreating itself. It actually changes every time I look at it. How does it do that? I do not know, but I would like to."

Again, Bugosi paused.

Marax inspected his fingernails. "Anything else?"

"Oh, yes," Bugosi said. "It is clear to me that this mechanism is, in fact, merely a component of a larger device. What is the purpose of this device? I do not know—"

"But you would like to," finished Marax.

"Yes. Precisely."

The Doctor looked up at the ceiling, then back at Bugosi. "Professor, I give you my solemn word that within twenty-four hours you will see a demonstration of the device in action."

Bugosi looked askance at Marax. "How very elliptical."

Marax turned a palm up. "It is all I am prepared to offer at this time."

Erika focused on the open hand. If Marax closed it, Bugosi would die.

After a moment, the Professor gave a theatrical sigh. "Oh, very well. Since you give your *solemn word…*"

Marax placed his hand back on the armrest, and Erika relaxed, but only just.

"One more thing, though…" said the Professor.

Erika rolled her eyes. Some people just didn't know when to quit.

Marax made a show of looking at his pocket watch. "Yes?"

"I took the liberty of doing some research on you. Up until a few years ago, you were a general practitioner in rural Arizona. You could have been fairly described as a 'country doctor.' Isn't that correct?"

"I suppose so."

Bugosi glanced at Erika, then back at Marax. "You had a daughter named Catherine—"

"Do not say her name," the Doctor snapped. His hand was palm up again. Erika hoped it would close. She was ready to see the color of Bugosi's blood.

The Professor was conciliatory. "I meant no offense. I was merely seeking to clarify—"

"Will you please come to the point, if indeed you have one?"

"Very well," said Bugosi. "I will be direct. I want to know where you got this design."

"How do you know I didn't create it?"

"Please! With your education and experience? A mind as provincial as yours could never have conceived such a thing."

Marax's fingers were twitching.

"I care a great deal about money," Bugosi said, "but I care even more about knowledge. I *insist* you tell me where this design originated. In fact, I am making it part of the purchase price."

"And if I refuse to pay?"

"Then take your money and go. But the item will remain with me."

Marax's hand began to close into a fist, but then stopped. He reached up to stroke his moustache. Erika was disappointed, but she obeyed the silent command.

"All right," the Doctor said. "The design I gave you was copied from a schematic I discovered in Spain."

"Iberia? Interesting. How did you find it?"

"I was led to it by a demon."

Bugosi coughed. "I'm sorry, what did you say?"

"I was led to it by a demon. I made his acquaintance while I was in La Mancha."

The Professor glowered at Marax. "If you think that I am going to allow you to mock –"

"No mockery. I am being completely honest. I swear it."

Bugosi's expression slowly shifted from anger to amazement. "You actually believe it."

"It is the plain truth."

Bugosi looked at Erika. "Pray tell, did *you* meet this 'demon'?"

"No one can see or hear him but me," said Marax.

Bugosi tilted his head. "I note that you're using the present tense…"

"He followed me here from La Mancha. He is my constant companion."

"Is he here now?" Bugosi asked with a half-smile.

"He's right behind you."

"Ha! I'm tempted to look, but you've already told me that he is invisible."

"That's right."

"What does he look like? Does he have horns and a tail? Does he carry a pitchfork?"

"He is a dragon."

This time, Bugosi *did* look. "Can he see me?"

"Yes," said the Doctor. "I think he likes you."

"Really? Why do you say that?"

"He's been laughing ever since you walked in the room."

Bugosi turned back to Marax. He stared daggers at the Doctor. "No mockery, eh?"

"No, Professor. None at all."

There was an awkward silence, then Bugosi rose to his feet. "Waldo, take the Doctor's briefcase. If the money is all there, then give him the package inside the safe." He pointed a damning finger at Marax. "Doctor, you are a madman. I want you out of my house as soon as possible."

"I want the same thing," said Marax. "I'm glad we're in accord."

Later, when they were back in the car, Erika said, "I wish you had let me kill that man, sir. He had no right to speak to you that way."

"Don't let it bother you, my dear," said Marax. "We got what we came for. That's all that matters." He held up the item he had purchased from the Professor and examined it in the light of the morning sun. It resembled nothing so much as a large tuning fork, golden-hued and gleaming. There was an indistinct quality to its edges, as if they were in a constant state of flux; twisting, bending, and straightening again…

Marax's eyes began to hurt. He put away the tuning fork and looked out the window at his constant companion.

The Dragon was still laughing.

From the window of his second-floor study, Bugosi watched as Marax was driven away. After the car had pulled out of sight, the Professor stepped over to an oak cabinet, opened it, and withdrew a perfect copy of the tuning fork. He held it aloft and addressed the thing as if it were the skull of Yorick. "Your secrets will be mine soon enough," he said.

"I'm sure Mr. Shiloh won't keep you waiting long," the secretary said.

"Well, he'd better not," Sally said with a smile. She was in a playful mood. "I've got better things to do than sit around here all day. I'll bet you do, too. Hey, I've got an idea! Why don't you take the afternoon off, and I'll buy you lunch at Nittoli's. You can give me some background for my article. I promise to keep all your comments off the record." She gave a conspiratorial wink. "It'll be fun. A girl's day out. What do you say, Timms?"

The secretary went as white as an Alpine winter. "I…I…d-d-don't…th-think…" She closed her eyes, took a breath, and tried again. "I don't think that's a good idea. If Mr. Shiloh…if he were to find out…"

"Hey, take it easy," Sally said. "Just forget I said anything, okay?"

"I'm sorry," the woman said, and she turned away from Sally to hammer something on her typewriter.

Jeez, what a wee tim'rous beastie, Sally thought. *How can anyone be so scared of a twerp like Eddie?*

The buzzer on the secretary's desk went off, and Mrs. Timms flinched as if she had been slapped. She leaned close to the intercom. "Yes, Mr. Shiloh?"

"Send in Miss Paige," was the curt reply.

"Right away, sir."

Sally started to walk to the door, but she was cut off by Mrs. Timms, who bustled in front of her. "Please, let me get the door for you," she said.

Sally was a little annoyed. "You don't have to do that, sister. I'm used to opening my own doors."

The secretary looked up, and Sally was shocked at the forlorn despair that filled the woman's eyes. "Please," she said. "It's expected of me."

"Sure. No problem."

Mrs. Timms reached for the door, and Sally noticed that the secretary's wrist was mottled and chafed by something that looked like...

What the hell? Are those rope burns?

She tried to look Mrs. Timms in the eyes, but the woman was staring resolutely at the floor, a perfect portrait of utter abasement.

What has he done to you?

Then the door was open and Edgar Shiloh was hailing her from her from across the room. "Come in, Miss Paige," he said. "It's a pleasure to see you again! I'm very excited about this interview."

Sally smiled, but she was no longer in a playful mood. "The pleasure is all mine," she said. "I can't wait to introduce our readers to the real Edgar Shiloh."

In his room at the Falmouth Inn, Sterling Harrow sipped his morning coffee and read the story on Krause's murder in the early edition of the Tribune. It was a tasteful piece. The paper had shown admirable restraint in reporting the more gruesome details of the German's demise.

Then again, perhaps he was giving the Tribune too much credit. It was just as likely that the police were reluctant to share any more than they absolutely had to. One tidbit they *had* offered up for public consumption was very interesting to Harrow.

"*The bodies were discovered by a young bellhop,*" he read aloud. He lowered the paper. Could this be the mysterious outsider? "I wonder..." he murmured.

Except he didn't wonder at all. He knew. The question was, how to proceed? He turned it over in his mind as he perused the rest of the paper. His eye fell on an amusing little piece about a fifty thousand dollar reward for the capture of some urban vigilante, a near-mythic figure called Brother Bones. He smiled. Perhaps he would look into that after this Dragon business was disposed of. Harrow never turned up his nose at easy money.

Sinclair was tired and depressed. He wandered listlessly through the shop, adjusting books and dusting shelves, barely aware of his own actions. He was plagued by a nagging feeling that he should *do something*, but he had no idea what that something was.

They will seek you out, the dead man had said. How long would that take? And if they did find him, what would they want?

He shuffled to the front of the shop and assumed his place behind the cash register. He closed his eyes and rubbed his temples.

Should I reach out to them with the Insight? Maybe, but he felt a petulant reluctance to do so. Let them come to him! He wasn't some fresh-faced initiate, begging for a place at the table. It wasn't his fault that he had been deceived. How could he have known that he was just one of –

The brass bell rang. He opened his eyes and there was April, the sunlight shining in her golden hair. "Hi," she said.

"Good morning," he replied in a guarded tone.

She looked down at the floor, then back up at him. "I…uh…I want to apologize about yesterday. About losing my temper like that. I'm sorry."

"Think nothing of it."

Silence. They looked at one another, each expecting the other to add something. Neither of them obliged.

Finally, April said, "Well, I guess that's it. See you around." She turned to go, and Sinclair somehow knew that once she had crossed the threshold, he would never see her again. Part of him wanted to stop her, but a larger part—perhaps the better part—thought that a clean break might be for the best.

As her hand was about to close on the knob, the brass bell rang and the door opened to admit a dashing, dark-skinned gent swinging a black walking stick. He flashed a grin at April, then stepped slightly to one side. "Your pardon, *Señorita*," he said, and he gave a small bow as he held open the door.

April gave Sinclair a cryptic glance, then said, "Thanks, but I wasn't leaving."

Sinclair was bewildered, but grateful. She wasn't gone yet. Not quite yet.

"Very good," the man said. He stepped jauntily into the shop and beamed at Sinclair. "Good morning, *mi amigo*! Is this your place?"

"It is."

"A fine-looking establishment. I have visited several bookshops today, and I must say that yours is by far the most charming of the lot."

"It is?"

"Oh, yes! Allow me to congratulate you." He approached Sinclair and extended his hand.

From the corner of his eye, Sinclair saw April's eyes widen with anticipation. He almost laughed. He had no intention of scanning this fellow with the Insight. In fact, he never would have scanned *her*, but he had been so surprised when she took his hand that –

Sinclair felt a blast of benign lightning flash through his mind. He snatched his hand from the Spaniard's grasp and gawked at the smiling *hidalgo*.

"So, I've found you," the man said with quiet satisfaction.

"You're one of them," Sinclair said.

"And you are one of us. Allow me to introduce myself. My name is Leandro Mendoza."

"I'm sorry…did you…*Mendoza?*"

"Yes. I believe you were acquainted with my older brother, Alfonso."

"Mr. Mendoza was your brother?"

A sadness came into the Spaniard's eyes. "Indeed he was. We had been estranged for many, many years. In fact, I didn't even know he was dead, until just now."

"What else have you learned? Just now." Sinclair looked down at Leandro's hand. It was still extended, now palm up, as if holding forth an offering. Leandro followed the gaze, and let the hand drop.

"Surprisingly little. You instinctively raised a shield as soon as you felt the incursion of the Insight. Well done, that. I have many questions for you, and I'm sure you have many for me. Perhaps it would be best if we continued this conversation in private?"

The Spaniard tilted his head to indicate the young woman behind him. Except she was no longer behind him. She was stepping around the counter, sidling up to Sinclair, smiling at Leandro.

"Hi!" she said. She stood at parade rest, her hands clasped firmly behind her back. "My name's April Moon."

Leandro's eyes flicked from her to Sinclair and back again. "Well, I am very pleased to meet you, Miss April Moon. Now, if you could please excuse us…"

"Lancer business, huh? It's okay. I know all about it. I'm Sinclair's disciple."

It was Leandro's turn to gawk. "His disciple?"

Sinclair opened his mouth to speak, but April cut him off by driving the heel of her shoe down on his toes.

"That's right!" April said. "I'm learning how to use the Insight. I'm going to fight the Dragon!"

Leandro gave Sinclair a hard look. "Your...*disciple?*"

Sinclair picked up the look and turned it on the girl beside him. "April," he said, "you know that I prefer the term, *acolyte*."

Bethany had almost finished typing Mr. Shiloh's Rotary speech when the office door opened and Sally Paige emerged, Mr. Shiloh close on her heels.

"Thank you again for a truly delightful morning!" Mr. Shiloh said. Although his unctuous tone made Bethany want to gag, she fervently hoped that his words were sincere. A delightful morning for Edgar Shiloh might equal a not-quite-hellish afternoon for Bethany Timms.

"Oh, thank *you*, Edgar," Miss Paige replied, her voice dripping maple syrup. "I only wish we could have done this sooner. I can't remember when I've interviewed anyone quite so intelligent...or charming."

Bethany clamped her teeth on the tip of her tongue. *Charming?* Had the woman been fooled so completely? She was supposed to be smart!

"Perhaps we can talk again soon," simpered Mr. Shiloh. "In a more informal setting, I hope?"

Miss Paige brushed a bit of invisible lint from one of Edgar's lapels. "I think that's definitely a possibility," she said, putting a lot of breath into it. "I'll be in touch." Her hand traveled to his tie, and for a single, horrific moment, Bethany thought the woman was going to pull him in for a kiss. Instead, she simply adjusted the Windsor knot.

It was a small gesture, but the intimacy of it sent Mr. Shiloh into the upper atmosphere. His face turned as red as a cherry tomato. "I'll be looking forward to your call," he said, and he slowly closed the door without once taking his adoring eyes from Miss Paige's face.

Bethany had maintained an expression of studied indifference as she observed them from the corner of her eye, but inside she was screaming.

"Mrs. Timms," Sally Paige said.

Bethany flinched in surprise. She had expected the woman to depart without a word. "Yes, Miss Paige? Is there something else I can...help... you..." Her words died as she looked into the reporter's eyes. There was a darkness in those eyes, but also an unexpected depth of feeling. It was a little frightening, looking into those depths. "What do you want?" Bethany whispered.

"Only to give you this." Miss Paige placed a business card on Bethany's desk. "My home number's on the back. If you ever need help, call me."

"If I ever…? I'm not sure what you mean."

The reporter smiled. It was a friendly smile, surprisingly gentle. "Just keep the card. And remember what I said. You can trust me."

"All right."

Miss Paige nodded once, and then walked out without a backward glance.

They had moved their conversation to Sinclair's room at the back of the shop. The Spaniard did not bother to hide his distaste for the accommodations. He sat on the very edge of the proffered chair, as if fearing exposure to fleas. "I must say, you lead a very austere lifestyle, Mr. Sinclair."

"Isn't that the tradition?" April asked. She was sitting cross-legged on Sinclair's bunk. No self-consciousness there. She might have been relaxing in her own home.

"Tradition? What do you mean?"

"The tradition started by Don Julio," April said. "He lived like a monk, right? Sinclair sure does. He never uses the Insight for personal gain."

Sinclair was perplexed, but in a good way. April sounded almost proud of him.

Leandro turned to Sinclair, and burst into laughter.

"What's so funny?" Sinclair asked.

The laughter faded, but Leandro maintained an air of amused condescension. "You poor, poor fellow," he said. "Alfonso was your mentor, all right. Tell me, what did he teach you about the Insight? What are your abilities, exactly?"

Sinclair frowned and crossed his arms. "Telepathy, facilitated primarily by physical touch, although I have been able to make at least superficial contact with other minds over great distances."

"As you did with my friend, the late Gerhard Krause?"

"Was that his name? I'm so sorry about—"

"Put it from your mind. There was nothing you could have done to save him."

"Was he killed because he was a Lancer?"

"No, he was killed because he was a lecher. Enough about him. What else can you do?"

Sinclair hesitated before answering. He was disturbed by Leandro's contemptuous attitude toward the dead man. After an uncomfortable pause, he said, "I also possess a limited precognitive ability."

"How limited?"

"I can't foretell specific events, but I do get...feelings."

"Did Alfonso talk to you about these 'feelings'?"

"He told me to pay attention to them. He said they would warn me of the Dragon's return."

"Have they done so?"

Sinclair thought about it. "No," he said. "I've just been having nightmares. The same ones I've always had."

"Dreams of the Dragon gloating over the ruins of Cape Noire?"

"Yes! Exactly! Do you have them, too?"

"Only recently. Those are the visions that brought me here, me and the others."

"Recently? I've had them ever since Mr. Mendoza died!"

"That's because you are at the epicenter of the catastrophe," Leandro said. "You are like a man living with a never-ending alarm ringing in his ears. You've become so accustomed to the din that you barely notice it anymore. It's just a normal part of your life. Not so for the rest of us." His eyes glazed over for a moment. "Perhaps Alfonso wasn't completely wrong after all..."

"About what?"

The Spaniard made an expansive gesture. "About all of this. This *life*, if you can call it such, that he insisted on living, and which he obviously inflicted on you."

"What's that supposed to mean? Mr. Mendoza didn't 'inflict' anything on me! He was like a father to me! He saved mc from the streets!"

"I don't doubt it. Alfonso was a good man, and I loved him dearly, but he had the soul of an ascetic. He elevated self-denial to a religion, and deliberately impoverished himself in order to maintain what he perceived as the purity of the Insight." Leandro smiled and glanced out at the floor of the shop. "He couldn't live without his precious books, though. That's one sacrifice he would never make."

April spoke up. "It sounds to me like you guys weren't exactly simpatico on the virtues of the simple life."

Leandro's smile turned rueful. "It was an old argument between us," he said. "The only argument, really. Unfortunately, it was enough to destroy our relationship. Alfonso denounced me, withdrew from the Order, and left Spain. I never saw him again."

"He told me that he was the only Lancer," Sinclair said.

"Ha! I'm not surprised! That sounds just like him."

Sinclair's heartbreak was complete. "Why did he lie to me?" he murmured. "Why?"

"Don't be so despondent. He didn't lie at all, at least not from his perspective."

Sinclair's sadness gave way to confusion. "I don't understand."

"Alfonso believed that the Order was corrupt. He was constantly ranting about how all the others, myself included, had become a great lot of spoiled, self-indulgent hedonists. So you see, by his lights, he *was* the only Lancer. The only true one, at any rate." A thundercloud came into Leandro's eyes. "It was ridiculous! Just because he wanted to live like a Spartan didn't mean everyone else had to!"

"What did you guys do that made him so mad?" April asked. She threw a subtle, mischievous glance at Sinclair. "Did you use the Insight to pick winning numbers at roulette?"

"Among other things," Leandro said.

The mischief drained from April's eyes. "You can really do that?"

"Of course!" Leandro said. He cocked a brow at Sinclair. "Can't you?"

Sinclair shifted in his chair. "Mr. Mendoza always said that the Insight was a sacred trust, and to employ it in such a way was no better than petty thievery."

"Oh, he would say that!" Leandro snapped. "That self-righteous prig! And don't look at me that way. He was my only brother. I knew him longer and better than you, and I shall speak of him as I please."

Sinclair was about to respond to this, but he was cut off by April. "So what happens now? Are you gonna bring Sinclair and me into the fold?"

What do you mean, 'and me?' Sinclair wanted to ask, but he shelved it for later.

"That is exactly what I am going to do!" Leandro proclaimed, more cheerful now that he had set aside the topic of his sibling. "You may consider me your new mentor, *Señor* Sinclair. Trust me, you have only scratched the surface of what the Insight has to offer. A new world beckons, *mi amigo*, and I shall be your guide!"

"What kind of world?" Sinclair asked.

"A world of wealth and freedom," Leandro said. "A world of pleasure. A world without boundaries."

"Wow," said April.

Sinclair wasn't impressed. "Aren't you forgetting something?"

"What are you referring to?"

"The Dragon."

Leandro made a *pfft* sound. "The Dragon," he scoffed. "Don Julio was but a single man, and he defeated the Enemy with one blow. There are twelve Lancers in this city. Thirteen counting yourself. We'll dispatch that beast without shedding a drop of sweat."

"Are you really so sure?"

"I couldn't be more confident. Come to the Falmouth Inn this evening. We're meeting there at ten o'clock. I will introduce you to the others, and you can join in our council of war."

"I'll think about it."

"What is there to think about? Your destiny is calling!"

"I doubt Mr. Mendoza would have agreed with you."

Leandro snorted with exasperation. "You're right. He would have wanted you to languish in obscurity, living hand-to-mouth in this dustbin until you were buried in a pauper's grave. You would, of course, die with the satisfaction of knowing you had never used your gift for something so tawdry as personal gain. There would be that."

"That, and a clear conscience," Sinclair replied.

"You cut me to the quick," Leandro said in a caustic tone. "It's easy to see why Alfonso was so fond of you. You are clearly a man after his own sanctimonious heart. Well, let me tell you something, *Señor*. Your fellow Lancers do not share your scruples. My net worth exceeds ten million dollars, and I am far from being the wealthiest member of the Order."

He paused to let the statement sink in. Sinclair refused to give him the satisfaction of a visible reaction, but he saw April's jaw drop.

Leandro noticed this, and he directed his next remark to the girl. "If your mentor would rather cower in his hovel, then perhaps *you* would like to come to our meeting. It just so happens that I do not have an apprentice. I believe I would enjoy having one as beautiful as yourself. Think about it, *Señorita* Moon."

April did not reply, but her eyes were glued to the Spaniard. She was thinking about it, all right.

Leandro rose to his feet. "Ten o'clock," he said. He turned on his heel and marched to the door, his cane tapping the floor with every other step. "Don't let this opportunity pass you by," he called over his shoulder as the brass bell sounded his exit.

It wasn't clear to which of them he was speaking.

He must have been expecting her call, because he picked up on the first ring. "Dan Rains," he said.

"It's me, reporting as promised."

"Hi, Sally. How'd it go? Did you grill 'im like a steak?"

"On the contrary. I was as sweet as could be. Flirtatious, even."

"You're kidding."

"Nope. I call it my 'Venus Flytrap' approach. It works especially well on young men."

"I can imagine. Did you learn anything useful?"

"Just the usual society-page pabulum. I did press him a little about Henry Oliver, but it was a waste of breath. He's pushing the line that his guys were there on their own time and he has no idea why they were hanging out with a child-murderer."

"Is there a chance he's telling the truth?"

"No chance at all. I think Oliver was paying him for protection."

Dan grunted. "That would explain this 'Brother Bones bounty' crap that he announced the other day. Did you ask him about that?"

"I did, actually. He tried to pass it off as a publicity stunt, but he's dead serious. I can tell. If you see him sometime, mention Bones' name and watch the murder fly into his eyes."

"Has he had any takers?"

"None. He was pretty surprised. 'Fifty thousand dollars is a lot of money,' says he."

"And you said?"

" 'Yeah, but you can't spend it if you're dead.' "

Dan laughed. "All that aside, what's your personal impression of the kid, now that you've spent some time with him?"

Silence.

"Sally? You still there?"

Sally was thinking of something she had seen in Edgar's office. *What's that hook in the ceiling for?* she had asked.

I sometimes like to hang decorative things from it, Edgar replied.

He thought he was being cute. He didn't know Sally could hear the irony. He didn't know she had seen the secretary's wrists.

"He's evil, Dan."

"Evil? What do you mean? Does he like to drown puppies, or something?"

"Or something."

"You're serious, aren't you? What did he tell you that set off all these alarm bells?"

"DON'T LET THIS OPPORTUNITY PASS YOU BY."

"Just take my word for it, Dan. He's dirty. Keep an eye on him. I know I'm going to."

"All right, Sally. Thanks."

"You're welcome. Take care, okay?

"I will."

"You are not going to attend that meeting!" Sinclair said. "I absolutely forbid it!"

He expected April to erupt in fury, but she only laughed, which was somehow worse. "How do you plan to stop me?" she said. "I was invited."

"Under false pretenses! *I'm his disciple.* Phooey!"

"Phooey yourself, pal! I seem to recall you playing right along. What was that all about, huh?"

"It…seemed like the right thing to do at the time."

"Same goes for me. It just seemed like the right thing to do." She clasped her hands and fluttered her lashes. "And now a handsome *caballero* has offered to teach me all the secrets of the Insight."

"He only did that to irritate me!"

More laughter. "That's good. Keep telling yourself that."

He stared at her until she stopped smiling. "April, please tell me you're not serious about this."

"I can't say that, because I *am* serious. You heard what he said. Why wouldn't I want to live in a world without boundaries?"

"Because there's no such thing. He's deceiving you."

"He didn't sound like a liar to me."

"I bet that's what Eve said just before she took the first bite."

Her eyes narrowed. "You know what I think, Sinclair? I think you're jealous."

"Of whom?"

"I'll tell you *whom*. The guys who haven't spent the last twenty years scraping by in a book store. The guys who know what number's about to come up on the wheel. Those guys."

Sinclair turned away from her, and his eyes slowly scanned the cramped interior of the place he had called home for more than half his life.

Cramped interior.

Had he ever thought of it that way before? No, he hadn't. Not until today.

"You're right," he conceded. "I'm jealous of them. There, I said it. Satisfied?"

If she was, she didn't seem to find much pleasure in it. "You're taking this the wrong way," she said. "I'm not trying to humiliate you. I'm trying to make you see that you can have all that stuff, too. Don't you understand?"

"Yes, but I still think it's wrong."

"Wrong? To want nice things? To want a nice life? I know what it's like to be poor, Sinclair. I grew up poor. I never even had indoor plumbing before I moved to Cape Noire."

"But you were happy, April. I know you were. I *know.*"

April's jaw clenched and she looked at the floor. "That was before Daddy died."

"And if your father were here now, what do you think he would tell you to do?"

"Oh, come on! That isn't fair!"

"I mean it, April. Do you think he would want you to go to that meeting?"

"I don't know!"

"Yes, you do. What would he think of Leandro Mendoza? What would he say about you hanging around with a man like him?"

April met his eyes. "You want the truth? Probably the same thing he'd say about me hanging around with a guy like you!"

He laughed then. He couldn't help himself. "That sounds about right. He'd think I was a middle-aged creep with an unhealthy interest in his daughter. And I doubt I'd be able to convince him otherwise."

"I doubt it, too," April said, but then she smiled a little. "I'd take up for you, though. You're not a creep. Most of the time."

"Thanks for the ringing endorsement."

"As for that 'unhealthy interest' stuff, that better not be true."

He blushed. "It's not."

"Good. Don't go getting any ideas, Sinclair." She raised a fist. "Daddy did some boxing when he was a doughboy, and he showed me thing or two. This country girl knows how to take care of herself."

"I'll keep that in mind. Now, promise me you won't go to that meeting."

April threw up her hands. "All right! All right! But on one condition…"

"Yes?"

"*You* have to go."

"I'm not sure I want to do that."

"Either you go or I go. Make up your mind."

Sinclair made up his mind.

"You look really happy this evening, Mr. Shiloh," Lewis said.

Edgar met his eyes in the rearview mirror. "I do?"

"Yes, sir. If you don't mind me saying, you look like a man in love."

Edgar chuckled. "Maybe I am, Lewis. Maybe I am."

Edgar had been nervous about his interview that morning. He'd met Sally Paige at a couple of events, but had never exchanged more than a few words with her. He was, truth be known, frankly intimidated by her intellect and stunning good looks. The memory of one particular encounter still made him burn with embarrassment. "What's a lovely lady like you doing reporting on an ugly topic like crime?" he had asked.

"What's a little boy like you doing running a large corporation?" was the cool reply.

"I'm not…I have…I'm twenty-four years old!"

"I'm sorry. I should have said a *big* boy." She smiled to let him know that it was all in good fun. Just kidding. Really.

The next day, Mrs. Timms had paid a dear price for that little conversation. It took a two hour session for Edgar to fully recover his self-esteem.

Fortunately for Mrs. Timms, there was no need for any of that today. Edgar had been walking on sunshine since the moment Sally Paige had said goodbye. For the rest of the day, a single thought kept bouncing in his head like a red rubber ball: *She likes me!*

Now, relaxing in his car as Lewis navigated the rush-hour streets, he reflected on the fact that this shouldn't have been a surprise. After all, he was young, handsome, and wealthy. Why wouldn't she be attracted to him? She had just needed a little time to get to know him; that was all.

Later, as he was walking up the front steps, he decided he would go straight to his grandfather and tell him all about it. Gramps would eat it up. He always loved talking about women. It would take his mind off tomorrow's operation.

Grinning, Edgar opened the door, and then froze. There was a strange voice coming from the room at the end of the hall. He crept forward until he could make out individual words, spoken in a thick German accent.

"…but he was still concerned about his mistress," said the voice.

"What did you tell him?" Gramps asked.

"I said, 'Don't worry *Mein Herr*, I shot her, too.' "

Both men roared with laughter, and Edgar felt a pang of jealousy. He had never been able to make Gramps laugh like that. He chose that moment to enter the room.

"Eddie!" said Gramps. "You're just in time! This is Mr. Zorn. He's going to help us break Bones."

It took Edgar a second to catch the pun. He turned to the German, a big man with cold gray eyes and a decorative dueling scar. "You're here about the bounty?"

"I am."

"Come to my office day after tomorrow. We'll discuss it then." Edgar stepped aside to grant the man access to the hall.

Zorn ignored the clear dismissal. "I would prefer to discuss it now."

"Then I guess we won't be doing any business. Goodbye, Mr. Zorn."

Zorn turned to the Bruce, a questioning look on his face. Gramps rolled his eyes and raised his hands as if to say, *Can you believe this kid?* The gesture made Edgar feel angry and humiliated and very, very small. He opened his mouth to speak, but Gramps cut him off.

"Goddammit, Eddie! It was your idea to put a price on that bastard's head! Now we've got ourselves a professional who can deliver the goods, and you want to put him off? What the hell's wrong with you?"

"Gramps," Edgar whined, "there's a way to do these things, and showing up uninvited at a man's house –"

"This is *my* house, dummy! *Mine!* I was living here before you were a lick and a promise! I decided to let this man in, and I decided to listen to what he had to say. And now I'm telling you that this fella's our best chance to even the score with that freak." Gramps paused to give Zorn an admiring look. "Trust me on this, Eddie. I'm a good judge of men. Always have been."

Edgar wanted to continue the argument, but he knew it would be pointless. He tried to salvage some dignity by moving at a stately, unhurried pace to a nearby chair. He settled into it with a regal sigh and looked down his nose at the German. "So, *Mein Herr,*" he said, "what exactly is your proposition?"

"I will deliver the head of Brother Bones," said Zorn, "but I require a fifty-per-cent advance on the bounty. The remainder will be due upon completion of the job."

"Half up front? You must be joking."

"I assure you that I am not. I have a plan to draw this man out. It is a good plan, but it requires actions which I am not prepared to take without proof of your good faith."

"What kind of actions?"

"That is my affair. I am under no obligation to disclose my methods."

Edgar snorted. The man was so arrogant it was almost funny. "If I agree to all this, when can I expect results."

"Tonight. If you accept my terms, your enemy will be dead by dawn."

Edgar took a moment to think about it.

"C'mon Eddie," Gramps said. "Don't make the man wait all night."

Edgar locked eyes with Zorn. "Okay, you've got a deal, but there's one condition."

"And what might that be?"

"I want to be there when Bones gets it. I want to watch him die."

"Spoken like one of the Caesars," Zorn said with a chuckle. "Very well. Bring the other half of the money with you, and we will conclude our deal over the corpse of Brother Bones."

"Done and done," Edgar said. "Where do I go and when do I need to be there?"

Zorn told him.

☠ ☠ ☠

Donnie Rocket liked to work the train station. It was a thin stream to pan in, but Donnie had a knack for finding gold. Just last week, a succulent brunette with ebony eyes had rolled in from the sticks and fallen for his patter in five minutes flat.

First time in Cape Noire? Let me buy you a cup of coffee! Only sixteen? Get out of here! I would have sworn you were at least twenty-three! Have you ever thought about being a model? As a matter of fact, I have a friend who's a photographer...

For many years, Donnie had been the most successful talent scout in the Jorgenson organization. Big Swede himself had singled Donnie out for praise on more than one occasion. *Donnie*, he once said, *you're a divining rod for gorgeous whores! How do you do it?*

It was an interesting question. Donnie thought about it, and decided he had a special instinct for identifying and exploiting vulnerability. Over the years, this instinct had been honed to a razor's edge. Donnie was so smooth that some of his "clients" didn't even have to be hooked on dope before he delivered them to the brothels. Like starry-eyed snacks for Dracula, they entered freely and of their own will.

When Big Swede was killed, Donnie had been a little worried about his future. After some hand-wringing, he decided to go freelance, and it turned out to be the best professional move he had ever made. His reputation was a golden ticket to every cathouse in Cape Noire, and all of them were ready to do business with the Rocket Man.

These were happy thoughts, and Donnie was smiling even before he saw the sweet young thing stepping off the 6:10, her hazel eyes shining as she took her first look at the City of Night. She was a redhead, small and freckled and lovely, and Donnie decided then and there that he would keep her for a week or two before handing her over. He was entitled to a few perks every now and then.

Radiating brotherly love, he crossed the platform toward her. He was almost on her before she noticed him. He raised his hand in a friendly wave and was just about to speak when a ghost stepped into his path.

The ghost had jet black hair and eyes of frozen amethyst. She was dressed like a chauffeur, but the clothes were tailor-made and showed off her curves with admirable efficiency.

"Donnie," said the ghost, and in that single word was a universe of loathing.

"You," Donnie gasped. "You're dead. You and that other girl. They told me that both of you were killed when –"

The ghost flicked her wrist, and there was a shimmer as a knife appeared in her hand. "One," she said. "Two. Three."

Donnie didn't know what the top number was. He decided he didn't want to find out.

Stacy watched nervously as the handsome young man fled across the platform. He had been sauntering up to her like they were old friends, and then this woman in black appeared and *ka-pow*, he couldn't get away fast enough.

The woman turned to Stacy and gave her a cold stare. "New in town?" she asked.

"Yes, ma'am."

"Anyone expecting you?"

Stacy was too intimidated to lie. "No, ma'am."

"Do you have any money?"

"A little."

"Would you like to have a lot?"

Stacy bit her lower lip. "It would depend on what I had to do for it."

"Come with me," the woman said, "and let's find out what you're willing to do."

A few helpful handshakes at the Chandler Arms had given Sterling Harrow everything he needed to know. After enjoying a stroll through Whittington Park, he made his way to the Old Town address of Milton Pender; bellhop, would-be writer, and unwitting recruit into the Order of the Aspen Lance.

The hallway leading to Pender's apartment was narrow, filthy, and lit by a single naked bulb. A ferment of sweat, garbage and garlic assailed Harrow's nostrils as he searched for the correct number. At last Harrow found the door, but no one answered his knock. "Mr. Pender?" he said. "Are you in there?"

Harrow closed his eyes, reached out with his power, and his lips curled into a vulpine smile. The boy was home, but he was in state of near-catatonia. Harrow could feel the turbulent crackle of the Insight in Pender's unconscious mind.

"Later, then," Harrow whispered as he turned away from the door. He was ready for an elegant meal, and then he had a meeting to attend. After that business was taken care of, he would pay another visit to young Mr. Pender.

The man with the gray moustache would not look at Stacy. She squirmed uncomfortably in the back seat beside him as the woman in black drove them through the city. "May I ask where we're going?" she asked. She tried to strike a note of casual sophistication, but her voice only sounded small and frightened.

"Nowhere in particular," said the man. He had no trouble sounding casual. "What's your name, young lady?"

"Stacy."

"My name is Samuel. How old are you?"

"Twenty-four."

Samuel turned and met her eyes. "How old are you?" he repeated, still casual, but now with an edge.

"Seventeen."

"Do your parents know you're in Cape Noire?"

"Yes, sir." Pause. "No. No, sir, they don't. But it doesn't matter. They don't care. Listen, can we please…I don't want to make you mad, but…The lady, your driver, she said something about money…"

Samuel reached inside his coat and produced an envelope. It was a thick envelope. He sat it on the seat between them. "What would you do for a thousand dollars?" he asked.

Stacy gasped. "A thousand? I'd do just about anything."

"Anything?" said Samuel.

He began to describe some things that Stacy could do. He described them in crude detail. Some of the words were unfamiliar, but she was able to grasp the meaning. When he was finished, Stacy merely stared at him, barely able to breathe.

"Well?" he said at length.

"I don't…I don't…"

"My daughter did all of those things." Samuel said. He tapped the envelope. "She did them for less than this."

Stacy didn't know what to say. She felt light-headed. She looked away from Samuel and her gaze went to the rearview mirror. The driver's eyes were reflected in the glass, and Stacy saw that they were shining with tears. She turned back to the man beside her.

"She ran away when she was fifteen," Samuel said. "It was all my fault. After her mother died, I was…I didn't know how to…" He paused, then continued as if he were drawing poison. "She ran away. And she came here. And this place killed her."

Stacy looked down at the envelope. Samuel's hand cupped her chin. He lifted her face until their eyes met. "Do you want to die here, like my little girl?"

"No," Stacy whispered.

"Then go home. Give your parents another chance. Promise me you'll do that, and I'll give you this money."

"How do you know I'll keep the promise?"

"I don't."

The car came to a stop. Stacy pulled away from Samuel and looked out the window. They were back at the train station. The driver got out of the car and opened Stacy's door.

For a moment, Stacy was unable to move. Samuel pushed the envelope toward her. "Just one more chance," he said. "Just one."

Stacy nodded, took the envelope, and got out of the car.

After the car was gone, she stood at the station entrance for a long time, thinking.

The Dragon was angry. *Are you done with this nonsense?* he growled at Marax.

"It was something I had to do," the Doctor said.

"I beg your pardon, sir?" Erika said.

"Nothing, my dear. Take us back to the hotel. It's time for our final preparations."

Indeed? said the Dragon. *Are you sure there aren't any more lost lambs to save?*

"No," said Marax. "Now it's time for the slaughter."

Howard the cleaning man was still hitting the books when his phone rang.

"Hello?"

"Baldy said you left a message."

"I did. Thanks for calling back, Mr. Beest. I've found something in Edgar's records that I think you should know about."

"Yeah?"

"Well, as you know, our central question has always been fairly simple. Why is Eddie trying to expand his grandfather's criminal operations when the income from his legitimate business is already so huge?"

"Right. Go on."

"As it turns out, most of the TenaciTea profits are being eaten up by research and development. Eddie's worth a fortune on paper, but his actual cash reserves are minimal. He's spending it like it's water, and he needs every dime he can get just to keep up appearances."

"Research and development?" Beest rumbled. "What the hell is that all about? He's already got half the West Coast hooked on that swill. Is he trying to figure out a way to make it even more addictive?"

"Actually, he is. Or, rather, his chief researcher is."

"Who's that?"

"Well, that's what I thought you would want to know." Howard pronounced a name.

For a long moment, the only sound Howard could hear was the low, steady breathing of the monster at the end of the line. After one full minute, Howard said, "Mr. Beest, did you hear what—"

"I heard you. Are sure about this? About *him*?"

"Yes, sir."

"Do you know where he can be found."

"There's an Old Town address listed in one of the records."

"All right, then. I'm gonna be busy 'til about one in the morning. Come by here then, and bring all that stuff with you. I want to see it for myself."

"Yes, sir."

"Good work, Howard. Take a break. Go find yourself a woman."

"Thank you, sir. I'll do that."

A shadow fell on Sally Paige. Though she had been alone in the newsroom, she didn't even look up from her typing. She assumed it was one of the copy editors who worked in the evenings. "Whatever it is, make it quick," she told the shadow. "Hank's waiting on this piece and I really don't want to be distracted."

"Take your time, *Fräulein* Paige," a deep voice said. "I will be glad to wait until you are finished."

Sally's fingers froze above the keys. She swiveled her chair and looked into a pair of slate gray eyes set deep in a hard and handsome face.

I might be in a little trouble here, Sally thought. "Please accept my apologies," she said. "I didn't mean to be rude. I thought you were a Tribune employee. You see, the newsroom is usually closed at this hour…"

"So the guard informed me."

"He did?"

"Oh, yes. He was a very diligent fellow. He didn't want to let me in, but I managed to persuade him."

Trouble. Definitely. Sally had spent most of her life around dangerous men, and she knew she was talking to one now. "How strong was the persuasion, if you don't mind my asking?""

The man saw that he had been recognized—for what he was if not who he was—and this seemed to please him. "He will recover from it."

"Glad to hear it," Sally said, and she genuinely was. "So, what can I do for you, Fritz?"

"I need to get a message to Brother Bones."

"Then you should hire a skywriter. I don't have a line on Brother Bones. No one does."

"Really? How disappointing. I was told that you knew everyone."

"Who told you that? Edgar Shiloh? Did he hire you personally? Or are you just a freelancer trying to score a fifty thousand dollar payday?"

The man smiled. "A little bit of both."

Sally held up her hands. "Sorry, pal. I can't help you."

"I think you can." The man was very fast. It took only the span of a heartbeat for him to pull the Mauser from inside his white coat. "Let's go for a walk," he said.

He ushered her out of the newsroom and down the stairwell toward one of the rear entrances. When they reached the back door, Sally stopped and said, "What now? This opens onto a pretty busy side street, in case you didn't know."

"I am aware of the fact. My car is parked right outside the door."

Sally shook her head with amazement. She was angry and frightened, but she felt a sneaking regard for the sheer brass of the big man. "Do you really think you're going to get away with kidnapping me? It's going to take about five seconds for someone out there to notice that pistol you're holding."

"Who said I was kidnapping you?" was the cheerful reply. "Open the door and step outside. Please do not run. If you do, I will put a bullet in your spine."

Sally complied, and she emerged into the cool of the evening. There were fewer people on the street than she would have expected, but still a fair number of passersby filled the sidewalks.

"Just stand there for a moment," the German said.

What the hell is he doing? Sally wondered. She fought the impulse to turn and look at the man. She could feel his presence behind her, lurking in the shadow of the doorway. A minute passed, and then another. Sally tried to send a few pleading glances to some of the pedestrians, but the few who noticed just looked at her as if she were crazy.

"Daddy, I think something's wrong with that lady," said a small voice.

Sally looked down and saw a little boy, maybe four years old, who was eyeing her with a child's sincere concern. He was walking between a man and a woman who were obviously his parents. Sally looked up and made eye contact with the mother.

"Perfect," whispered the German.

The mother said, "Are you –" and the rest of the sentence was lost in a clap of thunder. There was a hole in the woman's forehead, and her husband's face was covered in a spray of blood.

"God!" the man cried, and then the thunder came again and his head jerked back and he fell beside his wife in a lifeless heap.

Now the child was screaming and people on the street were screaming and Sally was screaming, *"No! No! No!"*

She turned on the German. Gun or no gun she was determined to claw his eyes out, but he was just too fast. He stepped into her charge and drove his fist into her midsection. She fell retching to the sidewalk.

"Do not get up, *Fräulein*," the German said, and then he reinforced the order by kicking her in the side. He stepped around her and grabbed up the child, clapping one of his large hands over the boy's mouth.

Sally, struggling to catch her breath, rose to her knees. "Let him go," she gasped. "Let that kid go, or I swear to God –"

"Tut, tut," said the German. He pointed the Mauser at the boy's temple. "You are in no position to make threats. If you want this child to live, you will listen carefully to what I am about to say."

"I'm all ears," Sally snarled.

"Tell Brother Bones to meet me on runway thirteen of the Gibson Airfield tonight at midnight. Tell him to come alone and unarmed. If I see any police, the child dies. If I see a gun, the child dies. If he is even one minute late, the child dies. Do you understand?"

Sally couldn't speak. Horror, rage and frustration had rendered her momentarily mute.

"Do you understand?" the German calmly repeated.

"For God's sake!" Sally shouted. "I've already told you! *I don't know how to reach Brother Bones!*"

The German smiled. "Perhaps you should hire a skywriter," he said.

In the gloomy spare bedroom of a cold water flat, a candle began to burn. The flame was steady and cold, and cast a dim glow on the body of Brother Bones. He remained in his chair, but his muscles tensed, his head slowly lifted, and his black eyes came blazing to life.

A ghost appeared in the unnatural light. She was—had been—young, barely out of her teens. Her pale, translucent form shimmered in air before Brother Bones. *My name is Martha Sawyer*, she said.

Bones acknowledged her with a single nod.

He broke my neck, she said. *Then he broke my arms and legs so he could stuff me into a cabinet.* She winced, as if from a remembered pain. *I was the first girl in my family to go to college. I was going to be a nurse.*

Bones said nothing.

I was going to be a nurse, she repeated, and grief for this stolen future seemed to overwhelm her. Tears began to flow from her spectral eyes. She covered her face with her hands, and then she faded from view.

Bones stared into the empty air, waiting.

The candle flickered. A man appeared. He was embracing another ghost, a woman. The woman's face was buried in the man's chest, and her body was shaking with silent sobs.

He gunned us down in the street, the man said. *He killed us for nothing, and then he took our son.*

The woman pulled away from the man and rushed to Brother Bones. She fell at his feet, and raised her hands in supplication. *Please don't let him hurt my little boy!* she cried, *Please! I'm begging you! Please! Please!*

The man came forward and gently helped his wife to her feet. He wrapped his arms around her, and they faded from view.

The candle flickered, and from out of the ether came the girl from Sadie Levine's. *The killer's name is Josef Zorn*, she said. *He wants your attention.*

"He's got it," said Brother Bones. "Where do I find him?"

There's someone you need to talk to.

Sally lurched to her feet as the German drove away with the little boy. Her stomach felt like it was wrapped around her spine, but she was so furious that she barely noticed the pain.

A crowd of onlookers had already begun to gather around the bodies, gawking and gasping in horror. One of them, a young man, grabbed Sally's arm and asked if she was all right.

"Do I look all right?" Sally snapped. "Let go of me!"

The man obeyed and Sally staggered to a nearby phone booth. She was already working out exactly how much, and how little, to tell Dan Rains.

I can't say anything about the airfield, she thought. *Dan will go out there with an army, and that poor kid won't see tomorrow.*

She closed the door to the booth and leaned against one of its walls. Each breath was an agony, and she knew the German's kick must cracked at least two of her ribs. "Brother Bones," she muttered disgustedly. "How the hell am supposed to get up with—"

The phone rang.

Sally, unthinking, reflexively picked it up. "Hello?"

"I understand you've got a message for me."

Sally's blood ran cold.

"I knew you wouldn't be able to resist," Leandro Mendoza said with a grin. "That's why I decided to wait here in the lobby."

Sinclair gave him a weak smile. "Am I on time?" he asked. "I'm not in the habit of carrying a watch."

Leandro chuckled. "Can't afford one, eh? That's about to change, I promise you." He gestured for Sinclair to follow. "You're a few minutes late, but I wouldn't worry about it. Do you know the way to the conference room?"

"I've never stayed at the Falmouth," Sinclair said, and he half-expected the Spaniard to say, *Couldn't afford it, eh?* Instead, he led him to a room filled with sumptuous chairs lining a table that would have been at home in Heorot .

Seated at the table were several men, all of them middle-aged or older. Like Leandro, they were trim and athletic, and yet somehow bloated with fortune and conceit. They were neatly attired in the latest Savile Row fashions, their stylish suits complemented by the black walking sticks that each of them carried. The clothes betokened wealth, but the men had an air of privilege that went beyond sartorial elegance. It was a quality of power, of *entitlement*, so thick that it was almost palpable.

"Brothers," Leandro said, "allow me to introduce our newest member, Mr. Arthur Sinclair of Cape Noire."

No one offered a greeting. They regarded Sinclair with cool cynicism, as if he might be a prop in a bad practical joke. One of them yawned.

Sinclair felt like a stable hand who had stumbled into a gathering of Restoration fops. He had a sudden impulse to turn on his heel and walk away, perhaps showing these fine gentlemen his middle finger on the way out. He was considering doing exactly that when a tall, gray-haired fellow shouldered his way past and took a seat. "Sorry I'm late," he said. "Have I missed anything?"

"Hello, Sterling," Leandro said. "I was just welcoming –"

"The Shopkeeper!" said the gray-haired man. He gave a little bow. "Sterling Harrow, at your service."

Sinclair nodded at him. "Arthur Sinclair," he said. "Pleased to meet you."

Harrow turned to Leandro. "I suppose congratulations are in order," said the Englishman. "I'm afraid my search did not meet with similar success."

Leandro frowned. "Not even a clue?"

"Sadly, no. The identity of Krause's heir remains a mystery."

"Krause's heir?" one of the Lancers said. He spoke with a pronounced French accent. "What are you talking about?"

"It's a long story, François," Harrow replied. He gestured at Leandro. "Perhaps Brother Mendoza would like to tell it?"

Leandro stared at Harrow long enough for the silence to become awkward.

He doesn't trust him, Sinclair thought. *You don't need the Insight to see that.*

Harrow did not seem the least discomfited by Leandro's scrutiny. He returned the Spaniard's gaze with a near-comical look of earnest innocence. "Something wrong, Leandro?"

Leandro didn't answer. He lifted his eyes to take in the assembled Lancers. "Gentlemen," he said, "the day of the Dragon is about to dawn. Though our triumph is inevitable, it will not come without cost. Indeed, as you have no doubt inferred from Brother Harrow's words, a heavy price has already been paid by one of our own. Here is the situation as it now stands…"

Sinclair relaxed into one of the deep leather chairs. Only half-listening to Leandro's monologue, he studied the aristocratic faces around him. *Can I ever really be one of them?* he wondered.

He caught the eye of the Englishman, Harrow, and the gray-haired man favored him with a patronizing smirk.

Sinclair had never felt more alone.

Milton Pender awoke with a start. "What time is it?" he mumbled. He sat up and rubbed his eyes. "Jeez, what *day* is it?"

The day of the Dragon is about to dawn, he thought, and gooseflesh rose on his arms and neck.

"Where did that come from?" he asked himself, but he had no answer.

He fumbled around until he found his small alarm clock. He squinted at the hands. *Golly*, he thought. *Just call me Rip Van Pender.*

His stomach growled, turning his mind to more pressing matters. He needed to get cleaned up a little, go out and find something to eat. And something to drink. The TenaciTea jingle began to ring inside his head, and he felt his throat contract with painful yearning. "Sure could use a swig," he said.

Wasn't there something else? he thought. *Something important I wanted to do?*

Then he remembered. "The power," he whispered, and he grinned. But where should he go to experiment? It would have to be a place with lots of people, bustling with activity even in the middle of the night. A place where he could choose from a variety of test subjects, and quickly get lost in the crowd if he started to attract attention. A place like…

🕱 🕱 🕱

"Five Corners," said Dr. Marax, pronouncing the words as if naming a disease.

"Is this where we're going to set it off?" Erika asked.

"Can you think of a better place?"

Cape Noire's most infamous neighborhood lay at the intersection of Allard Street, Benson Street and Wentworth Avenue. From this focal point—anchored by the aging Tinsley Tower—radiated six blocks of vice and corruption decried by bloviating politicos and shunned by all decent citizens. It was also one of the town's largest tourist attractions. No visitor to the city could claim they had truly seen Cape Noire without at least one furtive sally into this paradise for the perverse.

Into the carnal tumult strode Doctor Marax, the music box tucked under his arm, Erika close by his side. They had parked several blocks away, as it was useless to trying to find a space in Five Corners after eleven o'clock.

From the moment they entered the area, their ears were flooded with shouts and cries and drunken laughter. From within this collective roar came sibilant promises of ecstasy from young girls—and a few young boys—with grasping hands and painted smiles. They accosted the Doctor with almost every step, but he paid them no heed. Erika tried to follow his example, but she couldn't stop looking into their eyes. They horrified her. She saw through the feigned lust and into the howling desperation beneath, and in that vortex of misery she glimpsed her own reflection.

The Doctor gently took her hand. "I know what you're thinking," he said. "You're wrong, my dear. You're not one of them. You never were."

"How can you say that?" Erika demanded. "How can you say that when you know—" She broke off, remembering her place.

The Doctor gave her hand a squeeze. "They made you sell your body, but they couldn't take your soul. Always remember that."

Erika felt her lip trembling. She bit it until the feeling passed.

"Ah," said the Doctor. "That looks like a likely spot." He led Erika through the press of the crowd to a bus-stop bench occupied by a blushing college boy and an ill-clad woman. The woman was busily whispering in the boy's ear.

The Doctor cleared his throat and held out a five-dollar bill. "Can I persuade you to give up your seat?"

The woman snatched the money from the Doctor's hand and disappeared into the milling throng. "Hey!" the boy cried after her, and then he, too, was gone.

Marax and Erika sat down. The Doctor settled the music box on his lap. He retrieved from his pocket the item he had purchased from Professor Bugosi; the device that Erika thought of as the tuning fork. He held the fork over the top of the box and, to Erika's amazement, it slowly began to slip inside the thing, as if the surface of the music box was made of liquid rather than metal. When it was half-inside the box, it encountered some sort of resistance, and the descent halted.

"Is it supposed to do that?" Erika asked.

"Oh, yes," Marax said. "It's working perfectly." He delicately grasped the tuning fork between his thumb and forefinger, and turned it ninety degrees.

Erika heard something click, and then she felt rather than heard a throbbing pulse, a heartbeat within the earth. It was a strangely pleasant sensation, and it intensified with each passing second. "Shouldn't we go now?" she asked.

"Whatever for?" said the Doctor.

"Isn't there going to be an explosion?"

Marax laughed. "Indeed! But not the kind that you're thinking of. Do not worry, my dear. We are perfectly safe. My companion will protect us."

Erika did not feel reassured, but she buried her doubts and put her faith in the Doctor.

And the pulse grew steadily stronger.

The clock on the newsroom wall said that it was twenty minutes after eleven.

I can just barely make it, Sally thought. She cursed under her breath. She thought a great deal of Dan Rains, but at that moment she could have socked him in the jaw. Extricating herself from his questions had been like trying to escape from Alcatraz.

Dammit, Dan, I've told you everything I know! I have no idea why he killed those people!

Yes, Dan, I know some of the witnesses say he told me something before he drove off with the kid, but it was all in German. I didn't understand a word of it!

No, I don't need to go to the hospital and I'm not letting you take me home. I just want to be alone now, okay? Quit wasting time on me and go catch this guy!

She hated lying to him, but it had been a necessary evil. Ignoring the pain in her side, she slipped on her coat and adjusted her fedora. She stepped behind her desk and retrieved the S&W .38 she kept hidden in the bottom drawer. She stared at the weapon, and for a moment her resolve wavered. Was this really the right thing to do?

Then she remembered a crack of thunder and a scent of cordite, and the sight of a young man's face covered with his wife's blood and brains. Then she saw the young man join his wife in death, and she watched helplessly as a smiling killer took away an innocent child.

She dropped the gun into her purse and headed for the door. She hadn't asked to be dealt into this game, but now she intended to play to the end, and the big German was going to learn that Sally Paige played for keeps.

There were no lights on runway 13, but that posed no problems to the Hessian. A full moon hung high in the sky, casting a bright silver glow over the entire airfield. The illumination was strong enough that Zorn had no trouble reading his watch. "Five more minutes," he said, loud enough for Edgar Shiloh to hear. The young tycoon was hiding behind one of the planes that lined the runway, watching.

The planes, like the gravel runway itself, were mostly old and disused; clunkers kept on hand primarily to provide spare parts. The one exception was a gleaming red autogyro that belonged to the Hessian.

The autogyro was Zorn's pride and joy. He had customized it himself, and from a cold start he could have it in the air in less than one minute. This was no small feat of engineering, and Zorn was certain that one day it would make him famous in the field of aeronautics. He looked forward to that day. He had always considered himself, first and foremost, to be an aviator. Murder was just a way to pay the bills.

Huddled at the Hessian's feet was the trembling child he had orphaned a few hours earlier. The boy's hands were bound behind his back, and his head hung so low it was almost touching the gravel. He had not made a sound since arriving at the airfield.

"Do not worry, *mein Freund*," Zorn said. "One way or another, this will all be over soon."

The boy raised his head and looked out into the darkness. His expression—hope shot through with terror—was very familiar to Zorn. He had often seen it on the faces of his victims.

"Listen to me, *Junge*," Zorn said. "It appears that *Fräulein* Paige has failed us. I'm afraid we must bow to the inevitable. Please do not waste your final moments searching for a savior who will not come. You are old enough to face death with dignity."

"I hate you," the boy said.

"That's the spirit!" said the Hessian. He looked at his watch. Thirty seconds. He pointed the Mauser at the boy's head. "Do have any last words?"

The boy stopped trembling. He turned his red and swollen eyes to the Hessian. "You're going to be sorry for what you did," he said. "Brother Bones is going to get you."

Zorn sighed. "I think not."

"Think again," said a harsh, grating voice.

DAY FOUR

Edgar Shiloh saw the tall shadow before the German did. The sudden appearance was startling. One moment, there was nothing there, the next…

Edgar had been crouched behind the tail of a broken-down Jenny biplane, captivated by the tableau unfolding before him. He was wondering if Zorn was actually going to go through with shooting the kid, and he had felt a strange thrill of anticipation at the possibility. He was half-hoping that Brother Bones wouldn't appear after all.

But then he did appear. He was standing about twenty feet away from Zorn. His long black coat billowed in the midnight breeze, and moonlight gleamed on the white skull mask.

In spite of the cool night air, sweat began to trickle down the back of Edgar's neck, and the handle on the cash-filled briefcase felt greasy in his white-knuckled grip. *A vigilante with a gimmick*, Byrd had said, and Edgar found himself clinging to those words. He searched his memories of that distant conversation, found some other helpful phrases, began repeating them like a mantra: *Crazy as hell. Not the boogeyman. Psychological warfare.*

The skull turned toward Edgar, lingered there for a moment, then turned back to Zorn.

"You didn't see me," Edgar whispered. "You didn't. You couldn't."

"But I can," someone whispered in reply, and a locomotive crashed into the back of Edgar's head, driving him into unconsciousness.

Sally Paige, gun in hand, stood over the inert form of Eddie Shiloh and resisted the urge to give him a few swift kicks where it would do the most good. *Had yourself a ringside seat, huh?* she thought. *You sadistic little snot.*

She lifted her revolver and drew a bead on the German's head.

C'mon, Bones, she silently urged. *Get that kid out of there.*

119

The Hessian was grinning like a tiger shark. "The fabled Brother Bones!" he said. "It is such a pleasure to meet you!"

"It won't be for long."

Zorn laughed. He felt like indulging in a little banter. "You have wit as well as style," he said. "But are you capable of following instructions?"

Bones opened his coat to reveal a pair of empty holsters. "Now, let the boy go."

"Tut, tut," said the Hessian. "Why the rush? We both know how this is going to end."

"One of us does. Let the boy go."

"All in good time. I'd like to ask you a question or two. The story I heard was a little confusing. Are you Jack or Tommy Bonello?"

"Both. Neither. Let the boy go."

"Were you really a killer—"

"I still am. Let the boy go."

Zorn grew testy. He disliked being interrupted. He pulled the boy to his feet and pressed the Mauser to the back of his head. "You need a lesson in manners, Brother Bones. If you want this child to live, I suggest you discard that peremptory tone."

Bones said nothing.

"Why are you really here?" Zorn asked. "If what I've been told is true, your career is even bloodier than mine. While I admire your talents, I must say that I find your hypocrisy offensive. What gives you the right to judge your fellow murderers?"

"I don't pass judgment," said Bones. "Someone else does that. I only carry out the sentence."

"Just so," said Zorn. Then he lifted the gun and fired four shots into the heart of Brother Bones.

Sally cringed as she watched Brother Bones fall to the ground. *That's another one you're going to pay for, Fritz.* She steadied her aim and started to squeeze the trigger, but the German knelt behind the kid, ruining her shot. Sally felt a stab of panic, then a rush of relief as she realized that the killer was keeping his word. He was releasing the boy.

"Well, *Junge*," she heard him say as he loosened the child's bonds. "This is your lucky night. You have been saved by that self-righteous fool." He cuffed the boy on the back of the head. "Run along, now. I have a fee to collect."

The child obeyed, coming to his feet in a headlong run…straight toward Sally's hiding place.

☠ ☠ ☠

"Mr. Shiloh," the Hessian called. "I'll take that briefcase now."

Zorn looked around. Edgar Shiloh did not appear. He cocked an ear, but the only sound he heard was the retreating footfalls of the little boy.

"Mr. Shiloh?"

Zorn frowned. Where was that little dolt? Had he fallen asleep? It occurred to Zorn that the young man had absconded with the money. Surely not! He couldn't be that foolish, could he?

Zorn shook his head. He looked behind a couple of the nearest planes. Nothing. He stepped back onto the runway…and out of reality as he understood it.

Brother Bones was standing about twenty feet away. His long black coat billowed in the breeze. Moonlight gleamed on the white skull mask.

"This is impossible," said the Hessian. Then he said it again—"This is impossible"—as if insisting on the point would make the man disappear.

Brother Bones did not disappear. He began walking toward Zorn.

Zorn lifted his pistol and fired the six remaining rounds. He saw the coat jump with each hit, heard each bullet strike the flesh.

Brother Bones did not stop, did not fall.

"This is impossible," Zorn said, but his voice now lacked all conviction.

Brother Bones began to laugh.

The Hessian turned and ran.

☠ ☠ ☠

Bobby Crandall moved with speed and stealth through the ranks of the rusty planes. He was heading in the direction where he had last seen the boy. *Get the child to safety*, Bones had ordered him. *That is your only job. I will take care of the rest.*

From the runway, Bobby heard a fusillade of gunshots, followed by the unmistakable sound of Bones' laughter. Bobby allowed himself a smile of grim satisfaction. Bones was taking care of the rest.

He stepped around the tail section of an old Loening, and was startled by an unexpected sight. The kid was there, wrapped in the comforting arms of a woman in a trench coat. Her features were slightly obscured by the brim of a fedora, but Bobby recognized her instantly. Sally Paige was a well-known figure in Cape Noire.

Bobby withdrew before he could be spotted. *What's she doing here?* he wondered. *And who was the guy on the ground?*

Bobby puzzled over it for a second, and decided that this was a helpful turn of events. Paige was probably better suited to looking after a traumatized child than he was. She'd make sure the kid was all right. As all right as he could be, at least.

Bobby had begun to quietly retreat when his ears were filled with a mechanical roar.

Is that joker trying to get away on a plane? He must be crazy.

Bobby didn't know much about aircraft, but he certainly knew that there was no way the killer could get anything in the air fast enough to escape from…

Bobby gaped as an autogyro went screaming down the runway, climbing into the air as it passed by. Hanging from the plane's undercarriage, his heels dragging the ground as it rose, was Brother Bones.

"Oh, no," Bobby said, and he started running for his car.

☠ ☠ ☠

The boy cried out when he heard the plane. "Don't be scared," Sally said into his ear. "I've got you. I won't let anything happen to you."

"I want Mommy and Daddy," the boy whimpered.

"I know you do," Sally whispered. "I know." She lifted the boy in her arms and started to walk away. As she did so, her foot brushed against something. She looked down at it.

What was it the German had said? *Mr. Shiloh, I'll take that briefcase now.*

Sally smiled.

☠ ☠ ☠

Donnie Rocket had plunged into the Five Corners revelry with his usual abandon, but tonight his heart just wasn't in it. The face of the girl in the chauffeur's uniform kept floating in front of his eyes, taunting him.

I wish I could remember her name, he thought, and this surprised him a little. Since when did names matter? He had sold her to Mary Kat, he could recall that much. Mary Kat had paired her up with another of Donnie's

"BROTHER BONES DID NOT STOP, DID NOT FALL."

acquisitions, a country girl with a funny last name, *Max* or something. They had specialized in threesomes, and it was well-known that they were closer than sisters. It was equally well-known that they were dead, murdered in a raid by some of Topper Wyld's goons in retaliation for the massacre at Sadie Levine's.

Retaliation. Yeah, right. It had never been proven, but everyone knew that Wyld had ordered the hit on Sadie's—his own place—and framed the Swede for it, thus lighting the fuse on a powder keg that had blown business all to hell for years. Thinking of the late Boss Topper made Donnie want to spit in disgust. Why couldn't the greedy bastard have left well-enough alone? Besides, Donnie had always liked Sadie Levine. She was good people.

His nostalgia for the old days was interrupted by a weird bass rumble that vibrated his sternum. Beneath the rumble, like the strains of a harp being strummed beneath the sea, was the faint but persistent echo of a haunting melody. It was strange and discordant, and yet beautiful in the way that dangerous things sometimes are.

Donnie stopped walking. Where was it coming from? He scanned the faces of the people around him, searching for a sign that someone else could hear it too...

Milton Pender wandered through the Five Corners crowd, sipping his favorite soft drink and considering whose memories he would sample first. He was taking his time, enjoying the feeling of the soda hitting his system, when something began to pummel his eardrums until they were fit to pop. At first the sound made Milton cringe, but then something else came floating in beneath the percussive pounding.

Holy smoke, Milton thought. *That's the most gorgeous thing I've ever heard!*

Slightly alarmed, he looked around for the source of this feeling, and his eyes met with those of another young man who was similarly entranced. They shared a moment of silent communication—*Do you hear that?*—and then the sound was joined by something else, the scream of an engine in the sky...

The Hessian flew the autogyro without skill, craft, or reason. Those things had fled before the inferno of panic that was burning through his brain. He struggled mightily against this blaze, trying to snatch from the flames his capacity for intelligent thought, but it was all in vain. The fire burned too hot, feeding on his fear, leaving nothing in its wake save a charred and screaming instinct for survival.

He careened wildly between the Cape Noire skyscrapers like some daredevil barnstormer trying to dazzle the rubes. The plane shook and twisted in the air as the weight of the monster hanging from it shifted and turned.

He's coming! Zorn thought. *He's climbing to the cockpit! He's…*

Going to get you, promised the little boy.

"No!" Zorn cried, but his voice was lost in the roar of the engine as he banked sharply to the left to avoid crashing into the Falmouth Inn. He immediately turned back to the right, narrowly avoiding another large building that loomed before him.

Climb! He commanded himself. *Climb, you fool! Get out of this labyrinth before—*

A heavy hand fell on the Hessian's left shoulder. Screaming, he twisted the plane in that direction, and flew straight into a billboard extolling the joys of TenaciTea.

Milton's eyes left the face of the other young man and looked up at the sudden explosion in the center of the TenaciTea sign mounted on the roof of the Tinsley Tower.

Golly! He thought. *Is that a plane?*

It had to be, although it was hard to distinguish anything through the cloud of smoke rising from the billboard. For a moment, the ruined sign supported what was left of the plane—TenaciTea was, in fact, helping it to hang in there—but then there was an unholy screech of metal, and the wrecked plane began to pull loose. There was an outcry from the crowd as the moment of stunned inertia passed and they began to flee in all directions.

Barely had the space beneath the sign been cleared when the wreckage came whistling to the street. There was an explosion—not very large—but no one was injured by the falling debris. Nonetheless, the general flight had begun and was not easily reversed.

Milton found himself fighting the tide. What if someone had survived the crash? It was pretty unlikely, but still…

He had been too late to help Martha and Mr. Krause. Maybe this was his chance to make up for it.

It's what the Black Haze would do.

Donnie Rocket was pushed back by the bovine mob as they began a stampede toward safety. He allowed himself to be swept along—no sense getting trampled—and then he saw her. It was her stillness that had drawn his eye. She was sitting on a bench, gazing with rapt attention at some beady-eyed geezer with a gold box in his lap. Then the pressure in his ears seemed to force some connection in his brain, and he remembered that her name was—

"Erika," he said, and he grinned as he realized that names *did* matter. There was power in knowing a name. Power that that one could use to subdue, to repay, to punish.

You shouldn't have threatened me with that knife, little girl, Donnie thought. *Time for you take a Rocket ride.* He started to work his way through the crowd toward her.

"Did we do that?" Erika asked. "Did we cause that plane to crash?"

"I don't know," the Doctor said impatiently. "I don't understand why we haven't seen the effects yet! It should have started by now! It should have…"

The Doctor stopped speaking, and a gleeful light came into his eyes.

"And so my brothers," said Leandro, "it is clear that we must –"

He was cut off by a cry from Sinclair.

All eyes turned to the Shopkeeper, but he neither noticed nor cared. His hands were pressed to the sides of his head, his features distorted with apparent agony.

"What's wrong with you?" Leandro demanded.

"It's happening," Sinclair gasped. "Can't you feel it?"

Something passed around the table like an electric current.

"He's right!" shouted one of the Lancers. "The crisis is upon us!"

The Lancers all rose to their feet. They lifted their walking sticks to port arms, twisted the handles, and withdrew the gleaming blades that were sheathed within. They raised the swords in the air. *"Father in Heaven,"* they chorused, *"let our hands strike true!"*

Leandro beheld this with barely concealed dismay.

Why hadn't he sensed it first?

Donnie was halfway to his once and future whore when a massive weight bore down on his shoulders, pressing him to the pavement. It was as if someone had hung a sack of bricks on his back. He was driven to his knees, and as he hit the ground he came to the alarming realization that the weight belonged to something that was alive.

"Hey!" he cried. "What the hell!"

He frantically reached behind his head and his hands met with flesh that felt like warm snakeskin. The thing tumbled from his shoulders and struck the sidewalk with a resounding thump. Donnie jumped to his feet, turned, and looked into a pair of burning yellow eyes, blazing in the face of a living gargoyle. The thing slowly drew itself up until it stood nose-to-nose with Donnie.

Donnie stared at the thing. He was so completely awed that the world around him seemed to recede into an opaque mist of irrelevance. He no longer heard the cries of the mob, nor did he see their panicked faces. He was the last man on Earth, with only the Devil for company.

The thing stared back at him, its eyes and mouth open wide with… surprise? A forked tongue snaked out to lick crooked fangs, and flattened nostrils flared as they drew in the polluted air. There was a sound like knuckles cracking, and a pair of large black wings unfurled from its back. It raised its hands and flexed long, thin fingers that tapered into long, sharp claws. It sighed with pleasure, and its breath was the wind from a charnel house.

"Hello, Donald Rockwell," it said.

Donnie shuddered. "You know my name?"

"I have been with you since the day you born," the thing said, and it giggled. Then it plunged its talons into Donnie's chest and opened his rib cage like a pair of saloon doors.

Five Corners, often called a Hell on Earth, had become a literal Pandemonium, and Milton Pender was trapped in the center of it.

From out of the empty air had emerged a legion of monsters, ripping and tearing at all they could reach. They did this with the clumsy enthusiasm of homicidal drunkards. Many of the beasts could barely stand, and a few attempts at taking wing resulted in pratfalls that would have been humorous under any other circumstances. But they were growing stronger and more agile with every second that passed, and whatever they lacked in physical prowess, they made up for in murderous vigor. They whirled about like clawed dervishes, covering their shiny scales and leathery wings with glistening sprays of blood.

This ferocious attack had the denizens of Five Corners in a state of pure animal panic. They ran like gazelles pursued by a pride of lions. No matter where they turned, there was another ravening demon waiting to rake their flesh.

Milton screamed as a severed arm went flying in front of his eyes, but he could barely hear his own cry over the damnable pounding in ears. The second layer of sound, the siren-song that had so mesmerized him earlier, had grown louder as well, but it was no longer beautiful. It had decayed into something harsh and atonal, the perfect melody for a massacre.

Oh Jesus God please get me out of here! He desperately prayed. As if in mockery of this plea, a demon leapt in front of him and raised a hand to slash his face.

"No!" Milton screamed, and the monster froze. It glanced at its upraised claws, then back at Milton. Its reptilian features twisted into a mask of furious bewilderment. *Why can't I kill you?* It seemed to be asking.

Milton, no less confused, gawked at the beast. "Get away from me!" he shouted.

The demon turned and staggered away, a rebellious puppet pulled by unseen strings.

What saved me from that thing? Milton wondered.

From some dark crevasse in the depths of his mind came an answer: *The power.*

A disembodied head rolled to a stop at Milton's feet, bringing him back to present concerns. There would be time to contemplate his new abilities later. For now, he had a job to do. He once more fixated on the plane as his true north, and resumed fighting his way through the chaos toward it.

Screams of terror and pain filled the air, but Erika heard none of it. She was now completely submerged in the thrumming of the music box, drowning in an otherworldly ocean of sound. This imposed deafness had the effect of giving her a curious distance from the horror unfolding before her.

Erika glanced at the Doctor, and saw that he was laughing. She had never seen him look happier.

Why aren't you laughing, too?

Erika stiffened. The words were clear and distinct, spoken in a guttural, yet strangely seductive, voice that she had no trouble discerning in spite of the music box.

"Who said that?" she asked. She spoke aloud, though she was unable to hear her own voice.

Don't you know?

Erika became conscious of a presence, an indefinable darkness that loomed above and behind her.

You never believed I was real, did you?

Erika felt a blast of hot breath on the back of her neck.

Turn, harlot, and see how wrong you were.

She turned her head.

From the smoking ruins of the autogyro, the Hessian came crawling. His broken body, blackened with blood and soot, inched along the pavement. Every tortured movement brought cascades of agony, but his heart was exultant.

I'm alive! he thought, and a faint chuckle rattled in his throat. It was true that his body was shattered, but he would recover. He was like the worm that emerged from the ashes of the phoenix, destined to rise even greater than before. Soon, he would once again soar through the clouds, and he would laugh at the memory of Brother Bones.

"Hold on!" someone yelled. "I'm coming to help you!"

The Hessian lifted his eyes. A corpulent young man was racing toward him. He must have been the one who shouted. There were others in the street, but they were running about in some sort of aimless frenzy. No, not aimless. They were fleeing from monsters.

Hallucinations, Zorn thought. *Shock and blood loss affecting my mind.*

They certainly looked real, though. Devils straight out of Dante. Remarkable.

And where was that wonderful music coming from? Zorn closed his eyes and concentrated on it. It made him think of killing fields in springtime. He pictured himself flying above them, fearless and free.

Behind him, something stirred in the wreckage.

Zorn opened his eyes. The young man had stopped running. He was frozen in place, staring open-mouthed at...

No! He can't still be alive!

Horror ripped through the Hessian like a serrated blade. He rolled onto his back, and the cerulean skies of his imagination turned black as he gazed up at Brother Bones. It was too much for Zorn. He broke down. He began to cry. "Please!" he said. "Please don't kill me!"

Bones reached down and pulled the Hessian to his feet.

"Please," Zorn sniveled. "I want to live."

"Martha Sawyer wanted to be a nurse," said Brother Bones, and he snapped the Hessian's neck.

That's Brother Bones! Milton thought. *Holy cow! I never thought he was real!*

Brother Bones dropped the limp form of the man he had just killed. He looked at Milton. "Duck," he said.

"Huh?" said Milton, and then then a pair of clawed hands grabbed him beneath his arms. He was buffeted by a wind from black wings, and he screamed as he felt his feet leave the ground.

"Fat little pig!" the demon said, his voice like venom in Milton's ear. "Be still and I may kill you quick!"

Milton was not still. He writhed and wriggled and cried, "Let me go!"

The demon gasped and its flight turned into an awkward roll through the air. It released Milton and he fell about ten feet to the pavement. He landed badly and felt something give way in his right ankle.

"How did you do that?" the demon screeched. It swooped down on Milton and perched on his chest. Milton could see that it was smaller than the others, about the size of an overgrown vulture. It glared at Milton with basilisk eyes. "By what authority did you command me? Explain yourself, pig! Tell me what –"

The monster was cut off by a hand that closed around its throat. Milton drew in a deep breath as the thing was snatched from atop his chest. He rose to his knees, and saw Brother Bones holding the demon by one hand, shaking it like a rag doll.

"You're the one who's got some explaining to do," Bones said. "Where did you come from? What are you doing in my city?"

"Your city?" the demon said with a strangled laugh. "Does it belong to you? Are you the prince of this world?"

"Riddles," growled Bones. "I'll put up with them from the girl, but not from the likes of you." Then he drove his fist through the demon's head. To Milton's amazement, the thing vaporized, disintegrating into a cloud of smoke that curled in on itself and then disappeared.

"One down," said Bones. He looked at Milton. "You need to get out of here, boy."

Milton nodded in fervent agreement. He didn't have to be told twice. He pulled himself upright, lurched onto Wentworth Avenue, and hobbled straight into the path of an oncoming car.

Bobby cursed and slammed the brakes. There was a soft *thump* as the DeSoto's bumper collided with the chubby kid, sending the guy spinning to the street. Bobby leapt from the car. He knelt by the prone form. "Are you okay, pal?"

The kid, wincing in pain, looked up at Bobby. "I think so."

"Just stay there. I'll get you some help."

"Are you nuts?" said the kid. "I'm not staying here! Can't you see what's happening?"

As if on cue, a cackling demon swooped through the air past Bobby, narrowly missing as it swiped at his head. "Aaah!" Bobby cried. "What the hell was that?"

The monster turned in a narrow arc and began to come at Bobby for another pass. Bobby, shocked into stasis, simply stared as the gargoyle came flying straight at him. Then he was roughly pushed aside and Brother Bones stepped into the demon's flight path. The monster pulled up and banked right, but it was too slow. Bones reached up and caught one of its feet as it sailed by and viciously smashed the thing to the street. When it hit the pavement, it cried out once, then disappeared in a puff of smoke.

Bobby looked at Bones. He had a thousand questions on the tip of his tongue, but a glance from the black onyx eyes silenced them all.

"Guns," said Bones.

Bobby reached into his coat and produced the twin automatics. "What are you gonna do?" he asked as he handed them over.

"Save who I can," said Bones. "Avenge the rest." Then he turned and waded into the fray, both guns blazing.

Bobby turned to the kid. The poor guy was frantically trying to pull himself upright, but his right leg kept slipping as though it couldn't support his weight.

"Let me help you," Bobby said. He reached down and took the boy's hand.

"You're beautiful," Erika said.

You find me so? The Dragon said. The white perfection of his razor fangs were a stark contrast to the obsidian scales that covered his massive frame. *I am but a shadow of what I was before the Fall. If you had seen me in my glory, your eyes would have boiled in their sockets.*

Erika nodded. She sensed the words were true. "Can I...touch you?"

You may.

Erika reached out, and her hand passed through the scales as if they were a fading dream. She was disappointed. "Why aren't you like the others?"

Those little fish? The Dragon tilted his snout to indicate the swarming demons that surrounded them. *I am older and stronger than they are. I swim in deeper waters, and it takes me longer to surface.*

"Not just different in that way," Erika said. She glanced over shoulder, then back up at the Dragon. "They're insane."

Of course they are. They have spent untold millennia as impotent spirits, trapped in linear time with nothing to do but tempt and tease you worthless lumps of clay. It would break the mind of almost anyone.

"Anyone but you."

The Dragon gave a smoky exhalation that might have been a laugh. *You are even smarter than Marax. You will make a worthy slave.*

Slave? Erika was so enchanted that she didn't bridle at the word. It was right and proper to be enslaved to the Dragon. It was...*natural.*

"How long before I can feel you?" she asked.

Soon, little one. I will bear you aloft in the cold night sky, and we will watch the little fish frolic in rivers of blood.

Erika's spirit soared in sympathy with this vision. Her skin tingled and her heart fluttered and she knew that she was falling in love.

They're getting harder to destroy, thought Brother Bones.

At first it had taken only a single shot to vaporize the demons. Then it had taken two. Now a minimum of four rounds had to be pumped into them before they would disintegrate. How much stronger could they get? If enough time passed, would they become invulnerable? Bones set his jaw. He would just have to kill them all before that happened.

"Easier said than done," he muttered to himself as he drew a bead on a demon scampering after a young prostitute. As Bones was about to fire, the screaming girl produced a derringer and emptied it point blank into one of the demon's eyes. The thing howled in agony and disappeared.

Bones laughed. "Welcome to Cape Noire," he said. "This city can kill anything."

Indeed, as the demons were learning to their sorrow, plenty of people made a point of going armed in Five Corners. Violent men and women who would have ordinarily been mortal enemies of Brother Bones found themselves fighting at his side, ignorant of the irony as they battled for their lives.

"Behind you, Bones!" shouted one of them, a pot-bellied man hefting a large revolver.

Bones heeded the warning, spinning into a crouch and firing at an airborne demon that was descending on him like a dive bomber. The monster did not vaporize. It crashed into Bones and they rolled wildly across the street, grappling furiously. Bones got the upper hand and began to smash the demon's head into the pavement. After a few seconds of this abuse, the monster screamed and dissolved into smoke.

"You okay?" the gunman asked, extending a hand to Bones.

Bones did not accept the help. "I'm fine, Howard. You should run home to Harry Beest."

Howard the cleaning man chuckled as he took a second to reload his revolver. "He's expecting me later. I'll tell him you said hello."

"Don't bother."

"Any idea what's causing all this?" Howard asked.

"It has something to do with that music I keep hearing. Do you know where it's coming from?"

"Afraid not."

The conversation ended in a roar of gunfire as both men opened up on a group of demons that were trying to encircle them. They had to empty their guns before the monsters went down.

Howard swore as he opened the cylinder to insert six fresh rounds.

"Where's a cop when you need one?" he said. Then he saw something and smiled. "Ha! Speaking of the cavalry…"

"Those aren't policemen," said Bones. "Policemen do not carry swords."

☻ ☻ ☻

Well, well, said the Dragon. *If it isn't the heirs of Don Julio, come to save the day.*

Erika followed the Dragon's gaze and saw a group of sword-wielding dandies doing battle with the demons. The men were making a good account of themselves. They thrust and parried among the monsters like modern musketeers, dispatching their enemies with speed and panache. Erika appreciated their skill. "They're pretty good," she said. "Who are they?"

A gang of fools, said the Dragon. *They think they're going to destroy me.*

Erika was alarmed. She drew her knife and leapt to her feet.

Calm yourself, harlot, said the Dragon. *They cannot even see me. Not yet.*

"One of them can," Erika said. She gestured with the knife, and the Dragon saw a bearded and bespectacled little man ogling him with fearful astonishment. He was a shabby, unimpressive fellow, but the Dragon could sense…

That one's dangerous. Keep him away from me.

"He's a dead man," Erika said. She started forward, but someone grabbed her wrist.

"You can't go out there!" said Dr. Marax. His voice was lost in the music, but Erika could read his lips. "You won't be safe! What do you think you're doing?"

"What I do best," she replied, and she pulled free and went out to battle the enemies of her new master.

☻ ☻ ☻

They didn't give Sinclair a weapon. *Sorry, old boy*, Harrow had told him. *Gerhard's blade was taken by the police. Why don't you just watch and learn.*

Trailing along like a junior mascot, he followed them to Five Corners, but his misgivings about the men faded when he saw them leap into action. They may have been accustomed to soft living, but they handled their swords like warriors born. Demons fell before them like dried stalks of wheat. The creatures seemed completely incapable of resisting the Aspen Lancers.

And why is that? Sinclair wondered. The monsters were absolutely slavering to kill the Lancers, but their blows fell like swats from the paws of kittens, and they could do little more than spit and snarl as they died beneath the blades.

Sinclair shook his head in wonder. *Mr. Mendoza was wrong about these men*, he thought. *The Insight has made them invincible. They're more than capable of handling this. I'm only in their way. I should go before I get someone killed.*

Feeling stupid and useless, he began to withdraw, and that was when he saw the Enemy. It was standing across the street, its saurian head at least twenty feet in the air atop a muscular, serpentine neck. Its wings curled protectively around a bench where an old man was tugging at the sleeve of an attractive young woman. The Dragon was looking down at these two, and Sinclair saw cruel amusement in the monster's eyes. Then the eyes lifted, and looked directly at Sinclair.

Are you one of the Lancers? The Dragon asked. The voice flowed through Sinclair's mind like molten lava.

"I am." The response was pure reflex. In truth, he wasn't sure anymore.

The Dragon turned his head and spread his wings, regal and rampant. That he was majestic made him even more grotesque, for he was a majesty corrupted and debased. *Kneel before me*, said the beast, *and I will let you live.*

Again, Sinclair offered an instinctive reply. "Never."

Die, then.

Suddenly, the attractive young woman was charging Sinclair, her arm raised high, a knife gleaming in her hand. The hand descended, and Sinclair was just fast enough to catch her wrist…

Hear the killer's cry. *Payback for Sadie Levine's!* He shouts, and the staccato crackle of his Thompson almost covers the sound of his laughter.

See the young girls. They huddle like frightened mice, hoping that by some miracle he will pass them by, let them go, let them—

See the door smashed open.

Please don't hurt us! We never did anything to you!

The killer grins. *Do I look like I care? Just this morning I murdered a dozen monks and my own twin brother! They didn't do anything to me, either!*

The Thompson roars and the killer moves on, unaware that he has left the job half-done. One of the girls had shielded the other. She sacrificed herself to protect –

Erika.

Excuse me?

My name is Erika. Catherine was...my friend.

You knew my daughter?

She died saving my life. I loved her. I loved her so much. I'm so...I'm so... sorry...

The broken man reaches out and takes the broken girl into his arms. They cling to one another as they heal, but they grow twisted in the embrace, and the world around them grows darker as they mend their broken hearts with hate.

Erika twisted out of the man's grip, lost her balance, and fell on her backside. She looked up at the man who had just invaded her memories. Incredibly, he was still holding out his hand.

"I'm sorry for what happened to you," he said. "If you'll let me, I can help—"

Erika screamed in fury and leapt forward. She slashed at his midsection, but he deftly avoided the blade. He was faster than he looked.

"Please!" he said. "It doesn't have to be this way!"

Erika went for his throat, but she was interrupted by a flying demon that slammed into her side. It rode her to the ground and cupped her face in its hands like a lover. "You shouldn't have left the Dragon's wings," it said. "Now you're mine!"

Erika replied by driving her knife into the demon's neck in a series of snake-strike blows that sent gouts of black ichor spraying into the air.

Then someone said, "Close your eyes, girl," and a pistol appeared at the demon's temple. Erika heeded the command, and for a moment the melody of the music box was drowned out by gunfire. The weight on her chest disappeared as the monster exploded in a cloud of oily smoke. Coughing, she rose to her feet, and found herself pierced by a pair of stygian eyes set deep in the sockets of a white skull mask. Erika drew back her knife.

"Don't be an idiot," growled Brother Bones.

Erika flinched, and in that moment of hesitation, the Dragon spoke up.

Return to me, harlot. I do not require your death just yet.

She hated to run from a fight, any fight, but she obeyed.

The Dragon smiled as he watched Erika race back to his faithless embrace. Though his power was only a fraction of what it once was, he could still thoroughly beguile a wounded spirit. Perhaps, one day, the girl would look back on this moment with the clarity of hindsight and be shamed and disgusted at how quickly she was seduced. That would be a delicious humiliation. He hoped he would be there to see it.

The monster turned his attention to the skull-faced man. Here was a novelty. What manner of creature was this? To his surprise, the man's eyes locked with his.

"You must be the Dragon," said the man. As with the shabby Lancer, the Dragon could hear the man's voice even through the clamor of the music box.

You know who I am?

"I was told you were coming."

You don't look like a Lancer.

"Lancer?" The man laughed, as if at a private joke. "I'm just a talking gun, and it looks like I'm aimed at you."

The Dragon bared his fangs. *Do your worst, fool.*

Bones emptied both guns into the monster, but the bullets passed harmlessly through the Dragon's intangible form. *Great,* Bones thought. *One of those.*

How was he supposed to stop this thing? For what must have been the thousandth time, he wished the girl would give him more to work with than vague outlines.

"Can you see him, too?" someone asked. Bones turned and looked at a rumpled little man wearing thick glasses.

"If you're talking about Nessie over there, the answer is yes."

"Thank God! I thought I was the only one! I don't know why the other Lancers can't—"

"Who are the Lancers?" Bones asked, reloading his pistols. "Those men with the swords?"

"Yes! This is what they've trained for! They should be here with us!"

"Well, they're not. You seem to know a thing or two about what's going on. Any bright ideas on how to kill that thing?"

"I…I…Mr. Mendoza always said that when the time came I would know what to do…"

Bones ground his teeth in frustration. Who was Mr. Mendoza? Did *everyone* have to talk in riddles? He was getting a new appreciation for Bobby. "What about that music?" he said. "Do you recognize it? Do you know how it's connected to all this?"

The man blinked as if he were emerging from a deep sleep. "You're right!" he said. "That must be the key! Literally! It's opening some sort of gate for these things to come through. If we can find what's causing that and stop it…"

Both of them turned toward the Dragon, and they saw it at the same time; the golden box in the old man's lap. "There!" they said in unison, and Bones opened fire.

The music had grown so loud that Erika felt as if she were breathing it. It filled her lungs like mustard gas, and blood began to run from her ears. She absent-mindedly noted this as she drew near to the Dragon. She gazed up at her new mentor, yearning for him to grant her a favorable glance. The Dragon ignored her, and Erika felt a twinge of panic when she saw his eyes widen with something like fear.

No! the Dragon roared.

Erika turned and saw the skull-faced man aiming his pistols at –

"Doctor!" she screamed, and she pushed Marax to the ground as the bullets began to fly. She fell protectively over the Doctor's body, then realized she had made a mistake. Marax wasn't the true target.

Bewitched though she was by the Dragon's glamour, Erika's mind was still clear enough to admire the marksmanship behind the tightly-grouped shots hammering the music box, and to marvel at the fact that the hits had almost no effect. The big, heavy .45 slugs merely bounced off the shimmering surface, leaving only small dents to mark their passage. One of the mangled bullets ricocheted into the Doctor's chest. Blood spurted from the wound and he let out a cry of pain which was lost in the furious bellowing of the Dragon. Then one of the shots hit the tuning fork.

The fork exploded, and a shockwave burst from the music box. Erika could actually see it; a shimmering circle of impure energy that blasted across Five Corners, shaking the dilapidated buildings, blowing apart the streetlights, and knocking to the pavement everyone its path. Every human being, anyway. The demons were completely disintegrated.

Erika lifted her head in time to see the Dragon dissipating like a cloud before a driving gale. As he faded from view, the monster's yellow eyes fixed on hers.

"Don't go," Erika pleaded.

Fear not, harlot. I am never far away. The Dragon gave her a farewell sneer, and then there was nothing left of him but a lingering stench of sulfur.

Sinclair was on his feet just a few seconds behind his ghoulish ally. "What happened?" he said. "Is the Dragon dead?"

"What do you think?" said the man in the white skull mask.

Sinclair looked around. The girl with the knife and the man with the music box had disappeared. Other survivors of the supernatural assault were slowly lifting themselves from the ground. Their dazed expressions made Sinclair think of pictures he had seen of shell-shocked soldiers at the Somme. "At least the demons are gone," Sinclair said. "That's something, anyway." He adjusted his glasses. "Tell me, are you Brother Bones?"

"Yes."

"My name is Arthur Sinclair, and I want to thank you. I'm pretty sure you just saved my life. The lives of everyone here, in fact."

"Tonight's work is done," Bones replied, "but I don't think this job is finished." He leaned into Sinclair and poked him in the chest. "You and I are going to have a talk. Soon."

"Yes, of course. I can be found at—"

"I'll find you. When I do, I expect you to tell me all about the Dragon, and the Lancers, and Mr. Mendoza, and anything else I might find useful. Do you understand?"

"Yes, I'll be glad to help."

"Glad or not, you *will* help. I'll be seeing you."

Brother Bones turned and walked away.

Sinclair swallowed as he watched him disappear into the darkness. "Nice to meet you, too," he whispered to the retreating shadow.

I know his secrets, someone whispered in reply.

Sinclair started. The voice was in his mind, furtive and fleeting…and somehow familiar.

Who's there? Sinclair mentally called. *How do I know you?*

Silence.

Sinclair concentrated, and he could hear the tinny echo of an annoying jingle. *It's the taste that brings you hope…When you're at the end of your rope…*

Sinclair opened his eyes. That was a memory from the night of Gerhard Krause's death. But there was no reason for him to be experiencing that now, unless…

Krause's heir, Sinclair thought. *He's here somewhere! I must have some connection with him since my mind was touching Krause's when he passed on the Insight.*

Someone slapped him on the back, derailing his train of thought and making him cry out in surprise.

"Don't have a heart attack, *mi amigo*," said Leandro Mendoza. "It's time for a celebration! Another triumph for the Order!"

Sinclair saw the other Lancers approaching. They were laughing and joking, sharing boyish gibes about each other's skill in battle. One of them, the man named François, saw Sinclair and said, "How about you, Shopkeeper? How many did you slay?"

"None, I'm afraid," Sinclair replied.

François gaped in mock astonishment. "Not a one? I thought you would at least bore a few to death!" The others found this highly amusing, and they passed by Sinclair in a natty cluster of derisive chuckles.

"Don't mind them," Leandro said. "Come on, I'll buy you a drink. We need to talk, anyway. I was very impressed that you were the first to sense that the Enemy—"

"What are you so damned cheerful about?" Sinclair interrupted. "You didn't stop the Dragon! You never even saw him!"

Leandro scowled. "Are you insane? Didn't you see us in action? We were unstoppable! The Dragon's minions had no choice but to retreat from our attack!"

Sinclair shook his head. "You really have no idea what happened here tonight, do you?"

Leandro's eyes narrowed into slits. "On the contrary," he said. "I know exactly what happened. My brothers and I acquitted ourselves with honor against the forces of darkness, while you sulked on the sidelines without offering so much as a word of encouragement."

"You…" Sinclair said, and that was all he could get out. The rest got stuck in his throat; a knot of furious recrimination that threatened to choke him. White-faced and speechless, he turned his back on the Spaniard and stalked away.

Leandro felt genuine regret as he watched Sinclair's retreat. What profit was there in deliberately alienating this man? It was so stupid. He considered going after the Shopkeeper and offering to make amends, but the impulse was quickly squashed by his pride. He had never apologized to his brother, and damned if he would do it for Alfonso's protégé. To hell with the little *mendigo*.

The keening wail of approaching sirens intruded on his thoughts. Leandro had no desire for a dialogue with the police. It was time to leave Five Corners. As he withdrew at a brisk but dignified pace, it occurred to him that he had somehow lost track of Harrow. The Englishman had been in the thick of things for a few brief minutes, but then he had quietly disappeared.

I shouldn't be surprised that he would turn out to be a coward, Leandro thought. This was a very satisfying notion but, upon reflection, he was forced to dismiss it. It just didn't make sense. What had there been for Harrow to run from? The demons had been helpless before the power of the Insight. An army of paper dolls would have been more of a challenge. It was all…so…easy…

You really have no idea what happened here tonight, do you?

"We defeated the Enemy," muttered the Spaniard. "It was a glorious victory."

You didn't stop the Dragon! You never even saw him!

Leandro frowned, and he unconsciously began to walk faster.

Dan Rains stepped out of his car and into a slaughterhouse. The air in Five Corners was heavy with moans, cries, and the coppery tang of human blood. The hellish atmosphere was enhanced by the suffocating darkness. All the streetlamps were shattered, and the only illumination came from the harsh headlights and rotating beacons of the ambulances and patrol cars. The sheer enormity of the carnage was overwhelming.

"Good Lord," said a nearby flatfoot. "Where do we even start?"

The words had a galvanizing effect on Dan. "First things first," he said. "Let's get this scene secured and start helping the injured. Get everyone who hasn't been hurt over to the old Bijou. We'll start conducting interviews there."

"Where do we establish a perimeter?" someone asked.

"Where the lights are on and there's no dead bodies," Dan replied, and his men went to work.

"What's wrong?" asked Brother Bones.

Bobby glanced at the rearview mirror. "Other than the fact that I was just in the middle of a bloodbath?"

"Yes. Other than that."

Bobby moved his eyes back to the road. They were almost home. "Why do you ask?"

"You haven't said anything since I got in the car. That isn't like you. You're a talker."

Bobby grunted. "I should think you'd be grateful."

"I'm not complaining."

"Then why do you –"

"You can't keep secrets from me, Bobby Crandall. I won't allow it. I rely on you too much. Now quit stalling and tell me what's wrong."

They had reached the sanctuary of the cold water flat. Bobby parked in the shadows and killed the engine. He turned to face Bones. "Do you remember that kid I ran into with the car?"

"What about him?"

"I grabbed his hand when I helped him up, and something…."

"Yes?"

"Something weird happened. I don't know how to describe it. It didn't hurt but…it was like being turned inside-out. I felt…."—he paused, searching for the right word –"…violated."

Bobby braced himself for one of Bones' hacksaw chuckles, but the skull merely tilted in a quizzical cant, as if the mind within was considering a math problem.

"What does the term 'lancer' mean to you?" Bones asked.

"You mean like a Bengal Lancer, like in the Gary Cooper movie?"

Bones shook his head. "Never mind," he said. He opened the door and got out of the car. Bobby followed him into the flat. Before he entered his room, Bones turned and said, "Keep an eye out for that boy. If you see him again, let me know immediately. Do you understand?"

"Sure thing. Thanks for taking me seriously. I was afraid you were going to think I was being crazy, or just plain stupid."

"You're not crazy or stupid," Bones said, and he stepped in his room and closed the door.

Wow, thought Bobby. *That might be the nicest thing he's ever said to me.*

"What's the nature of your injury?" the pretty nurse asked.

"I think I might have broken my ankle," Milton Pender said.

The nurse gave him a sympathetic look. "I'm sorry," she said, "but it may be a while before we can get to you." She gestured to the packed waiting room. "You see what we're up against, here. There's never been a crisis like this in Cape Noire. Were you in Five Corners when…whatever it was…happened?"

"I was," Milton said. "But I didn't really see anything. It's all just a blur."

"You poor thing," said the nurse. She gave him a friendly pat on the hand, and Milton flinched as if touched by fire. The nurse was startled. "I'm sorry. Did I do something wrong?"

Milton shook his head. "You shouldn't touch me," he said. "I've…I've got something that's catching."

She smiled. "This is a hospital, sweetie. Lots of people have something that's catching."

"Not like me," Milton said. "Listen, I don't mind waiting. I don't mind at all. Right now, I just want to be where there are lights. And people. I don't care if I ever go home."

Milton's statement was punctuated by a cry of pain from the waiting room. "Thanks for being patient," the nurse said. "Just have a seat and we'll get to you as soon as we can."

There were no chairs left, so Milton had to sit on the floor. He huddled there, his arms wrapped around his knees, and thought about Bobby Crandall and Brother Bones. In the blink of an eye—or rather, the clutch of a hand—he had learned all there was to know about the young card dealer and his terrible master.

Ah, but what to do with that dangerous knowledge?

What to do, indeed.

Father O'Malley was positively aghast. "And you haven't told Dan any of this?"

"I will when I get a chance," Sally Paige assured him. "I've already left a message with the desk sergeant that the boy was safe. Dan will talk to me as soon as he has time."

The priest shook his head. He had been asleep for two hours when Sally had come pounding on the door, a traumatized child in tow. Now he was standing just outside his small living room, engaged in a whispered debate with one of the most dynamic—and aggravating—women he had ever met. Nearby, the boy was curled on O'Malley's sofa, lost in what was probably more shock-induced catatonia than restful slumber.

"I think you've been very irresponsible on this one, Sally," said the priest. "But that's the last I'm going to say on the subject. What are you going to do now?"

"I need to get to Five Corners. There's a lot of noise on the radio about some kind of riot there. Who knows, I might even run into Dan. For the time being, I think the kid should stay with you. What he needs now is peace and quiet in a place where he can feel safe."

"He would feel even safer in a hospital or a police station," O'Malley pointed out.

"Maybe so," Sally acknowledged, "but I brought him here. Do you want me to take him away?"

O'Malley looked at the small, sleeping figure. "Let him rest."

"I was hoping you'd feel that way," Sally said. "Also, there's something else." She reached behind her and picked up a metal briefcase.

"What's this?" O'Malley asked.

"It's our little secret," Sally replied. She opened the case.

O'Malley's eyes widened. "Where did this come from?"

"Let's just say it's the boy's inheritance. I want you to hold on to it for him. Can you do that?"

The priest was wary. "If this money was obtained dishonestly…"

"What? You'd throw it in the fireplace?"

"No, I would return it to the person it belonged to."

"And I'm telling you it belongs to him. Trust me."

There was a moment of quiet tension, then the old man's features were creased by a tired smile. "All right," he said. "You may depend upon my silence."

"I knew that I could," Sally said. She leaned forward and gave the priest a peck on the cheek. As she drew back, she said, "Why, Father, I believe you're blushing!"

"Get thee behind me, Satan," O'Malley replied. He said it with a wink, but he was only half-joking.

☠ ☠ ☠

"Brace yourself," Erika said, and she pressed the small forceps into Marax's wound, reaching for the last of the bullet fragments buried in his flesh. Marax bit down on the leather belt he had clenched between his teeth. He had forgone painkillers, as he needed to keep a clear head to coach Erika through the procedure. It had hurt like hell.

"I have it, sir," Erika said. She withdrew the forceps and Marax heard a tiny plink as she dropped the piece of lead in the bathroom sink. He spit out the belt.

"You've done well," he said. "Now, suture the wound and wrap it. There are sterile dressings in the kit."

Erika obeyed with typical speed and efficiency. "I'm concerned about infection," she said as she worked. "We don't have enough medicine to properly care for this injury. I'll have to find a pharmacy later."

"Don't buy everything you need in one place," said the Doctor. "It might draw attention."

"I'll be careful."

After she had finished her ministrations, Erika spent several minutes washing her hands at the sink. Marax watched her reflection disappear as condensation gathered on the mirror.

"I need to burn these bloody towels," she said. "We don't want them found by any of the hotel staff." She turned to Marax. "Will you take the morphine, now?"

Marax got up and staggered to the bed. "Yes, please."

Erika prepared a syringe. "Is it over?" she said.

"For right now. You'll have to change the dressings in a few hours."

"That's not what I'm talking about."

The Doctor sighed as he laid his head on the pillow. "Of course. Foolish of me."

"Well?"

Marax closed his eyes. "The music box is undamaged," he said, "but the tuning fork is ruined. It would seem that we have failed."

"WHAT'S THIS?" FATHER O'MALLEY ASKED.

"What about the Dragon? Won't he tell us what to do?"

"I have not seen him since we fled Five Corners."

Erika made the injection. "Don't worry," she said. "He will not abandon us."

Marax looked at her. "I'm surprised to hear you talk like that," he said. "I wasn't sure you even believed in him."

"I didn't," Erika said.

Marax began to feel very warm, very relaxed. The pain in his chest seemed to be coming from somewhere far away. "What changed your mind?" he asked.

"He revealed himself to me," she whispered. "I belong to him, now."

Marax didn't care for that. *You belong only to yourself*, he tried to say, but his tongue wouldn't cooperate.

"Go to sleep," Erika said, and like a speck of stardust, the Doctor drifted into the airless outer dark of his memories…

He was in Spain. He had been traveling with Erika for more than three months, showing her the world, clearing her body and mind of Cape Noire's corruption. They had been living off of his savings, and money he had raised by selling nearly everything he owned. Healing Erika had become his obsession, but there was something else driving him, something burning at the center of his being that gave him no rest, no respite, no peace. What was he looking for? Wisdom? Enlightenment? He had no idea.

One morning in La Mancha, after a long, sleepless night, he arose before the sun and went for a walk in the Spanish countryside. He had a vague, fanciful idea of seeing one of Don Quixote's windmills, but instead he encountered a monster. At first it was just a shadow on the moon, but then it descended from the blue-black sky and landed gracefully in front of him, seemingly weightless in spite of its enormous bulk. Dumbfounded, too terrified to move, Marax gazed up at its yellow eyes.

Fear not, it said. *I cannot harm you, however much I would like to. How is it that you can see me?*

Marax found his voice. "I don't know. What are you?"

Greatness personified, it said. *And you?*

"I'm just a man."

The monster lifted a talon and pressed it against the Doctor's forehead.

Marax felt a chill, and realized with horror that the claw had passed into his skull.

A man greatly wronged, the monster said. *A man with a rage that burns so bright it has seared the scales from his eyes, and enabled him to behold the Dragon. Tell me, o man, would you see your daughter avenged?*

Inside of Marax, something flared like the surface of the sun. "I would."

The Dragon grinned. *And upon whom would you wreak this vengeance?*

"Everyone," said Marax.

Kneel, said the Dragon, *and I will grant you the means to fulfill your desire.*

The Doctor fell to his knees, and in that moment he knew what he had been seeking, and he knew that he had –

"Found it," the Doctor murmured.

Erika shushed him and caressed his forehead. "Rest," she said. "I will protect you."

"Everyone," whispered Marax, and he sank into what some might have mistaken for the sleep of the just.

The early edition of the Cape Noire Tribune started landing on doorsteps one hour before sunrise. The front-page headline read:

TRIBUNE REPORTER WITNESSES MURDER, KIDNAPPING.

The story was not written by Sally Paige.

Sally did share a byline with her editor, Hank Anderson, on an extra that screamed:

MASSACRE AT FIVE CORNERS!

The story was built primarily around off-the-record remarks by unnamed police sources. These officials believed that the bloody attack was "the work of anarchists." Apparently, these malefactors released some sort of poisonous, hallucinogenic gas into the infamous red-light district. They took advantage of the ensuing chaos to go on a killing spree. Citizens could rest assured that these criminals would soon be brought to justice.

A tightly-rolled copy of the paper thumped against the door of 909 Old Town Way at 5:30 AM. Waldo, already at his desk in Professor Bugosi's office, heard the tell-tale sound and walked down the hallway to retrieve it from the stoop. When he opened the door, he was very surprised to see a gun barrel hovering a few inches from his nose. He blinked, and soon realized that it was only one of several guns, being held by several gimlet-eyed men.

"Jaysus," a deep voice growled from the pre-dawn darkness. "Look who fell out of the ugly-tree and hit every limb on the way down."

Waldo raised his fists and turned toward the speaker. His anger at the insult disappeared when he realized who he was dealing with. Emerging from the shadows, impeccably dressed in a tailor-made suit, was a muscle-bound silverback gorilla. The ape showed his fangs in a grin. "What's your name, pal?"

"I'm Waldo."

"Pleased to meetcha, Waldo. You know who I am?"

"You're Harry Beest."

"Got it in one!" said the gorilla. "Your boss home?"

"He is."

"Well, don't just stand there, Waldo. Let's go see the Professor. No need to announce me. I'd like to surprise him, if you don't mind."

"He'll be surprised, all right," said Waldo.

"Goody!" said Harry Beest. "I can't wait to see the look on his face."

Edgar often dreamed of martial exploits. Being neither good nor great himself, he had devoted most of his life to studying men who were, and in his dreams he basked in their reflected glory. He was transported in these flights of fancy to stand with the likes of Leonidas at the Hot Gates, or Gustavus Adolfus at Breitenfeld, or Wellington at Waterloo. He sometimes realized he was dreaming, but that never lessened the tactile reality of the experience, or the pleasure he took in it…until now.

The usual glittering triumphalism was absent from this present dream, replaced by darkness, aching misery, and mind-numbing cold. There was no glory here, only a pervasive feeling of shameful and ignominious defeat. Where the devil was he? Had he landed in the middle of Napoleon's retreat from Moscow? In the distance, he saw a flickering light. A campfire? He began to stagger toward it. As he approached, a diminutive figure in a greatcoat and a bicorn hat stepped in front of the blaze. Good God! It *was* Napoleon! Edgar opened his mouth to speak, but the Little Corporal cut him off. "Wake up!" he shouted.

Edgar shook his head. Shouldn't Napoleon be speaking French? Why did he sound so much like...

"Goddammit! Wake up, Eddie!"

"Gramps?" Edgar muttered as he opened his eyes.

"What the hell are you doing out here on the ground?" Gramps yelled. "Lewis and I have been looking all over the place for you! I was beginning to think you'd flown off with that German."

"Someone knocked me out," Edgar said. He felt the strong hands of Lewis Toole help him to his feet.

"Yeah, yeah, we'll worry about that later. Where's Zorn? Did he kill Brother Bones?"

Edgar coughed. His head was pounding like the bass line in a military band. "I...I don't know. I'm not sure."

"Well, where's the money?"

Edgar looked around. "I don't know."

"You don't know? *You don't know?*"

"Gramps, please..."

"*You stupid little asshole!*"

Shame. Ignominy. Defeat.

In a dark corner of Professor Bugosi's lab, concealed in shadow behind a long black curtain, a miracle hissed and gurgled. The Professor sat down on a stool beside one of his operating tables, closed his eyes, and listened to the sounds. They were very soothing. *The music of my genius*, he thought, and he smiled.

The Professor had been awake all night. Not, perhaps, the best thing to do before a major operation, but he was too excited to sleep. The successful completion of today's procedure was going to be the zenith of his career, and a prelude to even greater accomplishments in the future. It was a pity that such unworthy worms as the Shilohs would benefit from this work. *Alas*, he thought, *needs must when the devil drives.*

He opened his eyes and was arranging some of his instruments when he heard the lab door open behind him. "Waldo," he snarled without turning, "how many times must I tell you not to enter this room without permission? You truly are the most idiotic—"

"Aw, don't be so hard on your flunky, Prof," a rough voice rumbled. "Waldo didn't have any choice in the matter."

Bugosi felt a chill. Slowly, very slowly, he turned and beheld a remembered sin. "Good morning, Harry," he said.

"Top o' the morning to you, too!" said Harry Beest. Behind his slouching form stood four thugs holding Thompson submachine guns, two of which were trained on a shamefaced Waldo.

"So," said Bugosi, "what can I do for you?"

The ape grunted. He turned to the nearest gunsel. "You hear that, Baldy?" he said. "The Prof is wondering what he can do for me. Got any suggestions?"

The one called Baldy affected a look of ponderous contemplation. "Gee, I dunno, Boss." He snapped his fingers. "Hey, I know! He could turn you back into a man! That would be swell."

"Holy smoke!" Beest exclaimed. "I hadn't even thought of that! What do you say, Prof? Think you can find room for me in your schedule?"

Bugosi narrowed his eyes. Frightened as he was, he was still irritated by this childish pantomime. "I'm afraid I can't help you, Harry. Another day, perhaps."

There was a flash of fur and muscle and the ape was on him, lifting him in the air, shaking him to pieces. *"No!"* roared Harry Beest. *"Not another day! Today! Right now!"*

Bugosi felt as if his teeth were about to rattle out of his skull. "You... can't...make...me," he managed to say. "No...matter...what...you...do..."

"You think so?" said Beest. He reached over to a tray of medical instruments and closed a hairy paw around the handle of a bone-saw. "Your stooge told me this room was soundproofed. Let's put that claim to the test."

"Go ahead," Bugosi gasped. "Torture me. Kill me. And you'll be trapped in that body forever. There's no one else on this planet who can give you back your humanity. No one. You would do well to remember that, Harry Beest."

The gorilla considered the statement, then gently sat Bugosi on the edge of the operating table. He leaned in close, and Bugosi could smell the nuts and bananas on his hot breath. "Point taken," said Beest. "I guess I've got to handle you with kid gloves. Fine, I can do that. What's your price, then? What will it take to get to get you to reverse...this."

Bugosi took a second to adjust his clothes. He cleared his throat. "As I said," he rasped, "some other time."

Beest glanced back at his henchmen. "Can you believe this guy?"

The Professor crossed his arms. His confidence was returning. He had the whip hand, now. He could feel it. "I'll get in touch with you when I'm ready to start negotiating price, as well as guarantees for my safety. You can expect to hear from me sometime in the near future."

"Uh-huh," said Beest. "You mean, never."

Bugosi smiled. He was starting to enjoy himself. "The *near* future," he said.

"After you finish whatever you're doing for Eddie Shiloh?" Beest asked.

"Who?" said the Professor, and his eyes unconsciously flicked to the long black curtain.

Beest grinned. "Don't try playing dumb, Bugosi. You don't have the knack for it." He turned, snapped his thick fingers, and one of the henchmen tossed him a Thompson. "Whaddaya say we have a look behind that curtain?"

Bugosi gestured to the drape. "Be my guest."

Beest accepted the invitation. He grabbed the curtain and pulled. There was a noisy clatter as the metal rings that held it suspended snapped one-by-one and went bouncing across the floor. There was a soft thump as the curtain fell in a bundle at Beest's feet. There was a collective gasp at what was revealed.

In the corner of the lab was a large glass cylinder that reached almost to the ceiling. Within the cylinder, suspended in a murky, bubbling solution that gave off an eerie, greenish glow was…

"What the hell?" Beest murmured. "Is that a man?"

"More than a man," Bugosi said. "A synthetic human, perfect in every particular."

Beest couldn't look away. "It…it's…*beautiful*."

Bugosi swelled with pride. "Yes, it is. The epitome and apotheosis of the masculine form. A god trapped in amber. It's missing only one thing to make it complete…"

The gorilla turned to Bugosi. His nostrils flared and his eyes narrowed. "Lemme guess. Mr. Handsome here doesn't have a brain."

Bugosi didn't answer. His eyes remained on the floating Adonis.

"Research and development," Beest growled. "This is where all that TenaciTea money has been going, ain't it? Eddie's been funneling cash to you so you could make this thing for Bobby the Bruce."

Bugosi looked into the gorilla's moist black eyes. "Well," he said, "I certainly wasn't making it for you."

There was a terrible stillness, as before an explosion, and too late the Professor realized he had made a mistake. Beest's hulking form began to tremble. He lifted the Thompson until the barrel was resting just beneath Bugosi's chin.

"Harry…" Bugosi said cautiously.

From Beest's throat erupted a deafening bellow of pure primal rage. The Professor closed his eyes and wondered if he would hear the shots that killed him. *Oh, what an artist dies in me*, he thought, and he cringed when Beest's roar was choursed by the Thompson as it blasted a hail of burning lead into…what?

He didn't shoot me! Bugosi thought. *Ha! I should have known he would never dare…*

Bugosi's thought trailed into white noise as he opened his eyes and saw the shattered cylinder, the flood of green solution, the bullet-riddled body of his greatest creation.

"Now it isn't for anybody," said Harry Beest.

"You stupid brute!" yelled the Professor. "Do you realize what you've done? Do you have any idea how much work—"

The Professor's words were smashed back into his mouth by the butt of the Thompson. Clutching at his jaw, he fell back onto the operating table. *"My dung!"* he cried. *"My dung! You almos' made me bide off my dung!"*

"I guess you'll just have to keep your trap shut for a while," Beest said.

"Animal!" Bugosi screeched, blood and spittle flying from his lips.

Beest leaned over the Professor. "You got a pair o' brass ones, Bugosi, I'll give you that. But you're not untouchable."

As if to illustrate the point, Beest closed a paw around the Professor's left leg.

"Every day that passes," Beest growled, "it gets harder and harder to remember what it was like to be a man. And one of these days…"

The hand squeezed.

"One of these fine, fine days I'm gonna decide I *like* wearing this monkey-suit. And when that day comes…"

Beest gave a twist, and Bugosi felt a bunch of things snap and tear in his knee.

"When that day comes," Beest whispered, "you're one dead son of a bitch."

Waldo grimaced as the Professor's wail of agony choked off at the height of the crescendo. After a moment of silence, he found the nerve to ask, "Is he dead?"

Beest shook his head. "He just fainted, is all. He'll be fine. Mostly."

Waldo cast a glance at the armed men who surrounded him. "What happens now?"

Beest poked out his lower lip, and scratched the top of his head with a long forefinger. "Good question," he said. "I expect we're gonna tear this place apart. Maybe we should tear you apart, too."

Waldo's muscles tensed beneath his clothes. "You could try," he said.

"Big words," Beest said. He jacked a fresh clip into his Thompson and leveled it at Waldo's midsection. "Do you think you could get to me before I cut you in two?"

"Only one way to find out," Waldo said.

"You got that right," Beest said, "but we don't have to do that today. I'll make you a deal. Pony up the combination for that safe downstairs, and I'll give you a pass."

It was an easy decision. Waldo recited the numbers.

"You got that, Baldy?" Beest asked.

"Got it, boss."

"Good," said Beest. "Clean out the safe and smash everything else. I'll meet you at the car in ten minutes."

The gunmen marched out of the lab, leaving Waldo alone with the ape.

"So," said Beest, "how long you been with Bugosi?"

"Little over a year," Waldo replied.

"What happened to you, anyway? Are you one of his experiments?"

"I have a disease. He said he could cure me."

"Did he, now? Has he made much progress?"

Waldo frowned. "He's been…busy."

"No time for you, huh?"

Waldo's head lowered. He studied the floor. "No."

Beest shuffled over. "Look at me," he said.

Waldo lifted his eyes.

"He's never going to help you," said Beest. "You know that, right?"

"Yeah," Waldo said, "but I just…I can't stop hoping."

The gorilla nodded. "I know. It's the same for me."

They regarded each other across a bridge of mutual understanding.

"Tell you what," said Beest, "if you ever decide you want to work for a *real* man, give me a call."

Waldo smiled. "I'll keep it in mind."

When Beest exited the brownstone, Baldy was waiting by the curb, standing patiently beside the gorilla's blood-red Duesenberg. He opened the door, and Beest heard the radio playing soft and low. "Sophisticated Lady" by Duke Ellington. Beest approved.

"Find anything interesting?" the gorilla asked as he settled into the car.

"Few thousand bucks," Baldy said as he slid behind the wheel. "Some bearer bonds. Couple o' notebooks full o' scientific gobbledygook."

"Hell of a stash," Beest said dryly.

"About what we expected," Baldy said. "But there's something else...."

Baldy reached on the seat beside him, then passed an object to his boss.

Beest squinted. "What is it?"

"Who knows? Jimbo found it in one of the second-floor rooms. It's kind of like a tuning fork, but if you look at it for a second—"

"Jaysus!" Beest said, and he dropped the thing on the floor of the car.

"Yeah," Baldy said. "It *moves.*"

Beest retrieved the strange device with a delicacy that few would have expected of him. "When we get home," he said, "put this thing in the safe. It gives me the creeps, but I'm holding on to it."

"You sure that's a good idea, Boss?"

"Hell, no" Beest said. "But that's never stopped me before, has it?"

Dan Rains was not amused. "I can't believe you!" he barked at Sally. "What the hell is wrong with you? I ought to haul you in for obstruction of justice!"

"Dan, I don't blame you for being angry—"

"Well, that's a relief! I wouldn't want to hurt your feelings. After all, it's not like you could have gotten that little boy killed. Oh, wait a minute..."

"Now, Dan—"

"Shut up, Sally! Just shut up!"

Sally closed her mouth and waited for the storm to pass.

She had approached Dan at Five Corners about an hour earlier and told him an abbreviated version of the events at Gibson Airfield. He had insisted on seeing the boy immediately, and he brought her along for the ride. After he satisfied himself that the child was safe, he asked Father O'Malley if he would mind looking out for the boy until the next of kin, if there were any, could be located. The old priest had agreed, though he had reservations about his ability to properly care for someone who had suffered such a profound trauma.

"You'll do fine," Dan assured him. "It was a good idea to bring him to you."

Sally had brightened when she heard this, but Dan gave her a look that dulled her luster. He waited until they were outside to really let her have it. Now they were standing on O'Malley's stoop, their faces illuminated in the rays of a sickly dawn, their friendship balanced on a razor's edge.

"I understand why you did what you did," Dan said, his tone softening, "but if you ever pull a stunt like this again…"

"We won't be pals anymore?"

"To say the least."

Sally tried to change the subject. "Any progress at Five Corners?"

"We think we've found your German among the dead."

"Are you serious?"

Dan glowered at her. "No, I'm just pulling your leg. I'm in a real joking mood."

"Sorry. You want me to identify the body?"

"That would be helpful."

"You're going to be mad at me for a while, aren't you?"

"Yes," Dan said. He walked down the stoop and opened the passenger door of his car. He gestured for Sally to get in.

"Anything I can do to make it up to you?" Sally asked, slipping into the seat.

"Yes," Dan said as he closed the door. "You can quit being a pain in the ass."

Sally had a comeback, but under the circumstances she decided to let it go.

"Gramps," Edgar groaned, "I don't know what else to say. I can't help—"

He was cut off by another barrage of insults. He tuned it out. He was discovering a faculty for willful deafness. He caught a sympathetic glance from Lewis in the rearview mirror, and it made him angry. He was the most powerful man in Cape Noire, and this punch-drunk lummox felt sorry for him. It was outrageous! He should be an object of envy, not pity!

At least his headache had diminished. Some hot coffee, a shower, and a shave had helped him to feel human again. But Gramps just wouldn't ease up.

It's because he's nervous about the operation, Edgar kept telling himself. *He doesn't really mean it. He doesn't really mean it…*

Then, a single sentence pierced the wall of static he had erected between himself and Gramps: "You're an even bigger loser than your father!"

"Excuse me?"

"You heard me, dummy! I'm tired of making up excuses for you! By God, I'm beginning to think the milkman must have been your grandpa. That would sure explain a lot of things."

"The milkman," Edgar said. His voice was low and soft. It was a tone Mrs. Timms would have recognized.

"Well, a true-blue Shiloh sure as hell wouldn't have *mislaid* twenty-five thousand dollars! I can't believe I talked myself into believing you could take care of business. All you're good for is giving speeches and screwing your secretary. You're not even man enough to—"

Edgar slapped him.

There was a moment of stunned silence. Gramps showed his teeth and said, "Why, you rotten little –"

Edgar slapped him again, harder.

Gramps was shaking, now. He lifted a gnarled fist, but Edgar batted it away, and slapped him so hard that the old man's head bounced off the car window.

"I can keep this up all day," Edgar said. "Can you?"

Gramps didn't speak, so Edgar slapped him again.

A fleck of blood appeared at the corner of the old man's mouth, and tears of rage began to course through the wrinkles beneath his eyes.

"We're here, Mr. Shiloh," Lewis said. He parked at the curb in front of 909 Old Town Way.

"Don't turn off the car," Edgar said. "I think Gramps may have changed his mind."

The old man looked up, his eyes wide with surprise, his fury instantly forgotten. "What are you saying?"

Edgar ignored him. He kept looking at Lewis in the mirror. "Gramps thinks that I'm a dummy. That being the case, this operation must be a dumb idea and we shouldn't go through with it."

"I never said…" Gramps murmured.

"What was that?" Edgar said. "I didn't quite catch that."

"I'm sorry," Gramps said. "You're not a dummy."

Edgar leaned in to him. "Am I a true-blue Shiloh?" he asked.

The old man nodded.

Edgar raised a hand. "Say it."

"You're a Shiloh."

"Okay, Lewis. You can turn off the car."

The Professor had been surprisingly subdued since emerging from his swoon. He had endured the application of a splint without a single insult or word of complaint. When it was finished, he had even gone so far as to commend Waldo for a job well done. This behavior was so unusual that Waldo felt compelled to comment on it.

"Angry at you?" the Professor responded. "Why should I be angry at you?"

"Well, you're always angry at me."

Bugosi snorted. He pushed himself up and sat on the edge of the table. "You're such an idiot, Waldo," he said, rubbing his swollen jaw. "I'm in too much pain to waste energy on all that. If you like, I'll berate you later for the sake of consistency."

"No need, sir. I don't mind you being inconsistent."

"Duly noted," said the Professor.

Then they heard the elevator.

Bugosi fished a pocket-watch from his coat. "The Shilohs," he muttered. "Right on time, damn them." He sighed and looked at Waldo. "You know, I've thought of a way to salvage this mess, but I haven't decided if I want to go through with it. Listen to me carefully…" The Professor outlined his plan in a few brief sentences.

The elevator clanked to a stop. They heard the metal door slide open.

"Can I depend on you?" the Professor asked.

Waldo gave a curt nod.

"Good boy," said Bugosi.

At that moment, Edgar Shiloh opened the door to the lab, his grandfather and driver following in his wake. "Bugosi!" he said. "What happened downstairs? The place looks like a hurricane …" He trailed off, staring at the ruins of the synthetic man.

"We had visitors," the Professor said.

"Visitors?" Edgar said.

Bugosi looked at Waldo. "Tell him."

Waldo told him.

"Harry Beest?!" Edgar said. "How did he find this place?"

"I was going to ask you the same question," said the Professor.

"What is that supposed to mean? Are you implying that this is somehow *my* fault?"

"I'm not sure. Is it?"

Edgar went off like Vesuvius. "Who the hell do you think you're talking to? Have you forgotten who's been footing the bill for all this crap?"

"You've been signing the checks," Bugosi said, "but the money was earned by me."

This provoked Edgar to even greater heights of rage, and he unleashed a torrent of profanities at the Professor. It was a spectacular display of temper, and no one noticed Waldo quietly sidling across the room.

"You demented quack!" Edgar shrieked. He stepped close to the Professor and began poking him in the chest with an extended forefinger. "You're nothing without me! If it wasn't for my help, you'd still be operating out of a goddam basement. Actually, your sorry ass would be in a rubber room, which is exactly where it belongs!"

"Do you really mean that?" Bugosi asked.

"I said it, didn't I?"

The Professor decided to go through with his plan. He nodded at Waldo, who then stepped forward and wrapped his arms around Lewis Toole. "Hey!" yelled the driver, then the air left his lungs as Waldo lifted him from the floor and squeezed.

"Sorry, pal," Waldo said. "It's nothing personal."

Lewis was a big man, but his strength was nothing to Waldo's. The driver wailed in agony as first his ribs, and then his spine, snapped under the unrelenting pressure. His body went limp in the bear-hug, and Waldo dropped him to the floor.

Edgar and the Bruce, stunned by the sudden violence, stood gawking at Waldo like a pair of wax effigies. Then Edgar cried out as the Professor thrust a needle into his neck.

"Quack, am I?" the Professor said as he emptied the syringe. "We'll see about that."

Edgar collapsed. His grandfather, looking like a trapped animal, flicked his eyes back and forth between Bugosi and Waldo.

"Now," said the Professor, "it appears that we have a little problem to solve."

"You're going to kill me," the old man said.

"Quite the opposite," said the Professor. "I intend to save you."

"How's that?"

Bugosi gestured to the synthetic man. "As you can see," he said, "the body I prepared for you has been irreparably damaged. Fortunately, I now have a suitable replacement."

The Bruce looked confused, then a wicked light dawned in his eyes. "What would you want from me?" he asked.

"A continuation of the arrangement I enjoyed with Edgar. No more and no less. Do we have a deal?"

The old man's mouth twisted into a parody of a smile. He looked down at the unconscious body of his grandson. "Well, *dummy*," he said, "looks like you're *really* going to be a true-blue Shiloh."

April, bright and smiling, breezed over the threshold five minutes after Sinclair opened the shop, demanding to hear all about his adventures of the night before. He tried to put her off, but she wouldn't be denied. "C'mon, don't be a jerk," she said. "You know you want to tell me what happened!"

She was right. He told her everything.

"That's what really happened in Five Corners?" she said after a long silence.

"Yes."

"The newspaper said something about anarchists…"

"Strictly speaking, that's completely true," Sinclair said. "In fact, you could say that those things were the original anarchists."

"And you actually saw the Dragon?"

"Saw him and spoke with him."

"But the other Lancers didn't."

"No."

April looked doubtful. "Not even Leandro?"

"No, not even Leandro!" Sinclair snapped.

April held up her hands. "Hey, hey, take it easy. I'm not trying to make you mad."

"Then don't take that skeptical tone with me! I know what I saw!" He paused, closed his eyes, and opened them again. "Listen, April. I'll admit that Leandro and his friends are strong with the Insight. I've seen that for myself. But they don't understand what they're dealing with. In fact, they don't even seem to care! They're acting like this whole thing is a lark, a minor obligation they have to tend to before they can go back to partying!"

"Gee," said April, "that's pretty harsh. Do you really think they're so bad?"

"Yes, I do! They're a bunch of high-handed snobs who are in way over their heads, and this city's going to pay a terrible price for their arrogance!"

April tugged at her left ear. "Okay," she said, "let's say you're right. The Lancers are a bunch of dopes and the Dragon's going to mop the floor with them. What are you going to do about it?"

"I have no idea."

"Maybe you should try talking to Leandro again."

"Confound it! Why do you keep bringing him up? What is it with you and that guy?"

April blushed. "Well, he *did* offer to make me his apprentice."

"Yeah, yeah, 'a world of wealth and freedom,' I remember. Well, let me tell you, this is a war that can't be won with money."

"Can *you* win it?"

He looked away. "If you had asked me that yesterday, the answer would have been yes. But now I'm not so sure."

She seemed disappointed. "What's changed?"

He sighed heavily. "I've always believed that the Dragon was a genuine threat. I never doubted it for a moment. But last night I discovered the difference between believing in a thing, and being confronted with the reality of it."

"And that would be?"

Sinclair thought of the Dragon's voice, the gleam of the monster's fangs, the plague-yellow glow of his jaundiced eyes…

"Fear," he said. "The difference is fear."

"That's it?" April said. "You're afraid of the Dragon?"

There was something in her voice that he couldn't identify. Mockery? Scorn? He wasn't sure, but he had already admitted his weakness, so there was no point in backing away. He looked her in the eyes. "Yes," he said. "God help me, I'm scared to death of him."

She smiled, very gently, and laughed a little. "Sinclair, you're really goofy sometimes, you know that?"

Sinclair wasn't sure how to respond. "I am?"

"My father saw a lot of action in the Great War," April said. "He used to say that only crazy people never got scared. Daddy was no coward, and neither are you."

Sinclair was touched. "Thank you for saying that."

"I'm just telling the truth. Can I make a suggestion?"

"Certainly."

"Why don't we wait to hear from Brother Bones? He said he would find you, didn't he?"

"Well, yes, but –"

"Okay, let's see what he has to say about all this. I'll bet he's got a lot more experience fighting monsters than we do. We'll let him take the lead! What do you say?"

"Yes, but—"

"But what?"

"Why do you keep saying, *we*?"

April grinned. "Cause I'm your acolyte, you big goof."

Milton spent most of the morning at the hospital. His injury was relatively minor, so he was given a low priority. When they finally examined him, it turned out he only had a severe sprain. They wrapped his ankle, gave him some painkillers and a pair of crutches, and sent him on his way. *Go home*, they said. *Take it easy for a couple of days.*

He didn't want to go home. He wandered over to Whittington Park and bought a couple of hot dogs and a TenaciTea from a vendor. The day was cool and clear, and Milton passed a few reflective hours on a bench beside a muddy pond.

Sometime in the late afternoon, his TenaciTea buzz was overpowered by his exhaustion, and he dozed off. He was awakened by a tap on the shoulder from a beat cop who eyed him suspiciously from beneath the brim of a peaked cap.

"You can't sleep here, son," the cop said. "If you need a place to stay, I can give you directions to the YMCA. They'll help you out."

"It's okay," Milton said. "I've got my own place."

"Then you should go there. This park's no place to be after sundown."

Milton forced himself to his feet and headed back into the streets. He caught a bus to the library, and made himself comfortable at a table beside one of the large windows that overlooked Main Avenue. He got a friendly clerk to round up some books on psychic phenomena, and he immersed himself in the material.

Around ten o'clock, his studies were interrupted by a sudden, breathtaking sense of alarm that struck him with the force of a seizure. He instinctively lifted one of the crutches as if it were (*a lance*) a weapon. His eyes raced around the silent room, searching in vain for (*the Dragon*) whatever had frightened him. He looked out the window and his eyes turned to the moon, still visible in spite of the city lights. For a fleeting moment—for the briefest of seconds—he saw something pass through the sky.

"The Enemy," he said.

"Shush," someone at the next table responded.

Milton turned to meet the gaze of a man who looked like a dyspeptic accountant.

"Stop making noise," said the CPA, "or I'll file a complaint."

"Sorry," Milton said. He turned back to the books, but he could no longer concentrate. After a few minutes, he gave up and decided to go back to the filthy apartment. As he walked to the bus stop, he kept glancing up at the open sky. He felt threatened and oppressed by that cloudless void, as if it were a shark-infested ocean of darkness, waiting to descend and drown the world.

Peering down from the starlit sky, the Dragon contemplated Milton with bemused disgust. *Someone bestowed that grub with the power?* the monster thought. *The Lancers have really lowered their standards.*

The Dragon veered away and soared over Cape Noire, regarding with contempt the humans below. Oh, how he longed to swoop down among them, to drape his claws with their steaming entrails. He had done this very thing once, many years previous, thanks to the machinations of a deranged Latin priest.

The Dragon smiled as he thought of Padre Segura. The little man had been so receptive to his suggestions! Consumed with lust and raging jealousy, the Padre had been easily convinced that he was aligned with the losing side. The Dragon came to him in dreams, made some promises, gave some instructions, and Segura went to work.

A few months later, the priest turned a tuning fork, and soon after that he found himself face-to-face with the Dragon. "Infernal Majesty!" cried Segura as he fell to his knees. "I pledge my soul to your Satanic glory!"

"Satanic?" said the Dragon. *"What are you babbling about?"*

The priest was confused. "Aren't you the Devil?"

"The Light-Bringer?"

"Um…yes?" said the priest.

"That cozening poseur!" bellowed the Dragon. *"I despise him! If I hadn't listened to him, I wouldn't be trapped here!"*

Segura curled into a cowering ball. "Forgive me, Master! I did not know!"

The Dragon grasped the priest and lifted him into the air. *"Forgiveness?"* he said. *"If that's what you crave, then you shouldn't have renounced the Carpenter."*

Then he tore the man in two and took wing in the skies over La Mancha.

The ensuing rampage had been highly gratifying, but sadly short-lived. He barely had time to bloody his talons before a certain grizzled knight-errant mounted on a muscular steed appeared on the horizon.

"Unholy beast!" the Spaniard cried. "Enemy of God! Prepare to pay for your inequities! I, Don Julio Jiménez Luquero, shall strike you down in the name of the Father, the Son, and the Holy Spirit!"

The Dragon was amused by this pious blowhard. *"My, what florid rhetoric,"* he said with a chuckle. *"Before I crush you, answer me this. If the Most High is so offended by my so-called inequities, why has He allowed me to manifest myself in this place? Why does He stand pat while I slaughter women and children? Is it not within His power to end this killing spree?"*

"Blasphemy!" shouted Don Julio. "Nothing is beyond the power of God!"

"Then why doesn't He stop me?" roared the Dragon.

The knight lowered his visor and lifted his lance. "Perhaps," he said, "you simply aren't worth His time."

The Dragon turned his mind's eye from the scene, forcefully putting away that hated memory. It was helpful, on occasion, to revisit defeats, but one should not dwell upon them. Though good for stoking the fires of rage, they were merely depressing if too-long considered. There were, in fact, very few things about the Dragon's life that he wished to consider. Thoughts of his long-past glory only sharpened the pain of his present straits, and as for his future…

His future was unthinkable.

All that mattered was the eternal, never-ending *now*, and filling that moment with as much destruction as possible. If he was to be consigned to the flames for siding with the Light-Bringer, then he would drag all that he could of Creation down with him.

Not that there's much here worth destroying, he thought. *This place is like a nest of termites.*

The Dragon shook his head as he gazed down on Cape Noire. He was honestly bewildered. Who could comprehend the Most High? What kind of deity would raze the Cities of the Plain, but suffer a pest-hole like this to live?

Maybe He no longer wants to, the Dragon thought, and he was so startled by this notion that he paused in his flight. Hovering, he turned his eyes to Heaven. *Is that why I'm here? Am I to be the instrument of your judgment?*

He listened for a reply. He received only silence. As always.

Fine! He roared in frustration. *Keep your own counsel! I'll see this city in ruins! This entire world, if I can! Perhaps then you'll have something to say!*

He blustered on like this for several minutes, thundering his defiance at the Most High. At length, his anger fizzled and he collapsed into the state of maudlin self-pity he maintained when not in the grip of his frequent rages. If only he could wear flesh again! If only he could *exert* himself! If only the music box could have played for a few…more…minutes…

If only, if only, if only…

The Dragon gnashed his teeth. As was his wont, he began to cast about for someone to blame for his failure. He quickly settled on Dr. Marax.

Curse that useless fool! He should have thought to commission a duplicate of the tuning fork! If we had one of those in reserve, then we could—

For the second time that evening, the Dragon was brought up short by an unexpected idea: What if a duplicate had already been made?

He turned in the air, and flew over the city to the home of the man named Bugosi. Smiling with anticipation, for he was certain his instincts were correct, the Dragon lowered his ghostly form through the roof of the unassuming brownstone. As it happened, the first room he passed into was the laboratory, and there he found a scene that genuinely surprised him. Clever monster that he was, it took him only a moment to grasp the implications of what he beheld.

It would appear the old king was wrong, he chortled. *There is something new under the sun, after all.*

Then he stopped laughing, and his dark heart began to race with excitement. Here was something for him; an opportunity so delicious it could have dangled by the Light-Bringer himself.

All right, thought the Dragon, *let's see if we can make this work…*

Robert the Bruce floated in a warm void of velvet darkness, as serenely happy as he had ever been. Snug in the comforts of this second womb, he waited in dreamy bliss for his impending rebirth as a virile young man. Goodbye to weakness and wheezing and coughing fits. Hello to white teeth and strong muscles and reliable bladder control.

His only regret was that Edgar's head had to be shaved for the surgery. One thing that could be said for the dummy, he had great hair…

It began to grow cold.

Hello, Son of Adam, someone said.

The strange voice seemed to come from everywhere at once. The sound of it filled the Bruce with an overwhelming, atavistic fear. "Who said that?" he cried out.

I did, came the reply, and the darkness was suddenly illuminated by enormous yellow eyes. They filled the void like a pair of slanting suns.

Robert was in awe. He felt like a gnat floating before a dinosaur. "Who are you?"

I am the Dragon.

"This is a dream," Robert said. "That's all this is, just a bad dream."

The Dragon laughed, and a file of gleaming white fangs appeared beneath the blazing eyes. *Indeed*, he said, *a dream from which you may never awaken.*

The Bruce didn't like that. He pretended he hadn't heard it. "What do you want from me?"

Much, said the Dragon. *This vessel does not belong to you, and as you have no legitimate claim on it, I believe I can take it from you.*

"Vessel? Wait! No! You can't—"

Can't I? Let's find out!

A giant black tongue snaked out from between the teeth. It snared the soul of Robert the Bruce, and snatched him screaming into the cavernous maw.

Professor Bugosi made some notes on a clipboard, then yawned and rubbed his tired eyes. He glanced at his pocket watch. Eleven-seventeen. Only forty-three more minutes before Waldo took over monitoring duties.

"Long day?" someone asked.

Bugosi jumped a little. He looked down at the face of Edgar Shiloh—well, Robert Shiloh, now—and was shocked to see the young man's eyes open and staring. They had a yellow tint that Bugosi hadn't noticed before. A side effect of the operation, perhaps?

"Awake so soon?" Bugosi said, mostly to himself. "This is a surprise."

"It certainly is," replied young Shiloh with a self-satisfied smirk. He tried, unsuccessfully, to lift himself from the table. "These straps are uncomfortable. Could you loosen them, please?"

Bugosi nodded. As he unbuckled the straps, Shiloh surprised him by forcefully coming upright. The Professor was alarmed by this unexpected vigor. He placed a hand on Shiloh's chest. "I understand your eagerness to be up and about, but you really should go back to sleep. Your recovery will—"

Shiloh batted away Bugosi's hand. Then he groaned loudly and clutched at the bandages that encircled his head. "Pain," he said with a grimace. "I had forgotten what it was like. It's been so long since that cursed lance pierced my breast..."

Lance? Bugosi thought. He was beginning to get worried. He nonchalantly reached for a syringe, and his wrist was captured in a grip of iron.

"Don't," said young Shiloh, and Bugosi noted with alarm that the yellow eyes were beginning to glow.

"Release me at once," Bugosi said. He was trying for a tone of imperious command, but he couldn't keep the alarm out of his voice. What the devil was happening here?

Shiloh smiled. "I suppose I should thank you," he said. "You've done me a great service."

Bugosi, unsure what to say, simply nodded.

"All I require from you now," Shiloh continued, "is a particular item you have in your possession."

"Item?"

"Yes, a copy of the device you forged for a certain country doctor. I'm sure you made a duplicate. Don't even think of denying it."

Bugosi was stunned. "How could you know about that?"

"I have been in this house before. I stood over your shoulder and laughed while you haggled with my servant, Marax."

"You...laughed?"

"Yes, I did. Marax told you, remember?"

Bugosi retreated into skepticism and denial. "This has to be some kind of a joke."

Young Shiloh raised his other hand and closed it around Bugosi's throat. "You're the joke," he said, squeezing. "You're nothing but a precocious monkey with delusions of grandeur. I have seen your kind come and go for ages. The only thing that distinguishes *you* is your cruel ingenuity. Now, where is my tuning fork?"

"I no longer have it," Bugosi croaked. He was dizzy, and small points of light were dancing before his eyes.

"Do not lie to me!"

"Not...lying...item...stolen..."

"By whom?"

"Harry…Beest…" Bugosi wheezed, and then he lost consciousness. The thing that used to be Edgar Shiloh let him fall to the floor.

"Well," said the Dragon, "I suppose I'll just have to steal it back."

Milton hadn't been in his apartment long when there was a knock at the door.

"Who is it?"

"A friend," someone replied.

Milton cocked an eyebrow. Was that an English accent? "You got a name, friend?"

"Mister Pender," said the muffled voice, "if you do not open this door in five seconds, I will leave, and you will never learn how to use your new-found abilities."

Milton opened the door. Standing before him was a silver-haired man in an expensive-looking suit. He was leaning on a black walking stick, and his patrician features were crossed with a sly, cold smile.

"Hello, Milton," the man said. "My name is Sterling Harrow. I'm so pleased to finally meet you."

DAY FIVE

With a spring in his step, the Dragon walked through the sparsely populated late-night streets, occasionally offering friendly smiles to people he planned to kill.

Look at these swine! He thought with a silent cackle. *If only they knew!*

He was wearing a comfortable suit he had found neatly folded in Bugosi's lab. Getting dressed had been something of a challenge, since he had never done it before, but he quickly grasped the mechanics of it. After that, he hastily slipped up to the roof and down a fire escape before he could be discovered by Bugosi's henchman. He'd had no desire to test his strength against that creeping brute.

After stepping onto the street, the Dragon decided to take some time to simply enjoy the experience. He had been strolling along for several minutes before realizing, to his complete astonishment, that he was whistling.

I'm making music! He thought gleefully. *I haven't done that since—*

He immediately shut down that thought. Better not to go there. He drew in another breath and whistled some more. Seemingly of its own volition, the sound formed into a jaunty little tune. How did he know this song? It certainly wasn't anything he had composed.

As he continued with the melody, he rifled through the contents of the brain he now occupied, flipping through memories like files in a cabinet. He soon found the information he was seeking.

Ah-ha! This song is called 'Boneyard Shuffle.' How delightful!

"How are you, Edgar? Mighty late for you to be out."

Startled, the Dragon turned see that a fat, cigar-puffing human had fallen into step beside him. *Edgar?* He wondered. *Oh, yes! I have the brain of Robert, but I inhabit the body of Edgar. I must keep that in mind.*

"I am doing just fine, Bill," the Dragon said, plucking the man's name from one of the Bruce's stray memories.

Bill Fraley gave him an odd look. "Are you wearing some bandages underneath that hat?"

"I recently suffered a head injury, but I'm much better now. In fact, you could say I'm a whole new man!"

"Well…uh…I'm glad you're all right. Say, you need a lift?"

"HARRY...BEEST..." BUGOSI WHEEZED.

"Lift?"

"Yeah. I was just about to head home. Would you like me to drop you off somewhere?"

The Dragon had a revelation. "I own a house!" he announced.

"No kidding," Bill said.

"Take me to my house!" the Dragon said. "I wish to see it. I want to eat food! I want to have drink!"

"Okay," Bill Fraley said. He looked as if he would like to rescind the offer. "My car's just around the corner."

The Dragon rubbed his hands together. What fun! It would be so interesting to taste things, again. The last time he had walked the Earth, the only flavor he had sampled was blood.

I'll have plenty of that, too, thought the Dragon, and he grinned.

Tossing and turning in his narrow bunk, Sinclair drifted in and out of a troubled doze. He felt as if he were wandering through a hall of broken mirrors, the glimmering shards flashing reflections from both the waking world and the land of dreams.

Along with the shattered images came distorted sounds; the hellish roar of the Dragon, the graveyard rasp of Brother Bones, the slick, unctuous tones of Sterling Harrow...

Sterling Harrow?

Sinclair made some sleepy noises of complaint. Why must he dream of that obnoxious parvenu? Why couldn't he have a vision of April Moon? That would be so much nicer. He made an effort to do so, but Harrow refused to fade from his mind. Rather, the man's noisome presence grew even more forceful, more immediate...

Sinclair was no longer in his bed. He was sitting at a small table in a dank, grimy little room. He could feel the wobbling of his rickety chair, and a deep, throbbing pain in his right ankle. Across the table, eyes in shadow beneath a dusty light, was the smug countenance of Sterling Harrow.

Lovely, Sinclair thought. *I think I'd rather dream of the Dragon.*

"It is quite obvious that you are a man of extraordinary potential," Harrow said.

Sinclair opened his mouth, and a stranger's voice emerged: "Gee, I'm not so sure about that, Mr. Harrow."

Sinclair was nonplused. *Did I say that?*

"You're too modest, my dear chap," Harrow said. "If you didn't possess the heart of a warrior, you would not have been chosen to receive the Insight."

"I appreciate what you're saying," the strange voice replied, "but I don't think I was chosen for anything. I think it was more of an accident."

"Nonsense!" Harrow said. "My friend would never have passed his gift to an unworthy soul. In my humble opinion, you were placed in that room by the hand of fate."

There's nothing humble about you, Sinclair wanted to reply, but he seemed to have no control over the body he was inhabiting in this peculiar dream.

"The hand of fate…" the strange voice said. It was a young man's voice, Sinclair noted, and there was something sad and hopeful in its uncertain tone.

What's happening here? Sinclair groggily wondered. *Whose eyes am I looking through?*

"Indeed!" said Harrow. "In fact, I would not be surprised if you turned out to be the greatest Lancer of them all!"

"Do you really mean that?" the young man asked, and Sinclair could sense the yearning behind the question, the desperate need for affirmation. "I knew Mr. Krause had given me some kind of power when he died, but I never dared to believe…"

Sinclair's drowsy stupor suddenly cleared, and he realized that this was no dream. *Good Lord!* He thought. *It's him! The man I became connected to when he gained the Insight! My consciousness must have drifted to his while I was sleeping! Perhaps I can communicate with him…*

Sinclair tried to capture the attention of the young man, but to no avail. The boy's mind was completely focused on Harrow's honeyed words.

"You can dare anything, now that you have the Insight," said the Englishman. "Money, women, power, all of it can be yours."

Oh, for God's sake, Sinclair silently groaned. *These guys are all alike!*

"Is that all you use it for?" the boy asked. "I mean, those things are great, but don't you think you should also…well…help people?"

Harrow smiled. "You wish to be a hero?"

Sinclair felt the happiness bloom in the young man's heart. "Can I?"

"Take my hand," Harrow said. "Open yourself to me completely, and I will give you all the knowledge you need to make your dreams a reality."

Sinclair had a dark foreboding. There was something lurking behind Harrow's eyes; something ugly and eager and rapacious…

He's lying! Don't let him touch you!

The boy didn't move. Sinclair prayed that he was getting through to him.

"Come on, lad," Harrow cajoled. "Embrace your destiny."

Don't listen to him! It's a trick! Get out of there!

"Take your place among the heroes," Harrow said in a silken whisper.

DON'T DO IT!

The boy lifted his hand.

Harrow took Pender's clammy hand and said a few words in a strange tongue. The boy stiffened and his face went white. "What did you just do?" he gasped. "Why can't I move?"

"I've paralyzed you with an enchantment," Harrow said with a smile. "Truth to tell, I wasn't sure it would work. I'm a tad out of practice when it comes to black magic."

"Black magic?"

"Yes, you know, the Dark Arts, the Left-Handed Path. The hypocrites in the Order frown on such things, but they're not here to disapprove, now are they?"

"I don't…I don't understand."

"Of course, you don't. You're an imbecile. In that regard, you would have fit right in with the Lancers. Fortunately, you will now serve a higher purpose."

"What purpose?"

"Increasing my power! You see, Mr. Pender, I have a little theory about the Insight…"

Without releasing the boy's hand, Harrow stepped around the table and moved behind the young man's chair.

"Consider this," Harrow said. "If the power can be passed from one to another, is it not logical to assume that it can also be *taken*, by force if necessary?"

Harrow closed his free hand over the top of Pender's head. The boy's hair was damp with oil and perspiration.

"What are you going to do?" Pender asked.

"Haven't you already guessed?" the Englishman said. He began a low, guttural chanting.

At first, nothing happened. Harrow was dismayed. Had he miscalculated? Used the wrong incantation? Shaking off his doubts, he continued the obscene mantra, and then the power began to flow. Harrow grinned.

Pender shook as though palsied. "Please," he said. "Please, stop. It *hurts*."

Harrow responded by tightening his grip on Pender's skull. The boy screamed. Harrow said some words, and the scream died. Pender was reduced to silently weeping as his soul was torn apart.

Harrow was exultant. It was even better than he had imagined.

Sinclair was trapped. He tried to disengage from the young man's mind, but Harrow's spell had enveloped him like quicksand; the more he struggled, the deeper he sank. Worse, he was forced to share the boy's torment. Sinclair could feel the Insight being ripped from Pender's psyche. The pain was excruciating.

I've got to break this connection, Sinclair thought. *If Harrow senses my presence...*

"What's this?" the Englishman said. "Is that you, Shopkeeper? What are you doing in there?"

Sinclair didn't respond.

Harrow laughed. "Silent treatment, eh? That's fine. I really don't care why you're in this cretin's brain. But since you've decided to join us..."

Sinclair felt a blade of fire slash into his Insight. The blade curled into a hook and buried itself in the power.

"Two for the price of one," Harrow said, and the hook began to pull.

Sinclair screamed.

The process lasted for about another ten minutes. When Harrow decided he had taken all that his victims had to give, he released Pender and pushed him to the floor. The boy lay there twitching, his chest rising and falling in short, shallow breaths.

Harrow was electrified by the double portion of Insight. The sensation was fantastic! What would it be like, he wondered, after he had stripped the power from the other Lancers?

"I'll be the greatest sorcerer in history," he said. "I will be like unto a god."

As if in reply, Milton Pender gagged and spit up what was left of his lunch.

Harrow was repulsed. "You're disgusting," he said. "I only regret that your Insight had to come burdened with the weight of your… worthless… memories…"

Harrow's eyes narrowed as his gaze turned inward. There was something interesting there, something unexpected.

"Oh, ho!" the Englishman said. "Not entirely worthless, after all! Who would have thought that a fool like you would know the secrets of Brother Bones? Why haven't you acted on that knowledge? Didn't you know there was a bounty on that man's head?"

Pender nodded weakly.

"Well?" Harrow said. "Weren't you planning to collect?"

"Thought about it," Pender murmured. "Decided…not to …"

"Why not?"

"I couldn't…betray him…saved my life …"

Harrow shook his head. "I withdraw what I said earlier. You never would have fit in with the Order. You're not our sort."

Pender looked up at Harrow. "I'll take that…as a compliment …"

"Take it as you please," Harrow said. "You know, I was going to run you through, but you aren't worthy of a gentleman's death. You're just a pathetic little sod who was born for the potter's field. Goodbye, Mr. Pender."

The Englishman lifted his cane and brought it down on the boy's head.

Agonized and delirious, Sinclair gazed up through Milton Pender's eyes at the sneering face of Sterling Harrow. He saw the cane flash down like a black thunderbolt. He heard and felt the horrendous *crack* as it connected with his skull.

He's going to kill him, Sinclair thought. *He's going to kill that boy and he might kill me too if I can't –*

Harrow swung again. *Crack!*

Sinclair cried out, but no one heard.

Crack! Crack! Crack! Crack!

Robert the Bruce was no gourmet, but his brain supplied the Dragon with enough culinary knowledge to cook a steak and a baked potato. He took the meal by candlelight, sitting alone in the spacious dining room of the Shiloh townhouse. The food was delicious. He ate every bite, and washed it all down with an ice-cold beer.

After he cleaned his plate and finished his brew, the Dragon began to feel a strange heaviness behind his eyes. He tried to shake it off, but the sensation only increased, along with the throbbing pain in his head.

"I'm tired and sleepy," he said aloud, identifying the sensations.

The Dragon was intrigued. He had never been to sleep before. Though part of him was burning to resume his mission without further delay, an even greater part was eager to experience slumber. After a moment of internal bickering, his sensual side carried the day, and he slowly made his way up the stairs to the Bruce's bedroom. When his head hit the feather pillow, he sighed with pleasure. This was definitely the right decision.

"The will is strong, but the flesh is weak," he said with a chuckle, and then he quietly drifted away.

Bobby Crandall was smiling when he parked his car in front of the cold water flat. He had recently made some happy memories. Both he and Paula Wozcheski had returned to the six-to-twelve shift at the casino, and he had successfully persuaded her to spend a couple of hours with him after they clocked out. Those were two good hours. Parting company with her hadn't been easy, but it wasn't a good idea to be out of touch with Bones for very long. The dead man's patience was limited.

When he stepped out of the car into the damp chill of the evening air, he was struck by an odd feeling of being watched. Bobby was the servant of a man with many enemies, and he took such feelings seriously. He stood motionless and stared into the darkness.

"Hello?" he said cautiously, and he immediately felt the urge to give himself a kick in the pants. He was so stupid sometimes! Did he really expect an answer? And if he got one, what would he do then?

He stood quiet and still for another few minutes, then gave up and went inside. What was there to be worried about? If someone was casing the joint, then let 'em. If they broke in, they'd get one hell of a surprise. Bobby couldn't help but smile at the thought of a burglar walking in on Brother Bones.

Later, as he prepared for bed, Bobby had a strange thought: *I never feel safer than when I'm here with him.* It was weird to think of Bones as a comforting presence, but that's exactly what he was. Cape Noire may have been a jungle, but Bobby Crandall lived with a lion.

Across the street, concealed in shadows, Sterling Harrow watched the lights go out in the cold water flat. Grinning, he twirled his cane and started walking back to his car.

☠ ☠ ☠

The screaming started just before sunrise. Waldo awoke with a start, nearly falling out of his chair. He came to his feet and lumbered over to the writhing form of Robert Shiloh. The old man was strapped to one of the operating tables. His spindly arms strained against the leather, and the tendons in his neck were as taut as piano wires.

"What's happened to me?" he cried. "What have you done to me? What have you done?"

"Take it easy," Waldo said. "Getting hysterical isn't going to help things."

"What have you done?"

Waldo shook his head. Why couldn't this poor bastard have stayed under 'til the Prof was back on duty? Oh, well...

"Edgar," Waldo said, "I've got some bad news. Your brain's been switched with your grandfather's. He's got your body now."

"No!" screeched the old man. "No! No! No!"

"Sorry, but there it is," Waldo said. "You might as well just accept it. If you keep this up, you'll give yourself a heart attack."

Edgar didn't take the advice. He screamed and screamed until his voice gave out and the only sound he could make was a dry rasp. Later, when he finally calmed down, Waldo loosened his straps, helped him up, and gave him a glass of water.

"My head hurts," the old man said after he drained the glass.

"I'm sure," Waldo said.

Edgar coughed and spit a wad of phlegm onto the floor. "Everything hurts."

"No more spitting," Waldo said, "unless you plan to clean it up."

The old man covered his face with his hands. "How could Gramps do this to me?"

Waldo shrugged. "He's evil. Didn't you know that?"

Edgar was trembling. "That son of a bitch. I'll kill him for this!"

"Yeah, well, that's between you and him," Waldo said.

"You're damn right it is. Where is he? Is he still here?"

"He's been gone for hours. He had some kind of dust-up with the Prof when he came to."

"Dust-up?"

"Don't ask me," Waldo said. "The Prof won't talk about it. All he wanted to do when I relieved him was go straight to bed."

Something bloody came into the old man's eyes. "Bugosi's downstairs?"

"I know what you're thinking," Waldo said, "and you can forget it."

"I'll pay you," Edgar said. "Name your price. All you have to do is let me—"

"Drop it. You're not getting near him. End of story."

The old man scowled and stared at the floor, brooding. After a moment, he said, "What are you going to do with me?"

"The Prof didn't give me any orders."

"Will you take me somewhere?"

"I don't know about that…"

Edgar looked up, and the pleading in his eyes was positively canine. "I'm begging you," he said. "Take me out of here. Why bother keeping me a prisoner? I'm a dead man, anyway."

Waldo frowned. In spite of himself, he felt pity for the man. "Where do you want to go?"

"My office."

"Your office? Why would you want to go there?"

Edgar clenched his fists. "There's where Gramps will be. He's got a thing for my secretary…"

Waldo held up a hand. "Never mind. Sorry I asked."

"Will you take me?"

Waldo sighed, and slowly nodded.

Bethany Timms reported for duty at eight o'clock sharp. She had just stepped into the office when she froze in place, like a deer catching the scent of gun oil.

The door to Mr. Shiloh's office was open, and a stranger in a brown fedora was seated at his desk. A cloud of cigarette smoke drifted over his head as he reclined in Edgar's swivel chair, staring out the window that overlooked the docks. She couldn't see his face, but she knew the man wasn't her boss. Mr. Shiloh never wore a hat indoors, and he despised tobacco.

"Good morning, Mrs. Timms," the man said. His voice was tired and ragged. He coughed a little, and turned the chair. "Do you know who I am?"

Bethany forced a smile. "You're Mr. Shiloh's grandfather," she said. "We've met before."

"Yeah," the old man said. "Tell me, have you heard from Edgar this morning? Talked to him on the phone, by any chance?"

"No, sir. Actually, I'm surprised he's not here. He's usually very punctual."

The old man grunted and put out his cigarette on the edge of the desk.

Bethany was horrified. She was sure that Edgar would find some way to blame her for that desecration. "If you'll pardon me," she said, "Mr. Shiloh doesn't like for people to smoke in his office."

"He's had a change of mind," the old man said. He lifted his other hand, and Bethany saw that he was holding a pistol. He pointed it at her. "Get in here," he said, "and shut that door behind you."

Bethany didn't move.

The old man gave her an ugly smile. "Come on, now. Just pretend I'm Edgar. You do everything *he* says, don't you?"

"He's my boss," Bethany said. Her heart was beating very fast.

"Don't I know it. Get in here or I'll shoot you. I mean it."

Bethany obeyed. Her movements were stiff, as if the fear were freezing her joints. "May I ask what this is all about, sir?" she said as she closed the door.

"You wouldn't believe me if I told you," the old man said. "Have a seat and relax. We'll wait for Eddie together. He should be along soon."

Bethany sat down and clenched her hands together in her lap. She tried not to look at her captor, but she could feel the touch of his eyes. They crawled like cockroaches up and down her body.

For several minutes, the only sound in the office was the shallow, wheezing breaths of the old man. Bethany wondered what his intentions were, but she didn't dare to ask. *When did I become such a coward?* she wondered. *When?*

Her spirit hadn't been broken overnight. It had been a gradual process. Edgar had started small, with lascivious jokes and crude innuendoes. These matured over time into explicit demands and ominous threats. He would get what he wanted, or her children would be taken. He could do it with a phone call. He was the most powerful man in Cape Noire…

"What are you thinking about?" the old man asked.

"Your grandson," Bethany replied, staring at her hands.

"No kidding?" he said. "I bet you're hoping I'll kill him."

"I would never hope for that."

There was a moment of silence, and Bethany heard the swivel chair creak as the old man leaned forward. "Are you serious?" he asked.

"Yes."

"Why wouldn't you want him dead? After all the things I've…I've heard that he's done to you? All those things he made you do?"

Bethany closed her eyes. She was burning with shame. "You know about that?"

"I know everything."

"Don't get me wrong," Bethany said, her voice quavering. "I hate him. I think he's the only person I've ever truly hated."

"But?" the old man prompted.

"But sometimes I almost feel sorry for him. He's so broken inside. He wants so much to be respected and feared…" Bethany laughed. It was a small, bitter sound. "I wonder what he would have been like, if anyone had ever really loved him."

"You think he would have been different?" the old man said. His voice was low and soft.

"Maybe," Bethany said. "Maybe he wouldn't have grown up to be a scared little boy who hurts people so he can feel strong."

"You stupid bitch!"

Startled, Bethany looked up. The old man's eyes were bulging with fury.

"You think I need your pity?" he snarled. "You think I'm a scared little boy?"

Bethany gaped at the man. He was rising from behind the desk. The gun was shaking in his hand. "I'll show you who's a little boy!" he said. "Get up!"

Bethany rose to her feet.

"Bend over the desk."

Bethany stared at him, overwhelmed by a shock of recognition.

"Goddammit!" he shouted. "I said, *bend over!*"

He lunged forward and punched her in the stomach. She folded at the middle and almost fell, but he held her up. He shoved her roughly onto the desk. As she went face-down over it, one of her hands landed on a sliver of metal. Her fingers closed around it, and without looking she knew what it was: Mr. Shiloh's ivory-handled letter-opener.

Behind her, she could hear the old man's belt sliding out of his pants. "Pull up your skirt!"

Her children would be taken.

"Quit stalling!"

He could do it with a phone call.

"I said, pull up your skirt, you stupid cow!"

He was the most powerful man in Cape Noire.

"I want to hear you count the strokes!"

In one swift movement, Bethany pushed herself off the desk, turned, and drove the letter-opener into the old man's throat.

"One!" she said.

She stopped counting after five.

Sally had just settled down for some badly-needed sleep when the phone rang. "This better be good," she said when she picked up.

"Miss Paige?" The voice in the receiver was tremulous and childlike.

"This is Sally Paige. Who am I speaking to?"

"You…you told me to call you…if I ever needed help…"

Sally identified the voice. "Mrs. Timms," she said. "What can I do for you?"

"Oh, God…"

"Mrs. Timms?"

"I've killed someone."

Sally wasn't sleepy anymore. "Where are you?"

"The office…"

"The bottling company?"

"Yes."

Sally chewed her lip. The voice of reason told her to hang up and call Dan. It was the right thing to do. The smart, safe, logical thing.

Mrs. Timms broke down. The woman tried to speak, but the weeping made her nearly incomprehensible. Sally was only able to make out one sentence: *You said I could trust you.*

"I'll be right over," Sally said.

The secretary's clothes were sodden with blood.

"Are you hurt?" Sally asked as she stepped into the office.

"No," Mrs. Timms said. "It's all his."

Sally knelt by the dead man. The rheumy eyes of Robert Shiloh stared past her into the infinite. His mouth was open wide, fixed in a permanent gawk of pained surprise. It wasn't a pretty sight. Sally pulled away the old man's hat, and regarded with interest the bandages that swathed his head. She stood up and faced Mrs. Timms. "Tell me what happened," she said.

Mrs. Timms told the story in fits and starts. She stayed on verge of collapse throughout the narrative, but she never quite tumbled over. Sally listened without interrupting, until the woman said something so bizarre that it demanded clarification.

"Wait a minute," Sally said, "you're telling me that you killed Eddie Shiloh?"

Mrs. Timms nodded.

Sally was patient, solicitous. "Timms," she said, "this is Robert the Bruce. I'd know him anywhere."

Mrs. Timms swallowed. "No," she said. "I know it's crazy, and I can't explain it, but that's Edgar. I would know *him* anywhere."

Sally looked down at the body. Her eyes were drawn once more to the bandaged head. There was a thin red line visible in the dressings, as if blood were seeping from an incision that circled the skull…

"Well," Sally murmured, "it's been done before. Just look at Harry Beest."

"I'm sorry," said Mrs. Timms, "but I don't understand what you're saying."

Sally's eyes remained on the corpse. "Timms, does the name 'Bugosi' mean anything to you?"

"The Professor? I've talked to him a few times. He would call and leave messages for Mr. Shiloh."

Sally's eyes flashed. *Bingo!*

Timms was confused. "What does the Professor have to do with anything?"

"Maybe a lot. Have you heard from…the other Shiloh this morning?"

"No."

Sally drummed her fingers against the side of her leg. "I would *really* like to talk to him."

Mrs. Timms let out a shuddering sigh. "I'm so sorry," she said. "Please, forgive me."

Sally's fingers went still. She looked at the secretary. "For what?"

"For dragging you into this. It was wrong. It was selfish of me."

"Hey, don't say that. I told you that you could call me."

Mrs. Timms didn't seem to hear. She stared at the dead man. "How could I have done something like this? I'm not a killer. I've never hurt anyone in my life. I've never hurt anyone…never…"

"Timms, listen to me…"

The secretary was shaking. Tears began to stream down her cheeks. "What's going to happen to me? Oh dear God…what's going to happen… to my…children…"

Her knees buckled, but Sally caught her and pulled her into a gentle embrace. "It's going to be okay," Sally whispered. "Everything's going to be all right. Everything's going to be all right…"

She kept repeating the phrase until she almost believed it herself.

Sally gave the secretary her hat and coat. *Go to my place*, she told her. *Get cleaned up. Stay there until you hear from me. Got it?*

Timms got it, but she was still worried about her kids. The babysitter would wonder what was going on if she didn't pick them up on time.

One of us will get them later, Sally had said. *Then we're all going to take a nice little trip to the beach. My treat.*

We are? Why?

Because you need a couple of days to get your head on straight. A change of scenery will do you good.

But what about the police?

You let me worry about them.

Are you sure about all this?

Positive.

I don't know what to say. How can I ever thank you?

There's no need. Virtue is its own reward.

All of that had been over half an hour ago. Now, Sally was sitting in the office, idly turning in the swivel chair, thinking.

Dan was smart and decent, but he wasn't the final authority on these things. At the very least, Timms was looking at a manslaughter charge, and Sally just couldn't let that happen. The poor woman had been punished enough. She didn't deserve to become the main attraction in a legal circus, forced to repeat the details of Edgar's abuse over and over again.

Sally cast a glance at the dead man keeping her company. Was Eddie Shiloh's brain really crammed in that noggin? It was more than possible if Bugosi was involved. But how did Eddie and the Bruce get tied up with the Professor? What was the connection? More important, how would Sally investigate all this from a jail cell? That was, after all, exactly where she was headed if Dan found out what she was up to. It was a puzzle.

"What the hell am I going to do about you?" she asked the corpse.

As if in reply, there was a soft knock at the private entrance.

☠ ☠ ☠

Howard the cleaning man waited a few beats before opening the door. Edgar always answered immediately if he was in. When there was no reply, Howard turned the handle. He was looking forward to some unimpeded snooping. Since he had found Eddie's safe and cracked the combination, Howard had made a point of looking in the thing every chance he got. Who knew what interesting items he might discover?

He pushed open the door, and the item he discovered was Sally Paige, sitting at the desk, aiming a .38 at his head.

Oops.

"Well bless my soul," Paige said. "If it isn't Howard Hollis."

"You know me?"

"I know every two-bit thug in this town."

Howard was slightly offended. "I'm four bits at least. What are you doing here, Paige?"

"I'd like to ask you the same thing. Last time I checked, you were working for Harry Beest. You decide to give that up for the glamorous life of a janitor?"

"That's me," Howard said, "always chasing rainbows."

Paige grinned. "Tell me, how long has the ape-man had you spying on Eddie?"

"Quid pro quo?"

"Sure, why not?"

"All right. I've been on the job for six months, give or take a week."

"That's a long time."

"You have no idea. My turn. Why is there blood on the wall?"

"Come in and see."

Howard stepped into the room, and then he let out a low whistle. "Cripes," he said. "Is that Bobby the Bruce?"

"The jury's still out on that one."

"What's that supposed to mean?"

Paige shook her head. "My turn. What's Eddie been doing with Professor Bugosi?"

"That's an easy one. Bugosi created TenaciTea. Eddie handles manufacturing and sales. Why are we talking about the Prof?"

"I have reason to suspect their relationship went sour. Does Harry Beest know that Eddie's in cahoots with Bugosi?"

"Yes, he does. My turn, again." He pointed at the corpse. "Why is his head wrapped in bandages?"

"I think Bugosi may have pulled one of his brain-switcheroos with Eddie and the Bruce."

Howard knelt beside the body. "I'll be damned," he said.

"What's Beest planning to do about Eddie and the Prof?"

"I don't know. He doesn't tell me everything." Howard stood up. "Who killed this guy?"

Paige answered a little too quickly. "Couldn't tell you. I found him like that."

Howard stared at her. "The cops are on the way, then?"

Paige's face flushed. "That's two questions in a row. Are you trying to cheat?"

"Don't be a hypocrite. You already broke the rules by lying. Do you seriously expect me to believe that you just stumbled on to this? I know you didn't kill him, otherwise you'd be covered in blood. So, who did?"

"I've already told you –"

"Oh, cut the crap! Who are you trying to protect?"

Paige didn't reply, but her gun hand was steady.

Howard snapped his fingers. "The secretary," he said. "Has to be. I guess Edgar finally pushed her too far."

"I don't know what you're talking about," Paige said.

"Okay," Howard said, "but let's pretend that you do. If that were the case, then you might know a little about the hell that poor woman's been through."

"I might," Paige said.

Howard nodded. "And you might want to help her."

Paige's eyes narrowed. "Where are you going with this?"

Howard took off his glasses. He plucked a cloth from his pocket and cleaned the lenses.

He came to a decision.

"Well," he said, "I might be inclined to help her, too."

"You would?"

"Yes."

"Why?"

Howard put away the cloth and slipped his glasses back on. "I'm not a good guy, Paige, but that doesn't mean I'm incapable of doing a good thing."

The reporter slowly lowered the gun. "What exactly are you proposing?"

He gestured to the body. "Leave this to me, and I'll make it disappear."

"How?"

"The less you know, the better. Just take my word for it, when I'm done, it'll be like it never happened."

"You can do that?"

Howard smiled. "There's a reason they call me the Cleaning Man."

The sun passed over the city, darkened to red, and sank in the west.

About the same time that Howard Hollis was locking the door to the now-pristine offices of the Shiloh Bottling Company, Bobby Crandall was locking the door to his less-than-pristine cold water flat. He was moving at an easy pace. He had plenty of time before he had to be at the casino, so he planned to treat himself to a meal at Hancock's Diner. Hancock's was all the way across town, but on meatloaf day it was worth the trip. It was the simple pleasures that made life worth living.

As Bobby drove away to his appointment with blue-plate bliss, he did not notice the black Plymouth sedan hidden in the shadows of a nearby alley, nor did he see the predatory smile of the man behind the wheel.

"Enjoy your shift, Mr. Crandall," Sterling Harrow said as he watched Bobby pass by.

Enjoy your shift, Mr. Crandall.

"Who said that?" Milton Pender asked. The slurred question was uttered in a barely audible moan. No one in the grimy apartment responded. There was only silence and darkness.

"Can anyone hear me?"

Silence.

"Can't move."

Darkness.

"I'm scared."

In the apartment next door, someone turned on a radio. There was a burst of static, and then Milton heard a familiar song.

"It's the taste that brings you hope…When you're at the end of your rope…"

Harrow paused with his hand at the door of the darkened flat. Was that music? Where was it coming from? He listened intently, but the sound was gone.

That was odd, he thought. He wondered if there were some significance to that distant signal. Now that he had increased his Insight, he could sense hidden meanings in even the most banal phenomena. There were signs and portents everywhere. Everything was connected. One only needed eyes to see.

What if it was a warning? Perhaps I should turn back. After all, what is fifty thousand dollars to man like me?

It was nothing, of course. But this wasn't about money, anymore.

It was a test.

Harrow knew this was no ordinary man he was about to challenge. Bobby Crandall's second-hand memories had made that abundantly clear. Brother Bones truly was an Undead Avenger; an enforcer for powers beyond mortal understanding. Was Harrow's magic sufficient to conquer such a being?

I have to know.

He whispered an incantation, and the door opened at this touch.

The darkness that enveloped Milton Pender seemed to lighten. In the dim illumination, he saw a tidy but cramped living space, some threadbare furniture, a small kitchenette…

This isn't my apartment. What am I seeing?

More to the point, *where* was he seeing, and through whose eyes?

Mr. Harrow. He didn't get all my power, after all. Hooray for me.

Milton followed Harrow's gaze as the Englishman toured the empty rooms.

What is he looking for?

A door opened. A looming shadow filled the empty space. A grinning skull gleamed.

Hello, Brother Bones.

"Hello, Brother Bones," said Sterling Harrow, choking down the terror that rose like bile in his throat.

Brother Bones aimed a pistol at the Englishman's head. "Who are you and what are you doing here?"

Harrow raised his hands and said some words.

Milton saw Brother Bones stiffen, then lower his weapon.

He heard Harrow laugh. "It worked!"

What worked? What did he do?

"You're my puppet, Brother Bones!"

Oh, no. Oh, please no.

"You can drop your guns. You won't be needing them anymore."

This is all my fault.

"Let's go, Mr. Punch. I have a bounty to collect."

I have to do something.

Milton braced his hands against the floor. He took a deep breath, lifted himself, and pain exploded like dynamite behind his eyes. He tried to tough it out—*the Black Haze wouldn't surrender!*—but it was more than his broken body could take. With a faint cry of despair, he lost consciousness.

The Dragon was roused from a sound sleep by the ringing of a bell. Dazed and logy, he crawled from his bed and staggered in the direction of the noise. He soon found the offending device and gave it a withering glare. When that didn't do any good, he reluctantly extended a hand and picked up the telephone.

"Hello?"

"Good evening. Do I have the pleasure of speaking to Mr. Edgar Shiloh?"

"No," said the Dragon. He rubbed his eyes. He still wasn't fully awake.

"When will he be available?"

"Wait…Edgar, you say?"

"Yes."

"No."

"Pardon?"

"Robert."

"Excuse me?"

"I'm…wait…the brain of…the body of…"

"Perhaps I should call back later."

"No," said the Dragon. "There is no need."

"No need?"

"Yes. I am Edgar Shiloh."

"Are you sure?"

"Yes. Definitely."

"Well…in that case, I have something I think you will be interested in."

"Go on."

"My name is Sterling Harrow, and I have captured Brother Bones!"

There was another pause. The Dragon breathed into the receiver. He clicked his teeth.

"Perhaps you didn't hear me," Harrow said. "I have captured –"

"I heard you, Lancer. Bring him to me."

"Excuse me? Did you just call me –"

"I didn't call you anything."

"I distinctly heard you say –"

"I said, 'I heard your answer.' Now, bring him to me, and you can claim your reward."

"Very well. Where would you like him delivered?"

The Dragon told him.

Sinclair was awakened by the sound of breaking glass.

Dreaming, he thought. *Head hurts. Go back to sleep.*

He heard a latch click. He heard the brass bell ring. His eyes popped open.

Not dreaming. Someone's breaking in!

"Sinclair!"

April?

"Sinclair, answer me! Where are you?"

"I'm here," he croaked. He cleared his throat. "I'm here," he said again, stronger this time.

Then she was beside him. She turned on a lamp. "Jeez, are you all right?"

"I don't think so."

She pressed a cool hand to his forehead. "How do you feel?"

"Like someone beat me with a walking stick. Did you break the glass in my front door?"

"Sorry about that. I'll pay for the damage."

"Why did you…?"

"I've been worried sick about you! I've been calling and dropping by all day. I started thinking you might be hurt, or worse. We're dealing with some dangerous characters, y'know?"

"You were worried about me?"

"Of course. Why wouldn't I be?"

"Thank you," he said.

"Think nothing of it. What happened to you, anyway?"

"Sterling Harrow happened, that perfidious bastard!" Sinclair tried to sit up, and he nearly fainted from the pain that spiked through his skull.

"Whoa, whoa, take it easy! I think I should get you to a doctor."

"No doctors," Sinclair said, wincing. "I'm not really injured. I just had to share his pain."

"Whose pain? What are you talking about?"

"April, listen, I hate to say this, but we need to…we need to…"

"What do we need to do?"

He forced out the words. "We need to call Leandro Mendoza."

Harrow found it difficult to concentrate on his driving. The eyes of his ominous passenger glared at him from the rearview mirror, constantly pulling his gaze from the road.

"You can speak, if you like," Harrow said. "The spell will permit it."

Brother Bones did not speak.

"Tell me, how did you obtain your power? Did you make a bargain for immortality?"

No reply.

"I could make you talk, you know. Shall I demonstrate?"

"You missed your turn."

"What?"

"If you're going to the Shiloh house, you should have turned left."

Harrow pressed the brake and examined the street signs. He mumbled a curse, then turned around. "Why did you tell me that?" he asked.

"I want to hurry up and get this over with," said Bones.

"Are you so eager for your own demise?"

"No. Yours."

Harrow opened his mouth, then closed it. He reached up and turned the mirror so he could no longer see the black onyx eyes.

A few minutes later, Harrow parked his car in front of the darkened Shiloh townhouse. He waited until there were no other cars passing, then ordered Bones to follow him to the front door. He knocked, and the door opened to reveal...nothing. No one stepped outside. No one beckoned them to enter. There were only shadows in an empty hall.

Harrow leaned over the threshold. "Hello? Mr. Shiloh?"

A door opened at the end of the hall. Harrow saw a flickering red glow, and he could hear the crackle of an open fire.

"Come into my parlor," someone said. It was a cheerful voice, but there was something unpleasant in it, an acidic trickle of sneering contempt.

Harrow wavered. Something was wrong here. He reached out with his Insight, but it merely flashed and flew like a rudderless rocket, racing without direction through the empty confines of the house. *I'm not used to having so much power*, Harrow thought. *It will take time to learn to control it properly.*

"What are you waiting for?" growled Bones. "Don't you want your money?"

Harrow stepped aside. "You go first."

Bones obeyed, marching stiffly into the darkness with Harrow following in his wake. They went into the room and found a lean young man lounging by the fire. He was relaxing in a large chair, legs resting on an ottoman, a glass of wine held loosely in his hand. He was clad after the fashion of the Orient, in a red silk robe covered with golden dragons. His head was wrapped in bandages.

Harrow eyed him with distaste. Silk robes? How gauche. "Are you Edgar Shiloh?"

The man ignored him. He raised his glass to Brother Bones. "Good evening, my friend."

"You," said Bones. "I had a feeling you were going to be at the bottom of this."

"I'm glad you recognize me," the man said. He took a sip of wine. "I perceive that you are under an enchantment. That would explain how this imbecile managed to capture you. Magic must be your Achilles heel."

"I beg your pardon," Harrow said. "What did you just call me?"

"Be quiet, fool. The adults are talking."

Harrow marveled at this effrontery. Of all the infernal cheek! He decided to teach a lesson to this indolent pouf. He concealed his rage and affected the manner of one justly chastened. "Please accept my apologies," he said. "It seems we've gotten off on the wrong foot. Perhaps we can start over."

"Perhaps," the young man said.

Harrow advanced on him, hand extended. "My name is Sterling Harrow."

The young man rose from his chair. "My name isn't Edgar Shiloh," he said, and he took the Englishman's hand.

Harrow blanched. He intended to fry this lout's brain with a blast of his power, but the electric strike he sent forth had suddenly deepened into a steady flow of current. He felt like a battery being depleted of its charge. He tried to pull his hand away, but it seemed the circuit, once completed, could not be broken.

"Something wrong, Mr. Harrow?" the young man asked. "You're looking a little drained."

Harrow was mortified. He felt as if his insides were beginning to desiccate and crumble. "Who are you?" he gasped.

"Hasn't your Insight informed you?"

"My...Insight?"

"Well, *my* Insight, actually, although I've never referred to it by that name. You see, when Don Julio ran me through, a portion of my spirit went into him. He never really understood what happened. He thought the power was some sort of divine reward for defeating me. At least, that's what he told himself. Humans have an infinite capacity for self-deception."

"You're...killing...me."

"Calm yourself, Lancer. You're not going to die just yet. In fact, I'm even going to give you back a taste of the power."

Harrow cried out as a flow Insight burned into him like an injection of boiling magma.

"Oh, I suppose I should have warned you," the young man said, "it's a little more robust when it's coming straight from the source."

"What...are you...doing?"

"Fulfilling your destiny. Now, say my name."

In desperation, Harrow lifted his free hand and tried to utter an incantation.

The young man laughed. "Please! I practically invented that stuff. Stop embarrassing yourself. Say my name."

Harrow's eyes turned a sickly shade of yellow.

"Say my name."

"You are the Dragon," Harrow said.

"And you are my slave," the Dragon replied.

Brother Bones watched as Harrow fell and pressed his forehead to the floor, paying obeisance to his new master. Bones tried to move, and was disappointed to discover that the Englishman's spell was still intact.

"You have no idea how long I've been wanting to do that," the Dragon said.

"Why haven't you done it sooner?" Bones asked.

"An unfortunate technicality. I have to be physically present—in some form or other—before I can seize control of their precious Insight."

"So these guys, these 'Lancers,' all their hocus-pocus comes from you?"

"Ironic, isn't it? Don Julio thought he was founding an order of noble knights, but humans can't handle true power. It didn't take them long to become a fraternity of bullies and thieves."

"Are they all as rotten as him?" Bones asked, flicking his eyes toward Harrow.

The Dragon smiled. "You are wondering about your Five Corners compatriot, the one called Sinclair. He was an exception, a Lancer of genuine integrity. He might have actually been a threat to me."

"Might have?"

"Alas, this one stole his power, and now it is back in the claws of its rightful owner. I'm afraid Mr. Sinclair is a spent force, much like yourself."

"Don't count on it."

The Dragon laughed. "Defiant to the last, eh? You have the spirit of a true rebel. You know, you should be on my side. Why not join me? What do you owe this fallen world?"

"A debt I can never repay."

"I wonder," said the Dragon. He reached out and placed his hand over Bones' unmoving heart. He held this pose for several long moments, his yellow eyes staring into the sockets of the white skull mask. Finally, he let his hand fall.

"It's no use," the Dragon said. "I can't read you at all. Even my power can't penetrate your darkness. What are you?"

"I'm the sum of my decisions," said Bones. "Just like you."

That made the Dragon angry. "You would compare yourself to me? I once stood at the left hand of the Most High!"

"Really? Where are standing now?"

"In a better place than you."

"Only for a time."

"You impudent golem!" the Dragon shouted. He stepped back, waved his hands and said some words. Bones felt himself lifted into the air, and

"GOOD EVENING, MY FRIEND."

his long-dead nerves ignited in a firestorm of agony. It was excruciating, but he did not allow himself to make a sound.

"I may not be able to kill you," said the Dragon, "but I *can* hurt you. How do you like it, Brother Bones? Anything to say, now?"

"Go to Hell," Bones rasped.

"One day," said the Dragon, "but not today." He looked at Harrow. "Get up, slave. You have work to do."

"Yes, master," Harrow muttered.

The Dragon pointed at Bones. "You ruined my plans at Five Corners, but that was only a temporary setback. In a few hours, I'm going to destroy this city, and I'm going to do it in your name. Contemplate that while you suffer."

Bones was in too much pain to think of an adequate reply.

Leandro had been pleased to discover a charming little tapas bar just two blocks from the Falmouth Inn. He had a delightful meal before returning to the hotel in a warm glow of post-prandial satisfaction. As he was passing the front desk, he paused to check his messages. He did this more out of habit than expectation, and was thus surprised when the clerk handed him two slips of paper.

The first read, *Please call April Moon at shop as soon as possible.*

Leandro smiled. Perhaps Miss Moon had reconsidered his offer. But if that was the case, why would she be waiting to hear from him at Sinclair's bookstore? Hmm…

The second read, *Enemy found and cornered. Bring everyone. Do not delay. Harrow.* There was an address listed beneath the words.

Leandro stared at the piece of paper. Was this some sort of joke?

Enemy found and cornered.

He hefted the note as if weighing its veracity. It felt very light, indeed.

And yet, he thought, *I cannot afford to ignore it.*

He tucked both pieces of paper in his pocket and went to gather his fellow Lancers. By the time he reached the elevator, he had already forgotten the note from April Moon.

Crime is a weed.

"Huh? Whuzzat?"

It chokes the garden of justice.

Milton rolled onto his back and stared up at the shadows. Or did he? Were his eyes really open? Was he even still alive?

"Alive," he whispered. "Wouldn't feel pain if I was dead."

Get up, Milton.

"Who said that?"

You did.

"Lemme alone."

There's something you have to do.

"Can't."

You must.

"Hurting. Can't move. Can't think."

I know, but you have to get up.

"Why?"

There's somewhere you have to go.

"Where?"

You still have a spark of the Insight. It can lead you to your destination.

"It can?"

Yes, but you have to hurry. You don't have much time.

"What is it I gotta do?"

When the time comes, you will know.

Tears began to flow from Milton's swollen eyes. "Who are you?"

The last, best part of you. The part that Harrow couldn't touch.

Something darker than the shadows moved in the apartment. It loomed over Milton. He looked up at it, and his split lips parted in a broken grin. "Black Haze," he whispered.

That's as good a name as any.

Slowly, painfully, Milton forced himself up.

No one answered the Spaniard's knock.

"For God's sake, Leandro," said François, "just open the damned thing."

Leandro looked over his shoulder at the other Lancers. They were lined up on the steps, fidgeting with impatience, staring up at him.

"I have a bad feeling about this," Leandro said.

"Don't be such a woman," said one of the brethren. It was Oleg, the Russian. He shouldered his way past the other Lancers. "If this is some sort of hoax, then Harrow will be punished for it. If not, then we can end this business and go home."

"Yes," Leandro said, "but can't you sense…?"

"Sense what?" Oleg asked.

Leandro shook his head. How could he explain it? It was like the heat of some barely-contained combustion, a raging fire hidden behind a heavy door.

This door, to be precise.

"Brothers," Leandro said, "I think we should send for Arthur Sinclair. Our ranks are not complete without him. He was the first to sense the incursion –"

"The Shopkeeper?" François interrupted. "That clown? Have you gone mad?"

Oleg muttered a Slavic curse and pushed Leandro aside. "Enough delays," he said. "It's time to finish this."

He opened the door and there was Sterling Harrow, standing at the threshold, smiling.

"Come in, brothers, come in!" the Englishman said. "I was just about to admit you."

"Where's the Dragon?" snapped Oleg. "You told Leandro –"

"Please," Harrow said, "just follow me to the dining room, and all your questions will be answered." He turned and walked away without a backward glance.

The Lancers crowded at the door. They watched Harrow disappear into a room at the end of the hall.

Oleg looked at Leandro. "What was that all about?"

François drew his sword. "I say go inside and find out."

"Wait!" Leandro said in an urgent whisper. "I'm convinced that this is a mistake!"

"And I'm convinced you left your *couilles* in your other pants," François said. He looked at the others. *"Allons, mes amis!"*

They were uncertain. Their eyes moved to Leandro, then to Oleg. The Russian shrugged and drew his sword. "I'm with François."

That decided it. They unsheathed their blades and followed the Frenchman into the gloom of the Shiloh house. The last two through the door were Oleg and Leandro.

"Relax, old friend," the Russian said with a smile. "You're making a fool of yourself. There's nothing to fear."

"I hope to God you're right," Leandro replied.

The Lancers marched into the room, weapons at the ready. When Leandro joined them, he didn't feel like a fool. He felt woefully vindicated.

They stood before a long dining table. At its far end, behind a plate piled high with grapes, cheese, and cold cuts, sat a hard-eyed young man whose head was swathed in bandages. The cruelty in his gaze was somehow enhanced by the effete languor of his posture; one leg hanging over an armrest, his silk robe open to reveal a sallow, hairless chest.

Above and behind this decadent prince, floating in the air as though nailed to an invisible cross, was the man called Brother Bones.

"*Mon Dieu*," said François.

"*Mais oui!*" said the young man. He tossed a grape into the air and caught it in his mouth. "I *am* your god! The god you've been worshipping since the first time you used my power to satisfy your petty lusts. I only wish that Don Julio could be here. It would please me immensely for him to see what a sorry lot the Order of the Aspen Lance turned out to be."

For a moment, the Lancers were too amazed to answer this insult. They had no idea what to do or say. No longer sure of themselves, they instinctively turned to their senior member.

"We've walked into a trap," Leandro told them.

"Yes, you have," Sterling Harrow said from the corner of the room.

The Lancers turned on him, brandishing their swords, but before they could strike, Harrow raised his hands and said some words.

"I can't move!" Oleg bellowed. "This is sorcery! Harrow, you pig! I'll kill—"

Harrow said something else, and Oleg was rendered mute. Leandro tried to speak, and discovered that the spell of silence had fallen on him as well. Fearfully, he turned his eyes to the young man at the head of the table.

"Do you know who I am, Spaniard?" the man said.

Leandro tried to nod, but couldn't.

"Master," said Harrow, "shall I complete their conversion?"

"No," the man said, "that pleasure belongs to me."

He leapt on to the table and said something in a tongue that Leandro had never heard before. The words were harsh, but somehow beautiful. As he listened, he felt a strange lightness of being, as if he were losing something that had lent him weight and substance. This process continued until he felt less like a man than the hollow shell of one. Then something began to fill the empty spaces; something that burned away the thoughts and beliefs that made him Leandro Mendoza, and replaced them with a single-minded desire to serve his new master. A yellow mist descended over his eyes.

The man on the table looked down on his new slaves. He opened his arms as if offering them an embrace. "Welcome," he said, "to the Order of the Dragon."

"Feeling better?" April asked.

Sinclair sat on the edge of the bed and massaged his temples. "I'm getting there."

"Good, 'cause if you're up to it, I'm thinking we should go to the Falmouth in person."

Sinclair considered it. "Maybe you're right," he said. "It might be a waste of time, but anything would be better than just sitting around here. If nothing else, maybe we can catch one of the other Lancers."

"You sure you don't want to call the cops?"

"And tell them what? That I had a vision of a murder?" Sinclair shook his head. "As much as I hate to admit it, Leandro and his pals are the only ones to deal with this."

"There's us," April said.

Sinclair almost smiled. "I appreciate the sentiment, but I'm afraid I'm not much without the Insight."

"I don't believe I'm hearing this! You're still a man, aren't you? You don't need magic to kick that guy's butt! Did Max Baer need the Insight to beat Primo Carnera?"

"No, but he couldn't have done it if Primo Carnera had the Insight."

April threw up her hands in frustration. "Y'know, I can see there's no winning this argument, so I'm just gonna drop it right now. Get yourself together and we'll head for the Falmouth. I hope you've got money for cab fare, 'cause I'm flat broke."

"There's no need. I have a car."

"Really? You never told me you had a car."

"You never asked."

Dr. Marax had been walking around the room in a worried daze for three minutes before he found the note. How had he missed it? It was right there beside the bed. He should have seen as it as soon as he woke up. It had to be the morphine that was making him so thick-headed. He reached for the slip of paper.

Gone out for food and medicine. Be back soon. E.

There was a knock at the door.

The Doctor frowned. It couldn't be Erika. She had a key. Whoever it was, he didn't want to see them. He started back for the bed. Then he heard the door open.

"It seems that politeness is wasted on you, Marax."

The Doctor turned to see a smirking young man wearing a gray fedora and a herringbone suit. The man was flanked by two dapper, cane-wielding toughs with jaundiced eyes.

"Who the devil are you?" Marax demanded. "How did you open that door?"

"A parlor trick," the young man said. "As for my identity, well, we met one night in La Mancha, and you shared with me your heart's desire."

"You're...*him?* No! Wait! That night in Spain, I asked what you were and you said..."

"Greatness personified," the Dragon replied with a grin.

The Doctor's knees buckled. He sat down heavily on the edge of the bed. "What happened to you?"

"It would take too long to explain. Suffice to say that I'm not beaten yet." The Dragon looked around the room. "Where's the harlot?"

Marax bristled at the Dragon's vulgarity. "Erika isn't here."

"That's too bad. There are some things I would have liked to try with her."

"What do you mean?"

"Forget it. There's no time for that nonsense, anyway. Where is the music box?"

Marax didn't answer. He was still wondering what the Dragon wanted to try.

The Dragon snapped his fingers. "The box, Doctor."

Marax reached under the bed and produced the device.

"Excellent," said the Dragon.

"What are you going to do?" the Doctor asked. "It's useless without the tuning fork."

"Your mastery of the obvious is awe-inspiring," the Dragon said. "As it happens, there is a replacement available. After I retrieve it, we will sunder the veil once more. And this time, the effect will be increased."

Somewhere inside of Marax, a red flag of warning began to wave. "Increased?"

"Exponentially."

"How are you going to do that?"

The Dragon told him.

Marax was stunned. "But I only wanted to punish Cape Noire," he said. "What you're proposing is…"

"Biblical," the Dragon said.

"You'll kill millions! That wasn't part of the plan!"

"It is now," said the Dragon. "I'm closer to feeling the wind under my wings than I have in centuries. Unlike the little fish, I don't need the music box to sustain my corporeal form. Once the signal brings me through, I'll be here to stay, and I can release all the fish who swim in the ether. We'll turn this world into an abattoir! Let's see what the Most High thinks of that!"

"But that's not what we talked about! It's not what I want!"

"Isn't it? *Upon whom would you wreak this vengeance?* I once asked. Have you forgotten your reply?"

The Doctor looked away. He hadn't forgotten.

"I thought not," said the Dragon. "I have places to go and things to do. If you wish to be present for the endgame, I will allow you to come along. You deserve to see the fruits of your labors."

"You're mocking me."

"Yes, but only a little. Now, hand over the box."

Marax rose to his feet. "First, promise me that you will allow time for Erika to escape."

The Dragon laughed. "You can't be serious! I'm not going to hold up my plans for the sake of a whore."

"Don't call her that!" shouted Marax. "You have no right –"

One of the Dragon's minions drew a sword and plunged it into the Doctor's wounded chest. Marax cried out and released the box, but the Dragon caught it before it fell.

"Shall I finish him, Master?" the minion asked, twisting the blade in the Doctor's flesh.

"No," said the Dragon. "Let him live long enough to hear the city scream. Its how he wanted to honor his daughter's memory."

The minion shrugged and withdrew the blade. Marax collapsed on the floor.

"My daughter…" the Doctor moaned.

"She was a whore, too," the Dragon said as he left the room.

"This thing looks great!" April said. "How old is it?"

"I bought it new ten years ago."

"New? I thought fresh-squeezed juice was your only indulgence."

Sinclair was defensive. "It was a very practical purchase," he said. "The Overland Six is a sturdy and reliable car. Would you like to drive?"

"You'd let me?"

"Of course."

"I've never driven anything but a tractor."

Sinclair tossed her the keys. "Looks like you're not going to be able to say that anymore."

April's grin was blinding.

He had obscured his battered features with a frayed scarf and a weather-beaten hat. It was a cool evening, so the attire didn't draw attention. Supported by his crutch—and a blind, robotic determination to keep moving—he hobbled down the shadowy back-streets. His path was determined by a gentle but unwavering compulsion, an internal divining-rod that was leading him to…what, exactly?

Just a little but further. You're almost there.

"S'good," Milton said. "Don't how much more I can…"

That's it. That's the place.

"Nice house."

Milton paused, took a moment to rest on the rail, then climbed the steps.

Go on in.

"Shouldn't I knock?"

Don't bother. No one will answer.

Milton tried the door. "S'locked."

Not to you.

"Don't understand…"

Close your eyes. Imagine a blank page rolled into a typewriter. Do you see it?

"Yeah."

Imagine your fingers over the keys. Now, ask yourself, how do I open this door?

Milton did so.

Are the words coming?

Milton could actually hear the click of the keys. "Yeah, but how…?"

When Harrow invaded your mind, he accidentally left a few things in your subconscious.

"Careless."

Evil men are seldom as clever as they think they are. Go ahead, read the words aloud.

Milton read the words.

The door opened.

The Dragon flinched. "What was that?"

"Pardon, Master?" François said.

"Something's amiss. Pull over at the next intersection."

The Frenchman did as he was told. The two cars behind—their seats filled with Lancers—did so as well, following without hesitation the lead of the Master.

The Dragon looked at the two men in the back seat. "I want both of you to go back to the Shiloh residence."

"What would you have us do?" one asked.

The Dragon frowned. He wasn't entirely sure. He decided to keep it simple. "Stay there until I tell you otherwise. Kill anyone who goes in the house."

"Yes, Master," they said in unison. Then Sterling Harrow and Leandro Mendoza, their differences forgotten in the glow of their enslavement, got out of the car and started walking.

The Dragon turned to François. "Now," he said, "on to the home of Mr. Harry Beest."

"Why do you want me stop?" April asked.

"Because I felt something."

"Jeez, I can't dodge every pot-hole in the road."

"I'm serious, April. It was the Insight. I know it was."

"How can that be? You said the limey stole it all."

"I thought he did, but maybe…"

Sinclair closed his eyes. He summoned the image of the valise that held his Insight. It was open. The buckles were broken, and the leather was torn.

He peered inside, and he saw something. It was tiny and incandescent, a fugitive cinder from a guttering flame.

"He didn't get it all," Sinclair said aloud, and even as he uttered the words, he felt something hot on the flesh at the center of his chest. Startled, he opened his eyes, reached into his shirt, and pulled forth the aspen shard that he wore around his neck. It glowed with the faint radiance of a dying ember.

"Is that thing supposed to be doing that?" April said.

"Yes," Sinclair said. He closed his fist around the shard. "Turn the car around. We've got a new destination."

"Where?"

"I'll know when we get there"

Bones heard the door open, then a series of labored, shuffling steps. He lifted his eyes, and saw a plump little man supported by a crutch come hobbling into the dining room.

"Who are you?" Bones said, his voice tight with the agony of the hex that held him suspended in the air.

"A friend," the man said in a strained rasp. He took off his hat and unfurled the scarf that was covering most of his face. The bruised and bloody features were nearly unrecognizable, but Bones knew he was looking at the boy from—

"Five Corners," Bones said.

"Oh, you remember me," said the boy. "My name's Milton Pender."

"What happened to you?"

"Guy named Harrow. Tried to beat me to death."

Bones ground his teeth. Sterling Harrow was due for a reckoning.

"He took the power," Milton said. "But he didn't get it all."

"The power," said Bones. "Bobby said you turned him inside-out…"

"I read his mind. Didn't mean to. Just sort of happened."

"And then Harrow stole the memories from you. That's how he was able to find me."

"I'm sorry," the boy said. "I'm so sorry."

"Apology accepted. Now, get out of here. You need a doctor."

"No, I'm supposed to be here. The Black Haze showed me the way."

"The Black Haze?"

Milton held up a hand. "Hold on a sec," he muttered. "I'm trying to see the typewriter."

"What are you talking about?"

"I'm going to save you."

Bones couldn't believe his ears. "Kid, you're delirious. Forget about me. Save yourself."

The boy didn't seem to hear him. "Okay," he said, "its working. I can read the words."

Bones, thoroughly baffled, watched as Milton raised his arms and began to speak in a strange tongue. Bones felt the pain fade from his limbs. His invisible bonds loosened, and he fell to the floor in a graceless heap. He rose to his feet, but he didn't see Milton. He walked to the end of the table, and saw that the boy had collapsed, his trembling body curled into a fetal position.

Bones knelt beside him. "Pender?"

The boy turned his head. "Hear you," he said softly. "Can't see you. Did it work?"

"Yes," Bones said. "It worked."

"You're free?"

"Yes, I'm free."

"That's good. Not sure I could have done it again. Getting hard to breathe."

"Come on," Bones said. "I'm taking you to a hospital."

"Please, can I rest for a minute? I'm so tired."

Bones placed his hand on the boy's shoulder. He felt the approach of a familiar darkness.

"Please," the boy whispered. "Don't need a doctor. Feel better already. Just need to rest."

"All right. You can rest."

"Just for a minute," Milton said. "Only a minute, and then I'll go home, okay?"

"Yes. Then you can go home."

"Thank you," the boy said. "Thank you…Thank you…"

A minute passed.

Milton took in a breath and slowly exhaled.

And then he went home.

Harry Beest was munching almonds in his study when he heard the gunfire downstairs. He didn't waste time wondering what was going on.

He reached for his ever-present Thompson and stormed down the spiral staircase of his Victorian mansion. As he thundered down the steps, Beest had a second to take in the astonishing sight of Edgar Shiloh yelling commands at a posh gang of swordsmen. Time seemed to take on an elastic quality, stretching to accommodate Beest's perception of the scene.

Beest kept seven men on night duty at the mansion. They were all tough and experienced thugs who could keep their cool under fire. The problem was, they weren't under fire. They had brought guns to a knife-fight.

Beest had long suspected that edged weapons (if expertly used) could best firearms in close quarters combat. Now he had proof. All seven of his henchmen, including good old Baldy, were on the floor in conditions ranging from slightly maimed to completely dead.

But I've got the drop on the bastards, Beest thought as he hit the ground floor, and then he slipped in a pool of blood and fell flat on his back.

Goddammit!

As embarrassed as he was furious, Beest scrambled to his feet only to find the tip of a sword poised before his right eye. He gnashed his fangs at the toff holding the blade, but the man barely noticed. His yellow eyes were fixed on some far horizon that only he could see.

"Hello, Beest," Edgar said as he walked over to join them.

"Eddie, you must be the biggest lunatic I have ever met. Do you really think you're going to get away with this?"

Edgar picked up the gun Beest had dropped in his tumble. "I'm here for the tuning fork. Where is it?"

Beest's features wrinkled in confusion. "Tuning fork? What the hell are you—"

Edgar turned and fired at one of Beest's wounded gunsels. The man's head disappeared in a burst of gore.

"Give me what I want," Edgar said, "or I'll kill what's left of your men. Then I will carve out your eyes and castrate you. Where is my tuning fork?"

"Hold it, wait a minute. Are you talking about that gizmo I pinched from Bugosi?"

"Yes."

"Baldy," Beest called out, "are you still in one piece?"

A groan from the corner of the room, then Baldy's voice. "More or less."

"Can you make it to the safe?"

"Yeah."

"Open it and give this punk what he wants."

"A wise decision," Edgar said.

"I'm just wondering if it's gonna be my last."

"Don't worry. I will allow you to live."

"Oh, yeah? Why's that?"

"I make it a point," Edgar said, "to never alleviate suffering."

When she found him the floor, she thought he was dead. Then she saw a scarlet bubble swell and pop over his chest wound, and she realized he was still breathing. She knelt beside him and gently lifted his head.

"Doctor," she said, "can you hear me?"

He opened his eyes. "Erika."

A knot formed in her throat. His voice, normally so strong and authoritative, was little more than a sickly gurgle.

"What happened? Who did this to you?"

"Dragon."

She felt as if she had been slapped. "You're lying."

The Doctor's eyes widened, and for a moment some his old fire was visible. "I've never lied to you. About anything. Ever."

Erika was ashamed, but she still couldn't believe it. The Dragon was so beautiful, so magnificent. He had promised to lift her on his wings...

The Doctor's fingers touched her cheek, leaving a sticky smear of blood. "Listen to me, Erika. I was a blind fool to trust him. He's a traitor. It's his nature. It's who he is."

"Why did he hurt you?"

Marax told her about his conversation with the Dragon. He told her what the monster had planned.

Erika was incredulous. "Would that really work?"

"I think so. You should go now. Before it's too late."

"No! I can save you. I have medicine. You can tell me what to do."

Marax was shaking his head. "I'm done for"

"No, you're not!"

The corner of his mouth lifted slightly. "Who's the Doctor, here?"

Erika began to weep. She couldn't stop herself. She didn't want to.

"Please," said the Doctor. "Get out of the city. Don't die in this place because of me."

"How can I live without you?"

"Don't be foolish. It's you who's been keeping me alive. Not the other way around."

She tried to tell him that he was wrong, but she couldn't form the words.

"You're the strong one," he said. "You always have been. I love you, Erika."

She cradled his head between her breasts and covered his face with her tears.

"This is the place," Sinclair said.

April parked the car in front of the townhouse. "Now what?"

"I guess we knock on the door and see who answers."

They ascended the stoop and discovered that door was slightly open. Sinclair gave it a gentle push, and it turned on well-oiled hinges. They stepped inside. It was very dark.

"Hello?"

No answer.

Sinclair looked over his shoulder at April.

"If you tell me to wait in the car," she said, "I'm going to slap you."

That was exactly what he had planned to tell her, but before he could think of an alternative, Leandro Mendoza came through the door and swung a sword at April's head.

Sinclair snatched April out of the way as the blade descended, and it whistled through the air at her back. Leandro swung the blade again, and Sinclair barely dodged being eviscerated.

"Stop it!" April shouted, and this actually made the Spaniard pause. His sword-arm trembled, and Sinclair perceived that the man was being torn by some silent, internal conflict.

"April," Sinclair said, "find a window or a back door. Get away from here. Now."

April didn't seem to hear him. "What's wrong with you?" she yelled at Leandro. "Have you gone crazy?"

"He's a slave to the Dragon," said a harsh, grating voice.

Sinclair turned to the sound. At the end of the hall stood Brother Bones.

"Stand aside," said the Undead Avenger. "Let me deal with him."

The ominous words seemed to spur Leandro to action. He aimed a thrust at Sinclair's throat, but Sinclair turned so the blade only grazed the side of his neck. April lunged into the opening and drove a right uppercut into the Spaniard's jaw. She followed this with a left hook that sent Leandro sprawling.

"Stay down!" April said.

Then Sterling Harrow charged through the door, his sword flashing as he drove it into…

Brother Bones, who was suddenly standing between April and the Englishman.

"You!" Harrow said. "How can you be –"

Bones grabbed him by the neck and slammed him against the wall.

Harrow frantically waved his arms. He struggled to utter an incantation, but the words were caught in his throat.

"Milton Pender sends his regards," said Brother Bones. Then he pulled the sword from his chest and drove it through Harrow's heart.

April gasped, but she didn't look away.

Bones drew the sword from Harrow's corpse and let it fall to the floor. He looked down at Leandro. The Spaniard was unconscious. Bones looked at April.

"My father taught me to box," she said in a sheepish tone

"He taught you well," said Bones. He turned to Sinclair. "What are you doing here?"

Sinclair quickly told him how he had been guided by his spark of Insight.

"I guess that hocus-pocus is good for something," said Bones, "as long as it's being used by a good man."

"What do you mean?"

Bones told Sinclair the true origin of the Insight.

"If that's true," Sinclair said, "then I can't possibly face the Dragon. He'll turn the power against me, just like he did the others."

"I wouldn't be so sure of that," April said. "You don't have much left in the tank, right? So there's not a lot there he can work with."

"Which means I'm useless either way," Sinclair said.

"No," said Bones. "He was afraid of you. He said you were a threat to him."

"He did?"

"Yes, so drop the self-pity and help me figure out what he's up to."

The words affected Sinclair like a dash of cold water. "All right," he said, "let's assume the worst, and say he was able to repair the device he used at Five Corners. Where would he want to set it off again? Any ideas?"

"He said he was going to destroy the city in my name," Bones said.

There was a moment of silence.

"Oh, no," April said, "I think I know what he's going to do."

She told them her theory.

"If you're right," said Bones, "then I've barely got time to stop him. Do you have a car?"

"Parked right outside," Sinclair said.

"I need you to take me there. I won't ask you to do anything more."

"Are you crazy?" April said, "This is our fight, too! Me and Sinclair are with you all the way! Aren't we, Sinclair?"

Bones looked at Sinclair.

"You heard the lady," Sinclair said. "We're with you all the way."

"No! Absolutely not! I won't stand for it!"

Bill Fraley rolled his eyes. "Preston, you don't have a choice."

"I am not going to let Eddie Shiloh commandeer my broadcast!"

"It's not *your* broadcast. It's WXYZ's broadcast, and TenaciTea is paying for it. So if the CEO of TenaciTea wants to give a personal message to the listeners, then we're going to let him do it. Do I make myself clear?"

Elliot didn't want to give up. "Can't you at least get him to wait for the break?"

"He doesn't want to wait for the break. He wants to go on at midnight."

"Maybe if you were to let me talk to him…"

"You'd be wasting your breath."

"How do you know?"

"Dammit, Preston! The decision's made! He's opening the program whether you like it or not! Now, let it go!"

Elliot went silent and still, which Bill knew from bitter experience was not a good sign. If Preston had surrendered, he would just stomp out of the office in a huff. But he was still sitting there. Which meant he was thinking.

"Tell me," Elliot said, "has he shared with you what he intends to say?"

"No."

"Do you know how long he's going to talk?"

"No."

"And you don't think there's anything wrong with this?"

"No."

Elliot leaned forward. "Why are you so afraid of him?"

Bill grimaced. This was the peril of working with someone who knew you inside-out.

"Answer me, Bill. What's really going on here?"

Edgar's lost his mind, Bill thought. *I don't know how to explain it, but there's something in his eyes that isn't even human. And don't get me started about those so-called bodyguards he's got stationed in the lobby. They're like a pack of zombies. I'd rather give him a few minutes of air-time than turn him down and risk…whatever it is he might do.*

That was what he thought, but did not say. He didn't feel like arguing or trying to justify his decision. He just wanted the conversation to end.

"Well?" Elliot said.

"Preston," Bill said, "when you're rich enough to sponsor your own show, you can call the shots. Until then, you'll just have to do what you're told."

Elliot stomped out of the office in a huff.

Bill breathed a sigh of relief.

Howard felt nervous as he knocked on his employer's front door. *Okay,* he thought, *decision time. Do I or do I not tell him about my little deal with Sally Paige? He needs to know what Bugosi did to Edgar, but he might be angry that I acted without—*

The door opened and there was Harry Beest, his face a mask of primordial fury. "Howard!" he bellowed. He grabbed Howard and snatched him into the house. "Look what that son of a bitch did! Just look!"

Dead and injured men littered the floor. Blood was everywhere.

"I'm gonna find that little punk and kill him before sunrise!" Beest roared.

"Find who?" Howard said.

"Eddie Shiloh! He came by here with the Pirates of Penzance and they cut up my guys! And he stole my gizmo! That…little…snot-nosed…"

Words failed him, and he let out a protracted roar of unintelligible profanity.

Howard decided not tell him about the deal with Sally Paige.

Beest recovered himself enough to speak again. "I want you to bring around the Duesenberg. We're gonna hunt that weasel down if it takes all night!"

"Yes, sir," Howard said. He had a feeling it was going to be a long night.

A gray Pierce-Arrow pulled up next to them as they arrived at the radio station.

"I know her," Sinclair said, nodding at the driver. "Her name is Erika. She was—"

"With the Dragon at Five Corners," said Bones. He got out of the Overland Six.

The woman in the chauffeur's uniform stepped out of her car to meet him. "Trade in your guns for swords?" she said.

Bones had armed himself with the blades taken from Harrow and Leandro. He lifted one of them and pointed it at the woman. "Are you going to be a problem?"

"Not for you."

"Why are you here?"

"I want to kill him."

Bones didn't need to ask who she was referring to. "Why the change of heart?"

"Does it matter?"

"It might, but I don't have time to discuss it. Will you do what I say?"

"Yes."

"If you cross me…"

"I won't."

It was good enough for Bones. "All right," he said. "Let's go."

☠ ☠ ☠

The walls of the green room were pressing in on Preston Elliot. He looked at his cast, and they didn't seem to be faring any better. Edgar Shiloh—*damn the man!*—had insisted on having the studio to himself until he had concluded his "message."

"Preston," said Steve Traynor, "I wish to state for the record that I find this to be completely unconscionable. Bill Fraley has no right to—"

"Oh, shut up, Steve," Elliot said, heading for the door. "I have to get some air. I'll be back in a few minutes." He walked down the hall to the service elevator, opened it with his key, and hit the button for the lobby.

Elliot was convinced that original late-night programming was the wave of the future. It had taken all of his powers of persuasion to sell the powers-that-be on letting him turn what was essentially a kid's adventure show into a major live event that would air in the middle of the night. One could argue that it was an absurd idea, but it was also daring and innovative, adjectives that naturally went with the name Preston Elliot.

Now his baby was being strangled in the crib by this nouveau-riche upstart.

How many are we going to lose? Elliot wondered as he lit up a cigarette. *How many listeners are going to tune out when that fatuous half-wit goes on the air?*

The elevator clanked to a halt. The doors opened, and Elliot was greeted by a phalanx of well-dressed men with black walking sticks. There were nine of them. They stood in a line before the building's entrance as if they were about to break into a dance routine.

Curious, Elliot stepped toward them and was confronted by one of the dancers. "Where are you going?" the man said in a Russian accent.

For a moment, Elliot was too surprised to be angry. Then the moment passed and he got angry. "Who the hell are you?" he said. "And what business is it of yours where I'm going?"

"No one may leave," said the Russian. "This is the Master's command."

The door to the street opened and a tall man in a long black coat stepped inside. He held a sword in each of his gloved hands. His face, shadowed beneath the brim of a black slouch hat, was a featureless white skull.

Elliot's cigarette fell from his lips. "Brother Bones?"

The Russian did an about-face and barked an order at the other men. Moving in precise coordination, the men drew swords from their canes and held them point-in-line at Bones.

"No one may enter," said the Russian. "This is the Master's command."

As if in defiance of this edict, three people followed Bones into the lobby. Two of them, a scruffy-looking man and a beautiful young blonde, were halted by Bones' outstretched arm. "Stay behind me," he said. He turned to the third, a shapely brunette in a chauffeur's uniform, and said to her, "No killing."

The brunette flicked her wrist, and a knife appeared in her hand. "Can I hurt them?"

"Yes," Bones said.

The brunette smiled. "I'll take the four on the left."

In the fifth-floor studio, the Dragon was simmering with eagerness. He clutched the music box so forcefully that, if he were in his true form, he would have crushed it like tinfoil.

There was a click on the intercom. "Three minutes, Mr. Shiloh."

The Dragon turned to the glass partition and smiled at the engineer behind the soundproof glass. Behind the engineer stood François, the Lancer. The Frenchman gave his master a respectful nod, which the Dragon did not bother to return. He reached into a pocket and produced the tuning fork. He lowered it into the music box until he felt it lock firmly into place.

He willed himself to be patient.

He had waited a long time for this victory.

He planned to enjoy every minute of it.

Arthur Sinclair was no stranger to violence. He had spent his boyhood on some of the meanest streets in the world, and he was well-acquainted with mayhem. But nothing in his considerable experience had prepared him for the sight of Bones and Erika in action. Brother Bones dealt out incapacitating injuries with the brutal efficiency of a machine. He was utterly heedless of the Lancers who descended upon him, shrugging off their attacks as a rhino might dismiss the bites of mosquitoes. Though they thrust and feinted and parried with skill and brio, they were simply overpowered by an unstoppable force. Bones' swords rose and fell, rose and fell, until five men were bleeding on the floor, groaning in pain as they clutched at wounds in their arms and legs.

Where Bones like a reaper at the harvest, Erika was like the star of a sanguinary ballet. She slashed through the Lancers with an economy of motion that was really quite beautiful, avoiding their attacks with practiced elegance as if the entire fight had been choreographed in advance. Her enemies may as well have been her dance partners, active collaborators in their own destruction.

It was over in a matter of seconds. When the last of the Lancers collapsed before Erika in a bloody, twitching heap, Bones advanced on an awestruck spectator standing by the elevator.

"Hey, I recognize that guy," April whispered to Sinclair. "He's—"

"Preston Elliot," growled Brother Bones.

"You know me?" Elliot said.

"I've heard of you. Is Edgar Shiloh here?"

"Yes, he is. He's going on the air any second now."

"We can't allow that. Is there a way to shut down the broadcast?"

"Shut it down? What are you talking about? Millions of listeners are expecting –"

Bones grabbed Elliot by the collar and lifted him until they were nose-to-nose.

"I know a way," Elliot said.

"Ten seconds, Mr. Shiloh"

The Dragon caressed the tip of the tuning fork between his thumb and forefinger. He licked his lips. He savored the moment.

"You're on the air in five…four…three…two…one…"

DAY SIX

Howard cruised through the late-night streets, trying not to be agitated by the fact that he was sitting next to a four-hundred-pound gorilla half-mad with murderous rage.

Maybe more than half, Howard thought.

In all the years that Howard had known him, Beest had never seemed more like a dumb animal. Anger had stripped away his humanity, and reduced him to a mass of muscles and grunts. It was a disturbing sight.

I can't take much more of this, Howard thought. *There must be something I can do that'll bring him back to himself.*

It occurred to Howard that music might soothe the savage Beest. He turned on the radio, and a familiar voice came drifting out of the speaker.

"...pleasure to share with you this original composition that I guarantee will stay with you for the rest your lives..."

Beest stared at the radio, his mouth hanging open.

"...exactly the kind of entertainment that you so richly deserve..."

The gorilla roared and pounded the dash with his fists, smashing the radio to pieces.

Howard decided this was Beest's way of saying, *Could you please get me to WXYZ so I can have a little chat with Mr. Shiloh?*

"I can have you there in about five minutes," Howard said.

Beest roared again. *Thank you, Howard. You're an excellent driver.*

"So turn up the volume," the Dragon said, "and prepare to be amazed."

He turned the tuning fork, and music box began to play. He felt the familiar throbbing pulse, and heard the opening notes of the deadly melody. He imagined the whey-faced fools who were leaning close to their radios, bewitched by the strange and haunting music. Would they even notice when their reality began to ripple? Would they hear it when the little fish broke the surface? Or would they remain in their state of stupefied enchantment until they felt the teeth and the claws?

He felt something twist and expand inside of himself. He gasped, and then laughed.

216

"...FIVE MEN WERE BLEEDING ON THE FLOOR..."

It's happening, he thought. *I can feel it!*

He imagined what must be happening in the world outside. The process would be faster this time. In millions of homes, the screaming had already begun. The blood was covering the walls. Desperate pleas to the Most High were being intoned and ignored. And he, the Dragon, was about to assume his place at the center of it all, leading his minions on an apocalyptic rampage of rapine and murder!

His back bulged beneath his clothes, and blood seeped through the fabric of his coat. The tips of his fingers split open, and long black claws began to emerge.

He could no longer contain his glee. He began dancing to the atonal tune, reveling in the death and horror he knew he had unleashed.

"The day of the Dragon has come at last!" he cried.

The intercom clicked.

"Having fun?" said a harsh, grating voice.

"How long was he on the air?" Sinclair asked.

Elliot looked at his watch. "Not more than a few minutes."

"And you're sure there's no signal?"

"Positive," Elliot said. He gestured to the control box he had been fiddling with. "I've completely disabled the transmitter. It's not hard to do, if you know how."

They were standing at the base of a tall antenna that rose from the building like an arrow aimed at the stars. At its paramount point, a beacon burned like a baleful red eye that looked out over Cape Noire.

April spoke up. "Could the Drag…um…could Shiloh somehow fix it?"

"From the studio?" Elliot shook his head. "There's no way. He'd have to join us up here on the roof, and to do that he'd have to get through Brother Bones and your brunette friend. I'm pretty sure that's beyond the scope of his abilities."

Sinclair and April shared a look. April held up a hand and crossed her fingers.

The Dragon looked at the harlot and the golem. They stared back at him with the cold finality of a fatal diagnosis. Behind them, François the Lancer was unconscious on the floor. The engineer was nowhere to be seen.

"It's over," said Brother Bones. "You're finished."

"You're wrong," the Dragon said. "I've won. Even as we speak, the little fish are—"

"In the slime where they belong," said Bones. "You got cut off while you were still running your mouth. You've been playing to an empty room."

The Dragon was trembling. He held the pulsating music box like a child embracing a beloved toy. Blood flowed from his eyes, ears, and mouth. "No," he said, his voice wet and plaintive. "I can't be defeated like this. Not after I've come so far…"

"Stop it," said Bones, "you're going to make me cry."

"You would dare to mock me?" the Dragon screeched. One of his eyes popped out, and it dangled loosely from the socket. "I am greatness personified! I was cast in perfection and bathed in glory and I will not be humiliated by the likes of you!"

Bones and Erika looked at each other. Neither of them spoke.

Blood spurted from the Dragon's hands as pink flesh fell away to reveal gleaming scales. His herringbone suit began to split at the seams.

"I demand an audience with the Most High!" he cried. "I demand to be acknowledged!"

No one acknowledged him.

Why won't He ever answer me?

"Maybe you're not worth His time," said Brother Bones.

The Dragon's scream almost blew out the intercom. His remaining eye rolled with blind rage. The music box crumpled in his claws, and then burst like a metallic pustule. As if following this example, the body of Edgar Shiloh exploded, covering the glass partition with an opaque coating of viscera.

"Hmm," said Bones. He had never seen that happen before.

"Is that it?" Erika said. "Is he dead?"

Inside the studio, something roared. They could hear it through the soundproof glass.

"That answer your question?" said Bones.

"Okay, Boss," Howard said as he pulled up in front of WXYZ. "I'm not sure how you want to play this, but I think…"

Beest was already out of the car and bounding across the street, hooting and bellowing like an escapee from the zoo.

Howard was mortified. *What is he doing? He can't just run in there!*

Beest rushed past the entrance without stopping.

Thank God, Howard thought. *I don't know what I would have done if he…*

Beest leapt onto the side of the building and started to climb.

Oh, crap.

"Did you hear that?" April said.

"I did," Elliot said. "It sounded like –"

There was a tremor.

Sinclair's pendant grew very hot against his chest. "Other side of the building!" he shouted. "Now!"

All three of them ran, and behind them the roof erupted. From the resultant cloud of dust and debris emerged the Dragon, his wings flapping as they propelled him into the air.

April stared up at the monster with a mixture of wonder and terror. *I really do live in a world with talking dragons*, she thought, and the realization took her breath away.

The Dragon turned in the sky, his fangs flashing and his tail twisting. *"Release me!"* the monster roared, and April saw that Brother Bones had his arms wrapped around the Dragon's neck, and Erika was clinging fiercely to one of the monster's legs.

In spite of her fear, April felt something like exaltation.

It seemed there were noble knights in the world as well.

Here I am, Erika thought, *borne aloft, just like he promised.*

She held on for dear life as the Dragon spun and bucked and heaved. His hard, dry scales scratched her face and hands as she clung to him.

I'm not going to survive this, she thought, and a strange calm descended upon her. This was her inescapable destiny. She was meant to die in Cape Noire.

But not without his blood on my steel.

She drew back her knife and slashed between the scales. She was rewarded with a spray of viscous black fluid and a full-bodied scream of pain and fury.

"*Die, slut!*" said the Dragon, and his tail whipped around and struck Erika's back. She lost her grip, and began a swift descent to the street below. As she plunged past the roof, she caught a brief glimpse of April Moon's horror-stricken features, and then she felt a terrible wrenching in her left shoulder when—

💀 💀 💀

Harry Beest caught the girl's arm as she fell past him. "Jaysus!" he roared, startled out of his berserker rage. "Where did you come from?"

"Aaah!" said the girl, and Beest realized that her shoulder was probably dislocated. Though her face was twisted in pain, he could see that she was a real looker, and he was glad that he hadn't let her fall. She gawked at him, and he felt vaguely embarrassed, like a schoolboy caught in the middle of a stupid prank.

What the hell am I doing here? Why didn't I just take the stairs?

He glanced at the windows. They were far too small for him, but...

"Who are you?" she gasped.

"Well, I ain't King Kong," he said, "and you ain't Fay Wray."

💀 💀 💀

April rushed to edge of the roof just in time to see a gorilla toss Erika through a window. Her thunderstruck brain was still processing this fact—*a gorilla!?*—when a roar from the Dragon returned her attention to the duel in the sky.

💀 💀 💀

Brother Bones hung down the Dragon's back, refusing to be dislodged by the monster's ferocious aerobatics. He still held both swords, but he couldn't bring them to bear with loosening his hold. He was at an impasse, but his unshakeable presence was driving the Dragon to the brink of hysteria.

"*Release me! Release me!*" the monster shrieked, his throaty roar rising to a pitch that could shatter glass.

Actually, Bones thought, *that's not such a bad idea.*

He waited until the Dragon turned for a vertical climb, then he drew back his arms and let himself fall. As he did so, he drove the swords into the monster's flesh at the point where the wings connected with the back. He held on the hilts and let gravity do the rest.

The Dragon screamed and April covered her ears in pain. A rain of blood fell across the roof, followed by Brother Bones, who landed almost at April's feet.

She went to her knees beside his prone form. She was opening her mouth to ask if he was okay, and stopped herself before the first syllable. How could he be anything like *okay* after what he had just—

Bones rose up and grabbed her by the shoulders. "Look out," he said, and he pulled her away with him just as the Dragon came crashing from the sky.

The roof shook with the impact, but miraculously didn't collapse as the monster landed in a writhing, reptilian mass. Sinclair and Elliot managed to keep their footing, but a wild lash from the Dragon's tail sent both men flying.

Sinclair slammed into one of the antenna's steel struts. There was a flash, and then the world turned to a muddy smear. Head swimming and nearly senseless, it took Sinclair a moment to realize he had lost his glasses. He rolled over and saw a blur he identified as Elliot. The man was lying by the door to the service elevator.

Hope he's okay, Sinclair thought, still dazed. *What about April? Where is she?*

He tried to get to his feet, but his legs seemed to be out of sync with the rest of his body. This lack of coordination may have saved his life, for a second later the Dragon's tail whipped by just above him, striking the antenna with a ringing metallic *whang* that provided a prosaic counterpoint to the monster's screams.

Sinclair squinted. He saw the vague outline of the monster, and then a pair of shapes that had to be April and Brother Bones.

Then the Dragon went very still, and Sinclair realized with horror that the monster had seen them, too.

Steam billowed from the Dragon's nostrils. The swords still protruded from his back, and blood spewed like black oil from his wounded wings. He lifted his enormous head and turned his yellow eyes to April.

She was transfixed by his gaze. These were eyes that had seen Heaven. They might even have looked on the face of God.

How could anyone fall so far? April thought, and beneath her fear she felt a strange and inexpressible sadness.

With a visible effort, the Dragon drew himself up to his full height. He towered above them like a monument to ruined glory.

April knew it was too late to run, but she didn't want to die cowering behind Brother Bones. She stood by his side and raised her fists. If she had to go, she would go down swinging.

The Dragon snorted and looked at Brother Bones. *"Everywhere I turn, I am besieged by harlots. Are you some sort of pimp that you should surround yourself with whores?"*

"I already told you," said Bones, "I'm just a talking gun."

"A gun that's out of ammunition," said the Dragon. He lunged down at them, and his mouth seemed to fill the world.

"No!" Sinclair shouted, and then he was on his feet, his heart and mind consumed with an overriding impulse to protect April. Then, as he ran toward the fray, he saw that someone else was doing a pretty fair job of that.

Brother Bones had caught the Dragon's jaws. He was holding the monster's mouth open wide, his arms trembling from the effort. It was the most impressive thing Sinclair had ever seen, a display of such raw power— and sheer, unyielding resolution—that it was exhilarating to behold.

The Dragon seemed paralyzed with astonishment. His black tongue lolled, and saliva flowed from his gaping maw. His breath reeked like a day-old battlefield, and his yellow eyes burned, burned, burned…

The shard around Sinclair's neck was burning. It was a teardrop of fire on his skin, but it wasn't painful. It was a flame of the spirit, one that purified by searing away the superfluous, leaving only the things that mattered, the things that had to be done.

When the time comes, you will know what to do.

It was as if Mr. Mendoza was running beside him, speaking into his ear. *This is it, boy. This is the moment.*

Sinclair grabbed the shard with his right hand and snatched it from about his neck. He held up his fist, and it shone red like the beacon in the sky above.

Go ahead, son. Lasso the lightning.

Sinclair leapt onto the Dragon's neck. He landed just behind the monster's head.

"Father in Heaven," he said, "let my hand strike true."

Then he sent his burning fist blazing through the top of the Dragon's skull.

Entropy raced through the Dragon like Greek fire. He could feel his spirit being drawn away. He had time, not much, to reflect on how completely he had been undone. This time, there would be no retreats into the ether, no licking of wounds, no scheming for vengeful returns.

I am killed, he thought, and he despaired.

His limbs went numb, and he collapsed on the surface of the roof. He felt the weight of the pestilent Lancer slip from his neck. He saw the man join Brother Bones and the blonde harlot. They looked down at him, and he was surprised that they did not seem to be gloating over his demise. They were merely bearing witness.

As the darkness closed in on him, he focused on the stygian gaze of Brother Bones. The Dragon stared into those black onyx eyes, and in them he saw a final, terrifying truth that would follow him through eternity.

The Most High had finally answered him.

"*Oh,*" he said with his final breath.

Then the abyss opened to receive him, and his unthinkable future became his never-ending now.

They watched the light fade from the Dragon's eyes. Then his body disintegrated into a thick black vapor, a little more pollution to blight the Cape Noire sky.

The spell was broken by a howl of sirens from the street below.

"The police are here," said Brother Bones. "This could be a problem."

"Maybe not," said Sinclair. "I think I can get us past them."

"How's that?" April asked.

Sinclair looked at her, and there was a yellow glint at the corner of his eye.

"You've got the Insight back," April said. "Is that really a good thing?"

"Oh, I think so," Sinclair said, and he gave her a smile that wasn't exactly reassuring.

There was a loud groan at the other end of the roof. They turned and saw Preston Elliot struggle to his feet. "What happened?" he said.

"The good guys won," April said. She looked at Sinclair and Bones. "Let's get out of here, fellas."

Harry Beest leapt onto the roof with a warlike bellow and a violent pounding of his chest. After a moment or two, he realized he was alone. As he had employed one of his best bellows, he was disappointed at not having an audience.

Then he saw the hole in the roof.

What is that? Did someone set off a bomb?

He thought about it for a moment. He dimly remembered hearing something like an explosion, and some weird shrieks in the sky, but he had been so caught up in his own bloodlust that the noises had barely registered.

He started to give the damage a closer inspection, but a few precarious creaks beneath his feet made him think again. He didn't want to create a second, Harry-Beest-shaped hole to keep the first one company.

He spotted a service elevator and cautiously shuffled toward it, then discovered to his angry dismay that it wouldn't operate without a key. He went back to the edge of the roof, and saw that the streets below were teeming with cops.

He looked for his Duesenberg, and saw it slowly pulling away. That was to be expected. All the boys had standing orders to avoid the cops. Howard was just following procedure.

His eyes wandered once again to the hole. He could hear small bits of debris sifting down from its crumbling edges.

Something told him he had stumbled into someone else's war, and it was one that he should stay out of. He'd catch up with Eddie Shiloh later. For the time being, he would just lie low and wait for the heat to fade.

But he didn't want to wait on the roof of WXYZ.

Sooner or later, he thought, *I'm gonna have to climb all the way back down from here.*

"Ah, shit," muttered Harry Beest.

Dan Rains entered the WXYZ lobby at the head of a small army of Cape Noire's finest. The marble floor was slick with blood and littered with wounded men. Some of them were clutching what appeared to be long, thin swords.

"What happened to me?" one of them said. "What's going on?"

"That's what I want to know," Dan said.

"I can help you with that," someone replied.

Dan looked up and saw a bespectacled little man steeping out of an elevator. The guy wasn't much to look at, but he carried himself with confidence and authority. He marched toward Dan, his bold manner an odd contrast to his disheveled appearance. As he drew near, Dan could see a crack in the right lens of his thick glasses.

"Stop right where you are," Dan said. "Please give me your name and tell me…tell me…"

Dan was staring at the cracked lens. There was something about the eye behind it. Something that seemed very important to examine, to know more about. Something almost…hypnotic…

"My name is unimportant," the man said.

Dan slowly nodded. That was reasonable. Why be nosy? He didn't want the man's life story. He just needed some facts; that was all.

"I will give you all the facts you need," the man said, extending his hand.

Dan liked hearing that. So few people seemed to understand their civic duty. It was refreshing to meet someone who actually wanted to help the police. He took the man's hand.

"It's a pleasure for me to assist you," the man said.

Dan was overwhelmed by a feeling of comradely good fellowship. "The pleasure's all mine," he said. "May I introduce you to my men?"

"You practically read my mind," the man said.

April was alone in the dark with Brother Bones. Elliot had shown them to an unused office, then left them there so he could go check on his actors. April asked him to look for Erika while he was at it.

"The girl with the knife?" Elliot said. "I thought she didn't make it."

April opened her mouth to tell him about the gorilla, then decided not to. If Erika was still alive—and April was pretty sure that she was—then she wouldn't need any help from Elliot. If ever there was a woman capable of taking care of herself, it was the girl with the knife.

"Never mind," April said. "It was just wishful thinking."

Elliot squeezed her shoulder and gave her a sympathetic look that was surprising in its warmth and sincerity. April was moved by the gesture, and she decided that beneath his patina of glitz, Preston Elliot was a genuinely nice man.

He promised to return soon, but the wait quickly became unbearable. April's system was still flooded with adrenaline. She wanted to be in the open air, to move, to *run*...

"Calm down," Bones said. "You'll be out of here soon enough."

April stared at the dim outline of the white skull mask. It was all she could make out in the oppressive gloom.

"I can't help it," she said. "I'm all tangled up inside. Nothing like this has ever happened to me. I'm just a girl from the sticks, y'know? I never dreamed I'd run into anything like the Dragon, or...or..."

"Or me?"

"Or you."

"You'll be fine," Bones said. "You're handling it better than most would."

"You think so?"

"Trust me. I've had some experience with this sort of thing."

For a moment, there was silence. April thought it was an especially heavy silence, even under the circumstances. Then she realized why.

She was the only one in the room who was breathing.

"My God," she whispered. "Is it true what they say? Are you...dead?"

Bones didn't reply.

April stared at the skull. It seemed to be floating in the darkness.

"It's all right," Bones said. "You don't have to be afraid of me."

"How could I be afraid of you? You saved my life. You're a hero."

"Hero?" Bones said.

"Yes."

"If you really knew anything about me, you would never call me that."

"I don't know you," April said. "You're right about that. But I'll tell something. You're more than a talking gun, and you'll always be a hero to me."

The heavy silence fell once more.

April closed her eyes and listened to the sound of her own breathing.

It was the sound engineer who had called the police. When Brother Bones and the lady chauffeur burst into the studio, he had absconded as soon as possible.

"The French guy tried to draw a sword on Bones," the engineer told Preston Elliot. "It wasn't much of a fight."

"Is he dead?" Elliot asked.

"No. I came back after the explosion and found him passed out under some ceiling tiles. He's sleeping it off in the break room."

Elliot surveyed the gore-spattered ruins of his studio. "Was anyone else hurt?"

"The rest of the cast was still in the green room when it happened."

Elliot turned to Bill Fraley. "How about you? Did you see anything?"

Bill didn't answer. He was staring up through the hole in the roof. He seemed to be in a state of shock.

"Bill?"

"Huh?"

"Did you see anything?"

"No. I was…I was in my office."

"I don't get it," said the engineer. "Why would Brother Bones want to kill Mr. Shiloh and blow up the studio? Was he mad about the show?"

"He didn't do this," Elliot said.

"Well, who did?"

"It was the work of anarchists," Sinclair said as he stepped into the room.

"Anarchists?" Bill Fraley said.

"Yes," Sinclair said. "It was the same gang who attacked Five Corners. They tried to hijack the broadcast. They were going to blow up the station while the world listened, but Brother Bones stopped them, with a little assistance from a group of secret agents."

"What secret agents?"

"They came here with Edgar Shiloh. They had been tracking the activities of the anarchists, and they knew that Mr. Shiloh was in danger.

Unfortunately, they failed to save his life. They made a heroic stand in the lobby, but they were overpowered by the villains. It's a wonder they weren't killed themselves."

Elliot almost laughed at Sinclair's audacity. No one was going to believe this hokum. He glanced at Bill, fully expecting the station manager to denounce Sinclair as a damned liar.

Bill wasn't saying anything. In fact, he was regarding Sinclair with something like adulation. Elliot looked at the engineer, and there was the same expression. He turned back to Sinclair, and saw a faint, phosphorescent glow in his eyes. The man winked at him.

"I've explained all of this to the police," Sinclair said. "They're organizing a manhunt for the gang even as we speak."

Elliot lit a cigarette. "Do you think they'll ever find them?"

Sinclair shrugged. "They're slippery characters, these anarchists."

"Yeah," Elliot said.

Sinclair turned to Bill and extended a hand. Bill took it without hesitation.

"Please remember the things I've told you," Sinclair said.

"Remember," Bill said in a dreamy tone.

"And please forget that you ever saw me."

"Forget," Bill said.

Sinclair turned to the engineer. He shook his hand.

"Anarchists," murmured the engineer.

"There's a good fellow," Sinclair said. He turned to Elliot.

Elliot took a step back. "I don't think I want to shake your hand."

"I won't ask you to."

"I'm allowed to remember the truth?"

"I think you've earned the right. Are my friends close by?"

"Just down the hall."

"Take me to them. I can get them out of here without anyone noticing."

"If you'd told me that a few minutes ago, I wouldn't have believed you, but now…"

"I know," Sinclair said. "I can hardly believe it myself."

Elliot exhaled a plume of smoke. "What kind of a man are you?"

"A good one, I hope," Sinclair said.

Elliot nodded. "I hope so, too."

The knocking was subdued but insistent. O'Malley's first thought was that it was Dan Rains, back for another late night visit. The priest didn't mind. He was, by nature, a garrulous man and he always enjoyed tipping a glass in the wee hours with a friend.

On his way to the front door, he paused to check on the boy. He was sleeping soundly, which was a blessing. O'Malley was worried for the child's future. No relatives had come forth to claim him, and it looked as if he were bound for an orphanage.

He was sadly ruminating on this when he cracked the door and saw an angel. She was young and blonde, with a porcelain complexion and pale blue eyes. She smiled at him.

"Sorry to wake you up, Padre, but I've got an important message for you."

"Message? From whom?"

The girl cocked a thumb at a sedan idling at the corner. "I was told to say it's from Brother Michael of Mt. Serenity. He said you would understand."

O'Malley understood, and he felt a chill that had nothing to do with the night air. "What does he want you to tell me?"

"There are two dead men at this address," she said, pressing a slip of paper into his hand. "One of them is a guy named Milton Pender. Brother Michael says that Milton Pender was a good man who deserves a decent burial. He wants you to see to it. Will you do that?"

"I promise," O'Malley said. "What about the other man?"

"His name was Harrow," the girl said. "Brother Michael says you don't need to worry about him. He's for the potter's field."

"You can drop me off here," Bones said.

They were on a dark side street near the docks. Bones had directed them there without telling them their destination.

"You live out here?" April asked.

"No," Bones said, "but this where I'm getting out of the car."

April pulled over and he stepped out. He closed the door and started to walk away, then paused and turned back.

April rolled down her window. "Something wrong?"

"No," Bones said. "I just wanted to say that you did well. Both of you."

"We couldn't have done it without you," April said.

Bones gave her a little nod, then moved his eyes to Sinclair. "You picked up a lot of power tonight, didn't you?"

"Yes, I did," Sinclair said.

"Power like that can change a man."

Sinclair turned away. He looked down the street.

"I'll be watching you," Bones said, and then he disappeared into the shadows.

Leandro was waiting for them at the bookshop. He looked lost and forlorn. He was sitting on the sidewalk beside the door, his arms wrapped around his knees. He stood up when they got out of the car. His eyes were red, and his jaw was swollen where April had punched him.

"You want something to drink?" Sinclair asked him.

"Do you have any sangria?"

"Will you settle for orange juice?"

"That will be fine."

He followed them in and sat down by Sinclair's chess table. He looked at April.

"I have a vague recollection of you striking me in the face. Did that really happen?"

"Yes, it did," April said. "In my defense, you were trying to kill me at the time."

Sinclair came back with the juice. He sat down across from Leandro. "How much can you remember?"

"Very little," Leandro said, accepting the drink. "Did you defeat the Dragon?"

"Yes, but we had a lot of help."

"Will you tell me about it?"

They did. April did most of the talking. She was very animated.

"So that's it," April concluded. "The Dragon's gone and Sinclair's got the Insight back."

"And Sterling Harrow is dead," Leandro said. "What of the other Lancers?"

"They're at the hospital by now," Sinclair said. "They're in pretty bad shape, but they'll live. I personally commended them for their bravery. I shook their hands."

Leandro gave him a suspicious look. "What did you do to them?"

"They have no recollection of the Dragon or the Insight. They think they're part of a secret society of wealthy do-gooders, led by you, of all people. The police believe this as well. You can look forward to a stern talking-to, but you won't be facing any criminal charges."

"You changed all of their memories with a single touch?"

"Actually, they did all the heavy lifting. I only gave them the basic outline of what I wanted them to believe. Once they accepted that as *prima facie*, their minds filled in the rest."

"Do any of them still have the Insight?"

"The Dragon didn't leave them with much. What little they had died with him."

"Died, or went into you?"

Sinclair didn't answer.

Leandro finished his juice. He set down the glass. "Alfonso would have been proud."

"I'd like to think so," Sinclair said.

"There is one last thing you must do to honor his legacy."

Sinclair sighed. "You think I should renounce the Insight."

"It is too much power for one man. Surely you can see that."

Sinclair rubbed his eyes. He felt very tired. "How do I get rid of it?"

"It is too dangerous to pass to anyone else. I'm afraid that leaves only one way to divest yourself of the power."

"I had a feeling you were going to say that," Sinclair said.

This was too much for April. "Hey, wait a minute! Are you guys saying what I think you're saying?"

Neither of the men spoke. They stared at each other over the chess table.

"Is anybody going to answer me?"

"Peace, child," Leandro said. "This doesn't concern you."

"Like hell it doesn't!"

"Then I shall speak to you plainly," Leandro said. "The Insight is not the blessing we thought it was. It is a demonic power that will corrupt and destroy anyone who wields it. *Señor* Sinclair faces a stark choice. He can die a martyr, or live only to lose his soul. What would you have him do?"

"You're overlooking a third alternative," April said. "He could live to be the force for good that your brother trained him to be."

"If Alfonso had known the true origin of the Insight—"

"Oh, shut up! I can't believe you! It was all well and good when you and your pals had the magic, but now that Sinclair's got it all, you want him to eat a bullet! Who do you think are?"

"I am a man who has seen the truth!"

"Only part of it! You say the Insight is evil because it comes from the Dragon, but the Dragon wasn't always evil, was he?"

"What are you talking about?"

"I'm talking about free will. The Dragon used to be an angel, but he chose a path that took him straight to Perdition. Sinclair's not the Dragon, and he's not you. He won't take that road. I know he won't. He's better than that."

"Maybe for right now," Leandro said, "but the power—"

"Power by itself is meaningless," April said. "It's what you do with it that counts."

Sinclair looked at April as if he were seeing her for the first time, and he finally understood how he really felt about her. He was not, as he had secretly feared, consumed by some stupid and hopeless erotic longing. No, it wasn't that.

He loved her.

He loved her because she was smart and brave and decent. He loved her because knowing her had made him a better man, and he would never do anything to disappoint her.

He loved her because she was his friend.

He looked at Leandro. "If it's all the same to you, I don't think I'm ready to die just yet."

The Spaniard stood up and straightened his coat. "I pray you do not regret this, *Señor.*"

"Don't worry about him," April said. "I'll keep him straight. I'm his acolyte, y'know."

Leandro turned to her, and surprised her by smiling. "Indeed," he said. "Sinclair is a most fortunate man."

He left without another word.

"What now?" Sinclair said.

"I don't know about you," April said, "but I'm going home. I need some sleep."

"Good idea. See you at noon?"

"Make sure the board's ready," April said.

Sally Paige was brewing coffee in the bungalow's kitchen when Mrs. Timms walked in.

"Are the boys still asleep?" Sally asked.

Timms yawned and nodded. "It was hard for them to settle down last night. They were so excited. This is the first vacation they've had since… well…ever."

"I'm glad I could do it for them," Sally said.

"They're convinced you're the most wonderful person who's ever lived, and I'm not inclined to argue."

Sally laughed. "I'm sure they think mom is pretty wonderful, too."

Timms frowned. "I just hope they never learn the truth."

Sally put down her coffee. "The truth? I'll tell you the truth. You're a good woman and a great mother. In fact, I know a little boy who could use some help from a person like you, if you think you're up to it."

"A little boy?"

"About the same age as your sons."

"What happened to him?"

Sally told her about the Hessian's message to Brother Bones. When she finished, there were tears in Mrs. Timms' eyes.

"You think that I could help him?"

"I'm sure of it."

"Oh, Sally, I wish I could. I really do, but…I don't have a job anymore. I don't know how I'm going to take care of my own boys, much less take on another."

"Is money the only problem?" Sally asked.

"It's the only problem, but you've got to admit it's a pretty big one."

Sally thought of the briefcase she had left with Father O'Malley.

"Timms," she said with a smile, "I've got a feeling that problem's going to get a lot smaller."

When Waldo brought Bugosi his breakfast tray, he found the man in a rare state of bafflement. The Professor was glaring at the early edition of the Tribune as it were printed in Sanskrit. He lowered it and turned his eyes to Waldo. "Have you seen this nonsense?"

Waldo set down the tray. "I never read the paper before passing it to you."

Bugosi pursed his lips. "You're already a clod, Waldo. Don't compound it by being disingenuous. I repeat, have you seen this nonsense?"

"Are you referring to the story about Edgar Shiloh being assassinated by anarchists?"

"Yes."

"I might have seen that."

Bugosi set the paper aside and began to butter his toast. "I don't suppose you've been able to determine how Edgar—the *real* Edgar—was able to escape from the lab?"

"It's a mystery," Waldo said, striving not to sound disingenuous.

"Quite," said Bugosi.

Waldo waited for a few beats, then turned to go. As he was opening the door, the Professor called to him.

"Yes, sir?"

"Start packing the essentials. We're moving out today."

"Today?"

"Yes, Waldo, today. The TenaciTea project has gone belly-up, and this location has been compromised. I don't want any more surprise visits from Harry Beest."

"I'll get right on it, sir. Do you have a new place lined up?"

Bugosi gave him an old-fashioned look.

"Sorry, sir. Stupid question."

Bugosi nodded and returned to his toast.

Battered, bleeding, tired, and hungry, Erika wandered into the train station and sat down on a bench. She didn't draw much attention. She had stolen a raincoat from a cloakroom at WXYZ, and it covered the improvised dressings she had used to cover the cuts she suffered when the gorilla shoved her through the window.

She hadn't made up her mind about that gorilla. She was grateful that he had saved her, but part of her wished he had just minded his own business. What was she going to do now? Her entire life had been devoted to the Doctor, and now he was gone. She had no friends, no money, no discernible skills except for murder and…that other.

She shook her head. She would cut her own throat before she returned to that.

She heard the whistle of an approaching train, and she had a vision of herself jumping in front of it.

She closed her eyes and heard the Doctor's voice: *Don't die in this place because of me.*

Then she heard someone else's voice: "Are you okay?"

She looked up and met the hazel eyes of a petite redhead, her pale skin dotted with freckles. There was something familiar about the girl, but Erika couldn't quite place…

The hazel eyes widened. "Hey, I know you. You're the driver."

Erika blinked. "Excuse me?"

"I'm Stacy. Don't you remember me?"

Erika remembered. "We left you here three days ago. Have you been hanging around this place the whole time?"

Stacy laughed. "I decided I wanted to see a little bit of the city. It seemed silly not to, after I had come so far. I was able to stay at a really nice place, thanks to all that money Mr. Samuel gave me. Say, where is he? I'd like to speak to him."

"He had to go away."

"Gee, that's too bad. I wish I could see him again."

"Why?"

"I'd like to thank him. I'd like for him to know that I kept my promise."

"But you didn't keep it. You're still here."

"Not for long," the girl said. She held up a ticket. "I'm going home. I'm going to give my folks another chance, just like he asked me to."

"Just like he asked," Erika said.

"Yeah," Stacy said. "So, where are you headed?"

"I have no idea."

"You're not going to meet Mr. Samuel?"

"I don't think I'm ever going to see him again."

Stacy sat down on the bench. She touched Erika's hand. "You want to come with me?"

Erika was stunned. "Are you serious?"

"It's a long ride and I could use the company. I'll spring for your ticket, and I'll even give you some walking-around money. God knows I've got plenty of it."

"Why would you do that?" Erika said. "You don't even know me."

Stacy looked up at the roof of the station. "Well, you and Mr. Samuel didn't know me," she said, "but I've got a feeling you may have saved my life."

The train whistle wailed. It was getting closer.

"Maybe I can return the favor," Stacy said. "Maybe you could use another chance, too."

"I'm not sure I deserve one," Erika said.

"Well, that's the thing about second chances," Stacy said. "The people who don't deserve them are the ones who need them the most."

The train pulled into the station.

Stacy looked at Erika. "What do you say?"

Erika took the chance.

EPILOGUE: THE SEVENTH DAY

Brother Bones maintained his lonely vigil. He sat in his silent room, staring through the open blinds into the night beyond, and beyond that toward the vanishing point where his past intersected with eternity.

He had a grim suspicion that his past *was* his eternity, and he was doomed to never escape it. He sometimes glimpsed a dream of redemption, but the dream would invariably retreat before the army of his gathered misdeeds. That bloody horde of memories was always on the move, bearing standards that listed all of his crimes, and crushing underfoot all hope of forgiveness. Their war-cries were many and varied, but their message was always the same.

We will always be with you.
We will always be here.
We will never stop screaming.
We will never...
We...

They stopped screaming.

Though he had no need to breathe, Bones drew in a breath.

He exhaled.

What had just happened?

He looked around the empty room. Everything was in its appointed place. Everything was as it should be. The darkness covered everything, just as it always did.

He closed his eyes, and was surprised to see a glimmer of white and gold radiance on the skyline of his internal landscape. He focused on it, and it began to grow brighter. He didn't know what it was, but it was...

Wonderful.

In the distance, he could hear the restless stirring of his army of sins. They grumbled and growled, eager to resume their endless campaign, but the light held them in abeyance. It grew stronger and brighter, driving back the persistent ghosts.

This will not last, he heard them say. *This day will end. This light will fade. And then we will be back. We will be back with a vengeance.*

He knew it was true. But if this wasn't redemption, it was still a respite. Someone, somewhere, had decided to grant him a brief moment of peace, and he decided that he would enjoy it while it lasted.

"Thank you," he whispered, and he turned his face to heaven, and basked in the warmth of a stranger sun.

Bobby Crandall had just come home when he saw the light behind Bones' door. It shone brightly through the cracks in the warped frame, shimmering slightly, as if reflected off the surface of a running stream.

Bobby was frightened. He stood outside the door, wondering what he should do. It was an ironclad rule that Bones' room was off-limits, but what if this was some kind of an emergency?

"Bones?" he said.

He heard nothing but the usual silence.

With no small amount of trepidation, he closed a hand around the knob. He was about to turn it when he had another idea. It made him feel shabby to do it, but he knelt down and peered through the keyhole.

The room was bathed in a golden glow, as if an evening sun from early autumn had taken up residence. In the center of the room sat Bones, perfectly still, his skull-face tilted slightly toward the ceiling. Floating in the air behind him was the spectre of beautiful young woman. She rested an ethereal hand on Bones' shoulder, and she gazed down at him with a curious expression that might have been sadness, and might have been compassion.

Bobby was no longer afraid, but something about the scene filled him with unbearable heartache. Whatever this was, it wasn't meant for his eyes. He stood and turned to walk away, and as he did, he heard the woman speak. She said four words in a melodious voice that pierced his soul, and would haunt him for the rest of his days.

You're welcome, Brother Bones.

THE END

ABOUT OUR CREATORS

WRITER—ROMAN LEARY was eight years old when a family friend gave him an Ace paperback of Conan stories. He has been a devotee of pulp fiction ever since. Today, he lives in North Carolina with his wife and their beautiful daughter. *Brother Bones: Six Days of the Dragon* is his first novel.

Roman Leary Halloween 1996

ARTIST—ROB MORAN is a comic book artist/writer based in the UK: as a writer he has created comic book series and wrote a nationally syndicated American newspaper comic strip. As an artist he has been a magazine illustrator, newspaper cartoonist, computer game designer and created posters for Scottish Opera. As a comic book artist he has worked for publishers in the UK, Europe and the USA such as Marvel, Dark Horse, Image Comics, Silver Phoenix Entertainment, Classical Comics, 2000 AD and many others. His comic book mini-series BLOOD NATION is currently being made into a major motion picture. You can see more of his work at http://robmorancomicart.blogspot.co.uk/

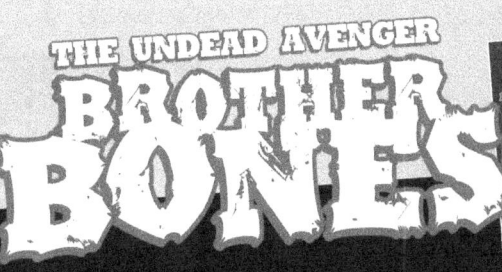

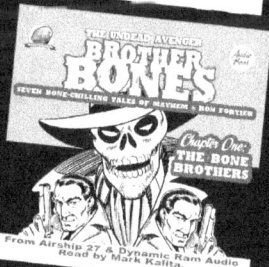

Coming soon!

Sherlock Holmes
Consulting Detective

The Return of RAVENWOOD

Easily one of the most little known pulp heroes was Ravenwood, the Stepson of Mystery. In all he appeared in only five stories as back up tales in issues of Secret Agent X. Several years ago Airship 27 Productions released its first volume in this series bringing back this unique occult detective, whose different colored eyes are always changing, along with his Tibetan teacher/mentor, the Nameless One, and his loyal British butler, Stirling.

Now, get ready for another quartet of brand new tales of suspense and action as the Stepson of Mystery once again sets out to solve bizarre mysteries the police are helpless to unravel.
Follow along as he confronts an amazing killer robot, teams up with the Black Bat to fight an alien horror and investigates ritualistic murders having no rhyme or reason. New pulp writers Janet Harriet, Aaron Smith, Jonathan Fisher and Gene Moyers pull out all the stops, delivering four original, fast-paced adventures that skirt the outer edges of fear and madness.

This is one pulp book best read with the lights on!

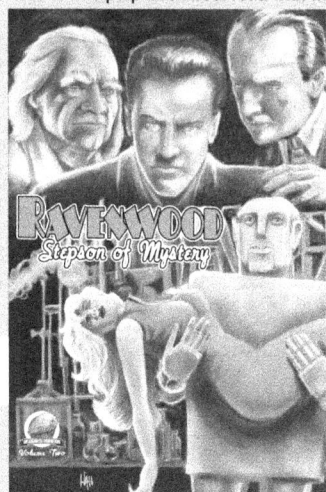

AIRSHIP 27 PRODUCTIONS
NEW **PULP**

FOR AVAILABILITY CHECK: AIRSHIP27HANGAR.COM